RUINED

Books by Amy Tintera

Reboot
Rebel

Ruined
Avenged

RUINED

AMY TINTERA

HARPER TEEN
An Imprint of HarperCollinsPublishers

HarperTeen is an imprint of HarperCollins Publishers.

Ruined

Copyright © 2016 by Amy Tintera

All rights reserved. Printed in the United States of America.
No part of this book may be used or reproduced in any manner
whatsoever without written permission except in the case of brief
quotations embodied in critical articles and reviews. For information
address HarperCollins Children's Books, a division of HarperCollins
Publishers, 195 Broadway, New York, NY 10007.
www.epicreads.com

Library of Congress Cataloging-in-Publication Data
Names: Tintera, Amy, author.
Title: Ruined / by Amy Tintera.
Description: First edition. | New York, NY : HarperTeen, an imprint of
    HarperCollinsPublishers [2016] | Summary: "Emelina Flores
    has nothing. Her home in Ruina has been ravaged by war; her
    parents were killed and her sister was kidnapped. Even though
    Em is only a useless Ruined—completely lacking any magic—
    she is determined to get revenge by infiltrating the enemy's
    kingdom, posing as the crown prince's betrothed"— Provided by
    publisher.
Identifiers: LCCN 2015029173 | ISBN 9780062396617
Subjects: | CYAC: Fantasy. | Revenge—Fiction. | Princesses—Fiction.
    | Love—Fiction. | BISAC: JUVENILE FICTION / Fantasy
    & Magic. | JUVENILE FICTION / Love & Romance. |
    JUVENILE FICTION / Royalty.
Classification: LCC PZ7.T4930 Ru 2016 | DDC [Fic]—dc23 LC record
    available at http://lccn.loc.gov/2015029173

Typography by Torborg Davern
18 19 20 21   PC/LSCC   10 9 8 7 6 5 4 3 2
❖
First paperback edition, 2017

RUINED

ONE

THE WHEELS OF the carriage creaked as they rolled across the dirt road. The noise echoed through the quiet forest.

Em crouched behind a tree, tightening each finger individually around her sword. A squirrel darted across the road and disappeared into the thick brush. She couldn't see the princess or her guards yet.

She glanced over her shoulder to find Damian hiding in a squat behind the bush, his body perfectly still. He didn't even appear to be breathing. That was Damian—incredibly fast or incredibly still, depending on what the situation called for.

Aren was in a tree on the other side of the road from Em, precariously perched atop a branch with his sword drawn.

Both boys stared at her, waiting for her signal.

Em pressed her hand to the tree trunk and peered around it. The sun was setting behind her, and she could see wisps of her breath in the air. She shivered.

The first guard rounded the corner on his horse, easily spotted in his bright yellow-and-black coat. Yellow was the official color of Vallos, the princess's home, but Em would have made them wear black. She would have insisted that several guards scout the area around the carriage.

Apparently the princess wasn't that smart. Or maybe she felt safe in her own country.

Em barely remembered what safe felt like.

She shivered again, but not because of the cold. Every nerve in her body was on high alert.

The carriage rolled down the road behind the first guard, pulled by four horses. There were five guards total. One in front, two on either side, and two in back. All of them were perched on top of horses, swords dangling from their belts. The princess must have been inside the carriage.

Six to three. Em, Damian, and Aren had faced much worse odds.

The guard in front said something to one of the men behind him, and they both laughed. The spot of blue on their chests wasn't clear from this distance, but Em knew what it was. Soldiers who had killed at least ten Ruined wore blue pins. For every ten killed, they received another pin.

The man in front had at least three.

She looked forward to wiping that smile off the guard's face.

Em returned her attention to Damian. She barely nodded.

He stood slowly, a dagger in one hand and a sword in the other. He lifted the dagger and narrowed his eyes at his target.

The blade sailed through the air.

Em jumped up. Damian's dagger sank into the throat of the guard at the side of the carriage; a scream ripped through the air. He toppled off his horse, and the other guards quickly dismounted, swords drawn. The horses neighed loudly, and one of them ran, hooves clomping as it disappeared into the trees.

Aren jumped from his tree and landed on top of two guards, his sword cutting through the air and finding his target.

Damian sprinted for the man trying to block the side door of the carriage. The guard's face was twisted in horror, his fear palpable.

That left only one man—the one in front—and he was staring straight at Em. She clenched her sword tighter as she raced toward him.

He grabbed something off his back. She barely had time to process the bow before the arrow was hurtling straight for her. She darted to one side, but the arrow sliced across her left arm. She gasped at the quick shot of pain, but she didn't have time to let it slow her down.

She broke into a run as he reached for another arrow. He aimed and she dashed out of the way, narrowly missing the second one.

Damian appeared behind him. He drove his sword into the guard's back. The man gasped and fell to his knees.

Em whirled around to find Princess Mary jumping out of the carriage, sword in hand.

A burst of relief exploded in Em's chest as she surveyed the princess. They had the same dark hair and olive skin. Mary had green eyes while Em's were dark. And Mary had small, delicate features, making her pretty in a way Em never would be. But from a distance, most people wouldn't be able to tell them apart.

Em lifted her sword as Mary rushed toward her, but the princess stumbled back suddenly, pulled by an invisible force. Her fingers sprang apart, her sword clattering to the ground.

Aren stood behind Mary, his gaze fixed on her as he used his Ruined magic to keep her in place.

Em had no magic. But she was better than almost anyone with a sword.

She shook her head at Aren, and he released his hold on Mary. She didn't need his help. Em took a small step back, allowing the princess to retrieve her sword.

She wanted to beat the princess, in every sense of the word. She wanted to see Mary's face when she realized Em had bested her.

The anger trickled in at first, hesitant, like perhaps fear was the better emotion right now. But Em embraced the anger, let it swirl and grow until it tightened around her chest and made it hard to breathe.

Em attacked first, and Mary raised her sword to block Em's. The princess kept watch on Damian, but Em knew neither of her friends would jump in to help again unless it was absolutely necessary. They knew she needed to do this herself.

Em lunged at Mary again, spraying dirt into the air. Mary raised her sword and Em ducked, letting the blade sail above her head. She bolted to her feet, slicing her sword across Mary's right arm.

The princess gasped and stumbled, and Em took advantage of the moment of weakness. She launched her sword against Mary's, knocking it out of the princess's hand.

Em took a step forward, aiming the tip of her blade at the princess's neck. Her hands shook, and she gripped her sword tighter. She'd imagined this part of the plan a hundred times, but she hadn't counted on the sick feeling in the pit of her stomach.

"Do you know who I am?" Em asked.

Mary shook her head, her chest heaving up and down.

"I believe you knew my father?" Em said. "You killed him and left his head on a stick for me to find."

Mary pressed her lips together, her eyes darting from Em to the blade at her neck. Her mouth opened, a squeak coming out before she spoke. "I—"

The princess cut herself off and ducked, grabbing for something on her ankle. She bolted upright, a dagger in one hand. She lunged for Em.

Em dove to one side. Panic seized her chest for a moment. If Mary killed her or escaped, the entire plan would crumble.

Mary swung at her again, and Em grabbed her wrist, yanking the arm with the dagger to the sky.

With her other hand, Em drove the sword into the princess's chest.

The blue pins hit the ground with a soft *clink*. Em counted as Damian and Aren ripped them off the coats of the dead Vallos guards. Nine pins total between them. Ninety Ruined killed, just by these five men.

She leaned down and scooped up the pins. The two inter-locking circles symbolized the union of two countries—Lera and Vallos—in their fight against the dangerous Ruined. The sword that cut across the circles symbolized their strength.

Em dropped five pins into Aren's hand. "Put them on your coat."

"But—"

"The Lera guard will respect you more. Actually—" She added one more. "Six. You'll be a star."

Aren's mouth twisted like he'd eaten something sour, but he put the pins back on one of the coats without protest. He slipped one arm through the yellow-and-black coat, then the other. He buttoned the five gold buttons and ran his hand down the front, straightening the material.

"Do I look like a Vallos guard?" He grabbed his sword. "Wait. It's more realistic when I swing my sword around like I have no idea how to use it. Now I look good, right?" He grinned too widely, showing off dimples on both cheeks.

She snorted. "Perfect." She pointed to where blood dotted his dark skin above his eyebrow. "You're bleeding."

Aren swiped at his forehead as Em dropped the remaining three pins in Damian's hand. "Get rid of those. We don't want hunters finding them and getting suspicious."

Damian slipped the pins into his pocket. "I'll burn them with the bodies."

Em's gaze slid to the wagon behind him, where the princess and her guards were piled. A piece of Mary's long dark hair stuck out from beneath the blanket at the back of the wagon, almost touching the dirt.

She looked away from the wagon. Her mother had always said that the only way to find peace was to kill everyone who threatened it. But the tight feeling in Em's chest remained.

"I should take care of the bodies as soon as possible," Damian said quietly.

Em nodded and turned to face Damian, then quickly focused on the ground. He had that expression, the one that made her heart squeeze painfully. It was a mix of sadness and hope and maybe even love.

He stepped forward and she wrapped her arms around him, the familiar smell of him enveloping her. He knew she wasn't capable of returning his feelings. Not now. Revenge swelled and twisted and burned inside of her and left room for nothing else. Sometimes it would simmer down for a while, and she would think it was gone, but it would always return. She would be back in her home, her lungs filled with smoke and her eyes watering as she peered around a corner. Staring as King Salomir pulled his bloody sword out of Em's mother's chest. Hearing her sister's screams as his soldiers dragged her away. Finding her father a few weeks later, after Princess Mary killed him.

Maybe when she killed the king and his family, she'd be able to feel something else. Maybe then she'd be able to look at Damian the same way he looked at her.

She tried to smile at him. A lump had formed in her throat, and the smile probably came out more like a grimace. She watched as Damian said good-bye to Aren.

"I should make it back to the Ruined camp by tomorrow evening," Damian said, stopping next to one of the horses pulling the wagon. He glanced at Em. "Are you sure you don't want me to tell them you're trying to find Olivia? They should know there's a chance their queen may return."

Em shook her head. "Not yet. They voted you as their leader, and they need someone to depend on now. Let's not get their hopes up yet."

Regret flashed across Damian's face at the word "leader." He was a good one, despite his young age. But he only had the position because the Ruined had turned their backs on Em. She might have been heir to the throne with her mother dead and sister missing, but she was useless. Powerless. *Not fit to lead*, a Ruined had said when they demanded Damian take over a year ago.

"Keep them safe," she said. "I'll wait to hear from you."

Damian climbed into the wagon, putting his right fist to his chest and tapping it once. The fist tap was the official Ruina salute to the queen, and something no one but Damian and Aren had ever done for her. Em blinked away tears.

She lifted her hand, waving good-bye, and Damian did the

same. The Ruined marks on his hand and wrist were visible, a reminder of why he couldn't even consider coming with them. The marks let the world know he was a Ruined with power. Em lacked power, so she also lacked Ruined marks.

It was completely dark now, and Damian's figure disappeared quickly, the clomping of hooves echoing through the night.

She turned back to Aren, who was pulling his collar away from his scarred neck. Aren had barely escaped the burning Ruina castle alive, and much of his upper body told the story. They also hid the story of his Ruined magic, as the fire had burned away all traces of his Ruined marks. His marks had been beautiful—white against his dark skin, the thin lines twisting together and creating spirals all over his arms and back and chest.

"Ready?" he asked quietly.

She grasped for her necklace and rubbed her thumb over the silver *O. No.* She'd been planning this for almost a year, but she'd never be ready.

"We should be able to make it to the Lera border by morning," Aren said as he walked to the carriage and climbed up. He gestured behind him. "Do you want to ride in the carriage like a real Vallos princess?"

Em headed for one of the horses. "Not yet. I'll ride a bit ahead and scout the area. I'll get in when we approach the Lera border." She swung one leg over the horse and settled onto the saddle. She glanced over at Aren to see her friend watching her, his head cocked to one side. "What?"

"Your mother would be proud, Em." He bowed his head

slightly at the mention of their dead queen.

"I hope so." The words came out as a whisper. She was certain her mother would be furious that Em had allowed her younger, powerful sister to be taken by the Lera king. Em was supposed to protect Olivia, and she'd failed.

But she would make it right. She would save her sister, and kill the man who had taken her and murdered their mother.

Make people fear you, Emelina. Her mother's words echoed in her head. *Stop worrying about what you don't have and start focusing on what you do. Make people tremble when they hear your name. Fear is your power.*

Wenda Flores had never known the days when the Ruined were feared for their powers and revered as gods, but she longed for those days. She wanted nothing more than to make the humans bow down in terror.

Em lifted her head, fixing her gaze straight ahead.

No one feared Emelina Flores, the useless daughter of the most powerful queen Ruina had ever known.

But they would.

TWO

CAS LEANED BACK, barely avoiding the sword aimed for his neck as he spun away from his opponent. His foot caught on a rock and he stumbled, throwing his arms out to keep from falling on his face.

His opponent's sword poked his chest. That was unfortunate.

"Dead." Galo grinned as he withdrew the dull blade. "Feeling tired, Your Highness?"

Cas took a step back, running a hand through his hair. The sun beat down on them in the castle gardens, and his hair was damp with sweat. "I am a bit tired. It must be from winning the first four times."

The guard spread his arms wide. He was still breathing heavily from the fight. "I like to lull you into a false sense of security first. Then I really start trying."

Cas laughed, transferring his sword to his left hand to roll up the sleeves of his white shirt. His jacket lay on the ground, covered in dirt they'd kicked around while sparring. His mother wasn't going to be pleased.

"Let's go again," he said, lifting his sword.

"Perhaps you should rest a moment." Galo placed his palms on his thighs, letting his sword dangle from his fingers. He let out a long breath. "You look exhausted."

"Yes. It's *me* who looks exhausted."

Galo straightened, glancing back at the castle. The white stone building loomed large next to them, casting a shadow across the gardens. Arched windows lined the rear of the castle, and a maid stuck her head out of one on the second floor, giving a rug a quick pound against the wall.

"Maybe we should stop." Galo gestured at the dusty jacket on the ground. "You're going to smell like dirt and sweat when your new bride arrives."

Cas dropped the sword on top of his jacket, messing it up further. "She's been traveling for days. I'm sure she'll smell as well. We'll be even."

"How very considerate of you, Your Highness."

Galo only called Cas "Your Highness" when he was making fun of him. Cas shot him a mildly amused look. Galo was two years older than him, and in his three years on the guard had become more of a friend than someone who should call him by his formal title.

"Did you hear that Olso warriors are coming to visit after the wedding?" Cas asked.

"I didn't hear that," Galo said, pushing a hand through his dark hair. "Why?"

"Negotiations. They have some issues with a treaty that gave Lera control of their main port after the last war. But I think my father agreed to the visit so he could show off."

"Show off what, exactly?"

"After I'm married, Lera will control Vallos as well as Ruina." Cas laughed. "It is impressive. He can't stop bragging that he's leaving me with two more kingdoms than his father left him. Of course, one of them is Ruina. That one isn't really something to brag about."

"Not unless you're a fan of dead crops and gray skies."

"I asked him if I could visit Ruina, see the mines, but . . ." Cas shrugged. "Maybe it's still too dangerous."

"It's definitely too dangerous," Galo said.

"Casimir? CASIMIR!"

Cas turned at the sound of his mother's voice from inside the castle. She swept out onto the patio of the second-floor library, the skirts of her light-blue dress swishing around her ankles. She planted her hands on her hips.

"She's been spotted at the end of the road," she said.

His heart dropped. "All right."

"You could at least pretend to be excited."

"I am simply alight with excitement and anticipation. I can hardly contain myself, really." He flashed a big fake smile. "How was that?"

Galo covered a laugh with a cough. His mother let out a deeply annoyed sigh and strode back inside.

"I'd better go," he said, grabbing his sword and handing it to Galo. He snatched his coat from the ground, shaking the dirt out.

"Good luck," Galo said, then frowned. "Is that the appropriate thing to say in this situation?"

Cas lifted one shoulder. There wasn't much to say to someone who was headed out to meet the woman he'd been ordered to marry. *Try not to vomit* might have been the best choice.

He gave Galo a tight smile and hopped up the steps, grabbing the handle of the tall wooden door. He threw it open, his eyes adjusting to the dim lighting in the staff dining room. To his left, a boy backed out of the kitchen door, the sound of clanging pans and yells drifting in from behind him. He held a tray of pastries, and he came to an abrupt stop when he spotted the prince.

Cas nodded at the boy, striding past him through the far door and into the hallway. Sunlight streamed in from the wide windows to his right, and the walls in this corridor were almost pink in the afternoon light. Later, they would look red. Every corridor was painted a different color, and when he turned a corner he found two staff members arranging bunches of yellow flowers against the bright-green walls.

The castle buzzed with noise as he walked into the foyer.

More flowers lined the banister of the staircase, and a staff member was wrapping blue ribbons around them. The air was full of anticipation and excitement as the castle staff prepared for the arrival of the new princess. Their bright faces just filled Cas with more dread.

His mother and father stood in front of the door at the main entrance, and he stopped next to them.

"You're all dirty," his mother said, taking his jacket from him. She beat at it with her hand, trying to remove lingering dirt. "Did you have to spar with that guard *before* she arrived?"

The king clapped his son on the arm. "He's just nervous. Working off some energy."

"I am not." Yes, he was.

Maybe *nervous* wasn't the right word. Cas had always known he'd marry someone his parents chose. He'd known, yet he hadn't quite prepared himself for how it would actually feel. Like his stomach was going to drop into his feet and his head would explode from the pounding.

What was the word for that?

"This is as good as it's going to get," his mother said, handing him his coat. He slipped it on.

"*Try* and talk to her?" the king said. "It makes people uncomfortable when you just stand there quietly."

"I don't always have something to say."

"Then think of something," his father said, exasperated.

The queen walked to the door, gesturing for them to follow.

"Come on. Both of you." She let the king slip past her and put a hand on Cas's arm. "Don't worry, Cas. I know she will be quite taken with you."

He shook her hand off but tried to smile like he believed her. *Quite taken with you.* How ridiculous. It was a treaty marriage, and Mary knew as much about him as he did about her. Nothing.

They marched outside into the sunlight, Cas trailing behind his parents. About ten staff members and several members of Cas's guard were waiting in two neat rows.

He walked down the castle steps and took his place next to his father as the gate began to open. He clasped his hands behind his back, then pulled on each finger of his left hand until he felt the knuckle crack. His heart was pounding so loudly it vibrated in his ears. He tried to fix his face into a neutral expression.

A dirt path ran from the castle to the front gate, flanked on either side by lush green grass and perfectly trimmed square hedges. Two guards pulled open the iron gate, scurrying out of the way as Lera's royal escorts came through on their horses.

Behind them was a small carriage that had seen better days. Dirt and mud stuck to the wheels, though that was to be expected after the journey through the Lera jungle. The body was plain gray, with a glass window on either side. The windows were open, and the one closest to Cas looked like it might fall off its hinges at any moment. A curtain had been pulled over the open space, obscuring the inside from view.

A young man in a Vallos uniform sat on the seat at the front of the carriage, reins in hand. Cas expected several more guards to follow him, but he was the only one in Vallos yellow. Strange. Cas always took several guards with him when he traveled.

The Vallos guard pulled the horses to a stop and jumped off the carriage, tugging on the ends of his jacket. His hands were covered in scars, like he'd been burned, and Cas tried not to stare as the man opened the door to the carriage. He'd never seen flesh that mangled before.

A hand emerged from the carriage first, and the guard took it, stepping back as a dark head appeared.

Princess Mary jumped out of the carriage, disregarding the step and kicking up some dirt in the process.

She was tall with long legs and wore a yellow dress that stretched tightly across her chest. It was also too short, revealing a bit of ankle, and Cas wondered if she'd recently grown taller or just had a terrible seamstress. A few strands of her dark hair had come loose from their tie, giving her a wild, disheveled look.

"Rumors of her beauty were . . . exaggerated," his father muttered.

Cas actually had known one thing about Mary, as her parents had written before they died, saying she was "beautiful" and "lovely" and "so pretty and delicate." But the girl in front of them wasn't any of those things. She was sharp angles and hard lines. Nothing about her seemed delicate at all.

The guard sort of waved his hand in Mary's direction. He clearly wasn't the one who usually introduced her. "Princess Mary Anselo of Vallos." Cas had thought they might refer to her as "Queen Mary," but technically she hadn't ascended to the

Vallos throne following her parents' death. Vallos belonged to Cas's father now.

Mary's gaze immediately slid to Cas. She had dark, intense eyes, framed by long lashes. The skin beneath them was a bit dark as well, making her look either tired or angry. Maybe both.

Cas bowed his head slightly in greeting, then focused his attention on the trees in the distance. He was less likely to jump out of his skin if he didn't make eye contact.

The herald stepped forward and swept his arm out toward the king. "His Majesty, King Salomir Gallegos. Her Majesty, Queen Fabiana Gallegos. And His Highness, Prince Casimir Gallegos."

"It's lovely to meet you, Mary," his mother said, bowing her head, then stepping forward and clasping Mary's hands in her own. The girl seemed surprised by this, and she leaned back, as if she wanted to run away.

Cas couldn't blame her. He was contemplating running himself.

"It's lovely to meet you as well," Mary said quietly.

The king beamed at her in that way he always did with women. "A pleasure."

One side of Mary's mouth turned up in something like a smile. Or a grimace. Cas found it difficult to read the expressions on her face.

"This is my guard, Aren," Mary said as the young man took a step forward.

"Did you bring only one?" The king's tone held a note of suspicion.

"Many of the Vallos guards have been sent to hunt down the Ruined," Mary said. "A few more escorted me to the Lera border, but I thought it best to send them back where they were needed." Her lips did something that still wasn't quite a smile. "You have so many excellent guards here in Lera."

"How true." The king grinned broadly as he beckoned to Julio, the captain of Cas's guard. "Take Aren inside and show him his quarters."

Aren threw his bag over his shoulder and followed Julio into the castle.

Both his parents turned to Cas, like they expected him to say something, and his mouth went dry.

Mary stared at him as if she expected something as well, and he had the sudden urge to never speak again. He squarely met her gaze and immediately felt as if they were having a competition to see who would become uncomfortable first. Cas was confident he would win that competition, every time.

"Excellent," the queen said. The king widened his eyes at his son. His mother extended her arm, slipping it through Mary's as she steered her toward the castle. "Will your things be along shortly?"

"Everything I have is in that carriage." She didn't say it like she was ashamed of it. Cas took another glance at the small carriage. There couldn't have been more than one trunk in there.

"That's all right, it's nice to start fresh," the queen said smoothly. "I'll have someone sent up immediately to get your measurements. I heard you're very fond of dresses?"

"Who isn't?" Mary asked.

Cas watched as they climbed the front steps and disappeared through the massive wooden doors. He'd said nothing to her at all, he realized. Maybe he should have at least asked her how her journey was, or if she needed anything.

The king sighed. "I suppose you could have done worse than Mary."

"We should ask the priest to say that at the wedding," Cas said. "'And now we unite Casimir and Mary. They both could have done worse.'"

THREE

A KNOCK ON the door made Em's eyes fly open. She gasped
and scrambled upright, the sheets tangled between her feet. She
rolled off the bed, yelping and hitting the ground with a thud.

She winced, pushing her hair out of her face. She was surprised she'd fallen asleep at all. She'd still been awake when the
sun started peeking through the curtains, unable to sleep in a
castle full of her enemies. She'd spent almost a year planning to
infiltrate the castle, but the reality of being surrounded by people
who would kill her if they discovered her true identity was more
unsettling than anticipated.

"Your Highness?" a voice called from behind the door.

She got to her feet, straightening her nightgown. "Yes?"

The door opened to reveal Davina, one of her maids, carrying a tray of food. *One* of her maids. The life these people led was ridiculous. Em's mother hadn't employed maids.

A maid is a potential spy, her mother used to say.

Davina held up the tray. "I brought your breakfast, Your Highness. And the queen has requested your presence." She put the tray on the table in the corner and turned back to Em, a smile on her young, pretty face. There was one knife on the tray, and Em studied it, trying to judge how sharp it was. Three quick steps across the room and she could reach around Davina for the knife to jab it in her throat before she knew what was happening. Five seconds, tops.

Em shook the thought away. She didn't need to kill her maid at the moment. "Requested my presence for what?"

"The wedding dress fitting, Your Highness."

"Oh. Right." She tried not to look like the thought of her wedding dress made her want to throw up.

"And the Union Battle is this afternoon," Davina said. "The queen wants to do the fitting first."

Was she supposed to know what the *Union Battle* was? It didn't sound good, whatever it was.

"Of course," Em said. "I'll get ready quickly."

Davina made a move like she was going to stay and help, and Em shook her head.

"I'm fine for now. I'll call you in when I'm almost ready?"

Davina hesitated, then walked to the door. "I'll wait right outside?"

"Yes, please," Em said.

Em sighed as Davina disappeared through the door. The maid had left tea and a thick slice of oddly colored bread on the tray. Em broke off a chunk and popped it in her mouth. It was sweet and delicious, and she quickly finished the whole piece. She hadn't had much good food for the past year.

She looked around her room. She'd rarely even had a bed for the past year, and now she had a sitting room, an office, and a bedroom. The large window on one wall showed off a lovely view of the gardens. The room had been decorated in blue, Lera's official color. The chair in the corner was blue, the tapestry on the wall was blue, and the sheets on the bed were blue.

It was all pristine and beautiful, and Em wanted to rip it to shreds. They lived like this while the Ruined were forced out of their homes and had to move camp every few days just to stay alive?

She'd have to make sure to burn down the castle before she was done. She could still smell the smoke from the day the king had burned her home to the ground, killed her mother, and taken her sister. It was only right to repay the favor.

She drained her tea and pulled out a hideous pink dress of Mary's. The weather in Vallos was much cooler than Lera, and the people were often completely covered from neck to toe. Mary's dresses were long-sleeved, stiff, and made more for function than fashion. They were wildly depressing.

Like the dress she'd worn yesterday, this one felt too short and tight as she pulled it on. But the fullness of the skirt hid the ill fit well enough.

Her necklace hung in the center of her chest, and she closed her fingers around it for a moment. The silver *O* was for Olivia, and she'd considered leaving it behind when she became Mary. But she'd worn the necklace every day since returning to the remains of her castle and finding it among the rubble. If she ever found Olivia, she would return it to her.

When she found Olivia. She didn't know why the king had taken her sister instead of simply killing her, but nothing would stop her from figuring it out and rescuing Olivia.

She let go of the necklace, the pendant falling against her chest. If anyone asked, she could simply say it was a circle. A gift from her parents.

She pulled her hair back, looping it into a simple knot behind her head. Davina returned and buttoned the back of the dress, then escorted her out of her rooms.

Aren stood near her door with two guards, outfitted in a blue-and-white Lera guard uniform. She had to resist the urge to rush over to him. Aren had been by her side constantly for the past year, and she felt as though she'd lost a limb without him nearby.

Em wanted to ask him how he was settling in, if he'd found out anything, if anyone suspected something odd, but Davina quickly brushed past him and the other guards. The maid did take a quick glance over her shoulder at Aren, a blush creeping over her cheeks when he smiled at them. Em suppressed a laugh. The list of girls blushing over Aren never ended.

Em and Davina rounded several corners, and Em immediately

lost track of where they were. The hallways were all the same except for the vibrant colors on the walls that changed each time they turned. The castle was laid out in a square, so at least it was a comfort to know that when she inevitably got lost, she could keep turning corners and end up back where she started.

Deep blue rugs ran down the center of the floors, and light spilled across the floors from the large windows. The windows were open and faced the east, so the ocean was barely visible. A cool, salty breeze blew through the hallways. Lera was much warmer than Vallos or Ruina, the sky completely cloudless. She could see why the people of Lera had forced out the Ruined generations ago so that they could remain. She wouldn't want to leave this place either.

Davina stopped and rapped on a large wooden door. It was quickly opened by a young woman, and the maid scurried away.

The woman escorted Em inside. The queen stood in the center of the room, her bright-red gown in contrast to the cream-colored outfits the two women next to her wore.

The large room featured racks of dresses, pants, blouses, and a wall entirely of shoes. The queen's closet. She couldn't help but hope that she'd get to experience that kind of wardrobe during her stay. If she had to deal with these people, she could at least wear some beautiful clothes while doing it.

Em scanned the room for weapons. A mirror was attached to one wall, but it was too large for her to break. There was a large platter of fruit on the table, and the white ceramic plate was likely sturdy enough to do some damage when smashed against a skull.

One, three, six steps and she could weave around the maids to get to the far corner of the room—grab the plate, duck a maid, smash it against the queen's head, spin around and push a maid away, use an edge of the broken plate to cut a jagged line across the queen's throat. Dead.

"Mary," the queen said, extending her arms to her.

Em clenched her fingers into a fist, fighting back the urge to scream. She hadn't counted on how difficult it would be to stand in the presence of the people who had destroyed her life. When she'd stepped out of the carriage yesterday, she'd almost grabbed Aren's sword and swung it at the king's head.

She took in a slow breath. Calm. Steady. Her mother was the scariest woman she'd ever known—the scariest woman most people had ever known—and it was partly because she never lost her temper. If she wanted to kill you, you didn't know it until the knife was already in your gut.

Em needed to be like her mother right now.

Perhaps the queen realized Em didn't want to be hugged, because she took both of Em's hands instead and squeezed them. When she smiled, the small half-circle scar on her left cheek moved. It was the only interesting thing on an otherwise boringly beautiful face.

"How was your first night? Were your rooms adequate?"

"They were perfect, Your Majesty," Em said.

"Please, call me Fabiana," the queen said, dropping Em's hands. "We'll be family soon."

"Of course." Fabiana was a terrible name, so Em would be

happy to call her by it.

"What do you think of Lera so far?" the queen asked. "Different than Vallos, isn't it? Less dreary."

"Much less," Em said, noting the subtle dig at Vallos. "And how does Lera compare to Olso? I hear it's cold there."

Fabiana barely lifted one eyebrow. "Lera is less . . . rigid."

"I'm sure it is." Em had never visited Olso, but she knew the warriors—the group of men and women who protected the country—well. Fabiana used to be one of them, before she defected to Lera, bringing secret information with her. She was probably the most famous traitor in all of Olso. Em had reminded the warriors of Fabiana's betrayal when she approached them about partnering with her. They'd happily agreed to join Em's mission.

The door opened, and a dark-haired girl stepped into the room.

"Jovita!" the queen exclaimed. "I'm glad you could join us."

Em took a long look at the king's niece. She was second in line to the Lera throne. Though she was around the same age as Em, something about the way she carried herself made her seem much older. She was a little shorter than Em but still had a formidable look about her. Her shoulders were broad and strong, her arm muscles rippling beneath her thin gray tunic every time she moved, and she didn't smile much, though Em didn't think it was because she was unhappy. She just seemed like the kind of girl who didn't smile simply to make others feel comfortable.

"I thought I'd stop by and see how our new princess is settling in." She strode across the room to the tray of fruit and popped a grape in her mouth. Em frowned. It would be very difficult to get to her weapon of choice with Jovita standing in front of it.

"Perfect timing. She's about to try on the dress." The queen gestured to the maids and one of the women scurried away, returning with a pile of blue material so high it almost covered her face.

"If you could take your clothes off, please, Mary," the queen said with a wave of her hand.

One of the girls began unbuttoning her pink monstrosity, and Em ducked her head to hide her flaming cheeks as the dress fell to the ground. Perhaps these women often undressed in front of total strangers, but Em had never been in her underwear in front of anyone but her mother and sister.

"We'll take your measurements and have some more clothes brought to you," the queen said as the girls took away Mary's dress. Em detected a hint of disdain as the queen examined the garment. She was suddenly very fond of it.

The girls held open the blue dress for Em and she quickly stepped in, eager to be covered again. The fabric was cool and smooth against her skin, and it flared out from her waist extravagantly. The ruched bodice hugged her torso, and a beautiful chain of beads wrapped around the waistline. It was elegant in its simplicity, and Em gingerly touched the soft fabric.

"Oh yes, that's lovely."

Em looked up to see the queen standing next to the mirror. She stepped in front of it and her reflection stared back at her. The dress was even more stunning when she could see it in its full glory. It was the most beautiful dress she'd ever seen. Olivia would have clapped and done a happy dance if she'd been there.

Tears pricked her eyes. "I'm sorry," she said as one slipped down her cheek. She quickly wiped it away.

"You wish your mother were here?" the queen guessed.

Em nodded. The real Mary probably would have cried for her dead family too. Perhaps any girl in this situation would have cried, regardless of the status of her mother. She had to marry Casimir, after all.

Cas. The name made her insides clench. They'd barely spoken yesterday, and she really hoped he planned to ignore her entirely. His parents had arranged this marriage; maybe he had a girl somewhere who he loved, and he would pretend Em didn't exist.

When she'd concocted this plan, she'd known, in the back of her mind, that she'd have to deal with the wedding night. Sex was generally expected immediately following a wedding, which meant that tomorrow night she'd have to be in Cas's bed. She'd never been in anyone's bed.

She just wouldn't think about it. She still had another day until the wedding, and pretending the issue didn't exist seemed the best course of action.

Perhaps she'd focus on her plan to kill him instead. She needed Cas, at least for a little while, but she hoped to dispose of him before leaving Lera. She'd kill him before the king and queen, so they could experience a bit of the pain she'd felt when her family died.

"I'm sorry," Em said, trying to compose herself. "I love the dress."

"Of course you do," the queen said. "I have excellent taste."

Em laughed despite herself, which earned a smile of approval from the queen.

The women took some measurements and put pins in the garment, then helped Em out of it.

"Have you spoken to Cas much since arriving?" the queen asked as Em slipped the pink dress back on.

"Only a little," Em replied. If him saying hello to her yesterday at dinner counted.

"Don't worry, you'll warm up to each other soon." The queen's lips twitched, as if she was thinking something she didn't want to share. "Have you been told about the Union Battle?"

"Not that I recall," Em said carefully, not sure if Mary was supposed to have that information. A maid pulled her dress tighter, trying to button it, and she sucked in a breath.

"It's a traditional part of a royal Lera wedding," the queen said. "The royal's intended battles someone of his or her choice for the entertainment of everyone. With dull blades, of course."

Em tried to hide a smile. That sounded exactly like her kind of wedding festivities.

"The point is to prove your worth and skill in battle," Jovita said. "I, for one, am looking forward to it. You know, the queen beat the captain of the king's guard at her battle. It was a very tough choice of competitor, and she demolished him. Everyone still talks about it."

"Jovita, stop," the queen said lightly. "You'll make her nervous." She patted Em's hand. "You're allowed to pick whomever you want, dear."

The condescension was so thick Em almost laughed. It was just like the Lera royal family to think they had everyone beat.

"I was ordered to kill the Ruined king in order to marry Cas. You don't think that proved my worth and skill in battle?" Em lied, swallowing down a wave of nausea. Mary murdering her father had been nothing more than a test to these people.

"Then I guess today won't be a challenge at all," Jovita said. Her smile didn't falter, but her eyes flicked to the queen's.

"Are you done?" the queen asked the maid who was fastening the last button. "Let's call for Cas."

"Oh, you don't have to do that," Em said quickly.

"We'll just have him escort you back to your room," the queen said with an amused expression. "He can't avoid you forever, after all." She told one of the maids to fetch him.

Em sighed and ran a hand over her hair. A glance in the mirror confirmed that she appeared tired and pale (and utterly ridiculous in the too-small pink dress), and she hoped Cas found her exceedingly unattractive.

The door opened only a few moments later to reveal Cas, wearing an expression like someone was poking him in the back with hot knives. He appeared angry, bored, or both. He glanced at her briefly but said nothing, and she shifted uncomfortably. She suspected he made everyone uncomfortable.

But he was handsome in a way that was hard to ignore,

unfortunately. He had his father's dark hair but his mother's blue eyes, and together the effect was striking. The king had an olive complexion much like Em's; the queen had slightly paler skin. Cas fell somewhere in the middle, his skin tanned from the constant Lera sun. He wore a thin white shirt with the sleeves rolled up to his elbows, and she could see muscle definition through the material. She quickly averted her gaze.

"You requested my presence, Mother?" When he finally spoke it was stiff, almost angry.

"I thought it would be nice if you escorted Mary back to her room. We've finished fitting her wedding dress."

Cas didn't glance at Em for even a moment. "Of course."

"Lovely talking with you, dear," the queen said. Jovita smirked, obviously still pleased with herself for throwing the new princess off balance.

Em murmured a polite reply as she stepped away from the mirror. Cas extended his arm out to her, and she took it, trying not to grimace at the contact.

Cas turned to the door so suddenly that Em almost stumbled when he tugged her forward. She grasped his arm tighter, quickly regaining her footing before she embarrassed herself by falling down at his feet.

"How was your journey to Lera?" he asked as he steered her down the hall.

"It was fine, thank you." Honestly, she was exhausted and her body still ached from days on the back of a horse. After meeting the Lera guards at the border, it had taken several days to get to the castle with that stupid heavy carriage in tow.

"And your rooms are adequate?" he asked.

"They're very nice."

He nodded once, and then didn't attempt any further conversation. Em didn't know whether to be relieved or think he was incredibly rude, so she kept her mouth shut as well.

Two guards and one maid passed them in the hallway, and she eyed the swords at the guards' hips. Disarming a member of the Lera guard wouldn't be easy. She'd probably have better luck yanking a rope off the curtains and using it to strangle Cas. Strangulation took awhile, so she'd have to pull him into a deserted room or corner for at least a full minute.

He stopped in front of her door, and she slipped her arm out of his. "Thank you," she said, grasping the door handle.

"You've been told about the Union Battle this afternoon?" he asked.

"I have. Sounds like fun."

He lifted one eyebrow, a hint of amusement crossing his face. "I'm glad you think so." He lowered his voice. "I have it on good authority that one of the guards drank too much last night and isn't feeling very well today. He has a red beard and a lot of freckles, if you're looking for an easy choice."

She blinked, unsure if this was some kind of trap. "Am I supposed to want the easy choice?" The queen and Jovita had just given her the opposite impression.

"Well, it will make you look good." He took a step back. His face was far less annoying when he smiled. "I won't tell, I promise."

"Th-thank you?" This felt like a trick. King Salomir seized every opportunity to prove Lera was the best, and it seemed this was no exception. They wanted her to fail so they could all laugh about her lack of skills in battle.

The edges of Cas's mouth twitched, further convincing her that this tip was his way of trying to embarrass her in front of everyone.

"I'll keep that in mind." She wrapped her fingers around his arm and gazed at him steadily. "How kind of you to help me."

He took a step back, clearing his throat. "Uh, sure. I'll see you later." He turned on his heel and strode down the hallway.

She smirked at his back. He was going to have to work much harder to fool her.

FOUR

THE UNION BATTLE was held in the Glory Ballroom, which Davina explained to Em was the smallest of the three ballrooms. It was still impressively big, with a square wooden floor in the center and purple carpet along the sides. Members of the guard were already lined up along the walls, and spectators stood in front of them. The only chairs were the large ones at the front of the room that were obviously for the royal family. The kitchen staff was outside, ready to bring in food and drink after the battle.

Em had changed into black pants and a formfitting black shirt for the occasion. They were her own clothes, and she stretched her arms out with a relieved sigh, the soft fabric moving with her.

Swords hung off the hips of every member of the guard. There were fifty guards in the room, easily. Even if she surprised one and took his sword, she'd probably kill one or two—at most—before they cut her down. She swallowed and tried not to think about it.

She found Aren in the crowd. He seemed calm, his expression neutral as a guard said something to him.

His brown eyes were bright, though, alive in a way Em hadn't seen since . . . ever, actually. A Ruined was fueled by the energy around him or her, and in Aren's case, the energy of every human in the castle. After a few weeks he'd probably be able to crush the bones of ten men before his energy was drained. That was the hope, anyway.

Various maps hung on the walls. She stood on her toes to peer at the one closest to her. It was dated around the same time as the war between Lera and Olso two generations ago. All four countries were on this map—Lera to the east, Vallos just below it, and Olso to the west of Lera. To the south of Olso was her home, Ruina.

It seemed unlikely they'd just write *Olivia* on a map to advertise her location, but she squinted at it anyway, just to be sure. She moved to the next one.

"Mary!" The queen stood in the doorway of the ballroom, an annoyed expression on her face. "Please come out here. You'll make an entrance with Cas."

Em walked to the door, brushing past the queen to find Cas leaning against the wall, his arms crossed over his chest. He still looked as though someone was poking him with hot knives, but now he'd grown bored of it. Painful boredom. That was the prince.

"If you don't know where to put her, don't just dump her any-where," the queen chastised Davina, who was wringing her hands at Fabiana's side. "Bring her to me, if you must."

"Yes, Your Majesty."

The queen disappeared into the ballroom, the maids scur-rying after her. Em watched the doors swing closed, silence descending onto the hallway.

"We'll go in when my father arrives." Cas leaned away from the wall and glanced both ways, like he hoped that moment was now.

She nodded, rubbing her thumb across her necklace. He watched her, his eyes flicking from her face to her hand.

"Are you nervous?" he asked.

She quickly dropped the necklace, sliding her hands into her pockets instead. "No."

"This doesn't really mean anything. It's just tradition."

"If it didn't mean anything, you wouldn't do it." She met his gaze. "Have you always used dull blades?"

"Of course."

"Why? Are you afraid the bride or groom will win, and one of your own will die?"

"I think we're more concerned that they'd lose, and we'd have to find a replacement."

His mouth twitched, and she almost laughed. "Me bleeding out on the floor would put a damper on the wedding tomorrow," she said.

Amusement crossed his features, and he hesitated for a beat

too long. Perhaps he was reconsidering the use of dull blades. "Yes, it would."

"Mary!"

Em's heart jumped at the sound of the king's booming voice. He strode down the hallway, his lips pulled into an almost comically wide grin. His smile was too big, like it was trying to conquer the rest of his features.

King Salomir and Cas were about the same height, but the king was larger and broader, with a neat dark beard. Some would find him handsome. Em did not.

"Are you ready for the battle?" he asked.

"Looking forward to it."

He laughed and clapped a hand on her shoulder. She considered breaking a few of his fingers.

He dropped the hand and headed for the ballroom, beckoning for them to follow him. He threw open the door in a dramatic fashion, sweeping his arms out like his admirers were free to adore him now. "Welcome to the Union Battle!" he yelled.

Cheers erupted from the crowd. Em trailed behind Cas and his father as they crossed the room. The king gestured for her to stop in the middle of the floor. He and Cas continued to the front of the room, standing with the queen and Jovita.

The king waited for the cheers to die down before he spoke again. "Today we celebrate the union of my son, Prince Casimir, and Princess Mary of Vallos. If this is your first Union Battle, the rules are simple. Our future princess will pick someone to battle. They will use swords only. The first one to make three fatal strikes will be the winner. I will call out each strike as they are made." He looked at Em. "Mary, you have your choice of any member of my or Cas's guard as your opponent. Or"—his lips quivered with amusement—"you can pick any member of the royal family, with the exception of Cas. But be warned, those who pick a member of the royal family usually live to regret it. If you have any doubt about your skills, I don't recommend it."

That last statement was a challenge. Em knew it. Every person in the room knew it.

She surveyed the guard. She found the man with a red beard and freckles. He was a bit pale.

She turned back to the front. She could take the king up on his own challenge. Or the queen, who'd been trained as a warrior in Olso.

Or Jovita. Em knew less about her skills, though as a member of the Lera royal family she would have had intense training in every type of combat. She'd certainly made her doubts about Em's skills clear.

Jovita raised both eyebrows as Em stared at her. The king laughed.

She glanced back down the line to see Cas subtly shaking his head at her.

The point is to prove your worth and skill in battle—

"Jovita," she said quickly.

The king laughed again. "A bold choice. You'll be nursing your bruises all night, I suspect."

"Yes, she will," Jovita said with a grin. She walked across the wood floor, stopping in front of Em. "Don't worry," she whispered. "I'll keep the bruises to the lower half of your body, so you'll still look pretty for your wedding day."

"Good luck trying."

Jovita smirked as a man brought them dull swords. Em took hers, relieved to have a sword again, even if it wasn't a real one.

"And I'd like to remind you that this is supposed to be entertaining, so please, make it a bit theatrical," the king said as he sat down in his chair.

Em gripped the sword, getting a feel for the weapon. It was heavier than the one she'd had to leave with Damian, but not by much. Jovita took a few steps around in a circle, swinging the blade back and forth.

Em glanced at the three people sitting at the front of the room. The king sat back in his chair, a wide smile plastered across his face. The queen was vaguely interested, her hands folded in her lap.

Cas leaned forward, his eyes bright as he nodded at her. Was he giving her encouragement? She wished he'd stop.

"On the count of three," the king said.

Em focused her attention on Jovita. If she didn't win this battle, she was going to have to look at that cocky expression for the rest of her stay in Lera. She needed to win. She needed to see Jovita down on her knees, a sword pressed to her throat.

"Three . . . two . . . one."

Em stepped to her left as Jovita approached. It was a slow, careful approach, like the kind Em often saw the most skilled hunters use. The new ones charged her; the veterans took their time.

They circled for only a moment before Em made the first strike. The room was quiet, the sound of metal meeting metal echoing through the room.

Someone cheered as they began, and others joined in. Jovita took two quick steps forward, and Em barely blocked the sword before it swiped across her neck. She jumped backward, ducking Jovita's second attack and rolling across the floor to move to the other side of her. She darted forward, tapping the blade to the center of the girl's back.

"One for Mary," the king said, a hint of surprise in his tone. The crowd cheered.

One. The first one. Em bounced on the balls of her feet. She'd needed to be first.

Jovita's amused expression had faded when she whirled around. She had clearly decided to take Em seriously, and a thrill of excitement ran down Em's spine.

She blocked Jovita's next attack, the crowd roaring as the women circled around, barely blocking each other's blades. When Jovita faked right, Em fell for it, and the girl jabbed her sword into Em's chest.

"One for Jovita."

Em barely had time to take a breath before Jovita was coming for her again. The faces and noise around her started to fade away, her focus entirely on the girl in front of her. Her mother had made her practice different types of combat every day when she was younger, and she found fighting almost comforting.

You were born useless, but you don't have to be helpless, her mother used to say.

Em saw an opening and poked her sword straight at Jovita's stomach, narrowly missing getting a jab in the neck.

"Two for Mary," the king said.

She took a step back, darting away from Jovita. She skirted around the edge of the floor until Jovita growled in frustration. Em darted back into the fight. Sometimes a moment to clear her head was helpful.

Jovita came at her so quickly she barely saw the movement. The blade was pointed straight at her forehead.

"Two for Jovita."

So much for clearing her head.

She spun around, getting a better place on the floor so Jovita wouldn't be able to back her into a corner. She was breathing a bit heavily now, but she was more relaxed than she'd been since her arrival yesterday. She'd have to find someone to spar with every day, or she might lose her mind in this castle.

Em blocked Jovita's sword once, twice, three times. Em ducked and dodged, suddenly feeling better than when she'd begun to fight. She darted around the floor, a smile starting to appear on her face.

When she saw the opening, she used one quick well-placed kick to the legs to bring Jovita down to her knees. Em jumped in front of her, aiming her blade directly at Jovita's neck. Cheers and applause erupted around the room.

"Mary wins," the king yelled over the noise.

Em kept her sword at Jovita's neck a beat longer than was necessary. She couldn't kill her with this sword, but she pictured it for a moment.

Em swallowed, stepping back and lowering her sword. Jovita got to her feet, a hint of amusement on her face.

"I suppose it serves me right for underestimating you?"

Em laughed, pretending to be good-natured about it. She turned away from the girl.

"Yes, it does," she muttered under her breath.

FIVE

CAS WAS SWEATING under his suit. The windows to the Grand Hall were open and a cool ocean breeze blew through them, but he was stuck in the small, stuffy waiting room right next door with his parents. He thought he might melt before the wedding began.

"You look nervous," his father said as he adjusted his son's collar.

"I do not."

"Well, you have no expression on your face at all, which means you're nervous."

Cas cocked an eyebrow. His father had a way of making everyone smile, and he tried not to give in too easily.

"I don't think she likes you much," the king said with a chuckle.

The queen let out an annoyed breath and patted her elaborate hairdo. Her dark hair was piled so high on her head, it must have been painful. "She likes him fine. Just yesterday she was asking if I thought he liked her."

"And what did you say?" the king asked.

"I told her the truth. That I didn't think he'd decided."

His father took his mother's arm. "That must have made her feel much better."

It was not unlike his mother to be brutally honest, though she also knew the value of a well-timed lie. Cas was surprised she hadn't reassured Mary with a lie about how he'd been instantly taken with her and was too shy to say so.

But perhaps it didn't matter if she knew the truth. They were getting married, regardless of whether or not he liked her.

Or whether or not she liked him. She'd looked at him like he was a bug under her shoe yesterday when he'd given her the tip about the Union Battle.

The priest opened the door, his bright-orange robes swinging around his ankles. "We're ready to begin."

Cas turned away from his parents and marched past the priest and into the Grand Hall. The room featured an impressive view of Lera all the way to the ocean through the floor-to-ceiling windows to his left, and flowers and sheer white ribbons lined each of the packed benches down the center.

He entered so suddenly that the rows of people all jumped to their feet at once, the wooden benches creaking and feet scrambling against the floor. He clasped his hand around his other arm and faced the aisle. He hoped she walked quickly.

His parents entered behind him and took their seats on the front bench, next to Jovita. All three of them had expressions on their faces like they were happy about something. Cas tried not to look at them.

The guests shuffled back into their seats, and Cas surveyed the room. Each guest held a cup of wine, which wasn't customary, but his father must have thought the ceremony could use some livening up. He wasn't wrong.

The guests were smiling and whispering, and it smelled like the end of a party, not the beginning. Like alcohol and disappointment and a reminder that tomorrow held a hangover and the usual drudgery.

How appropriate, Cas thought.

The door at the back of the room opened, and everyone stood and turned to face Mary. Her gown was a deep, vibrant blue that caught the light as she walked, and her dark hair was piled on top of her head with an intricate series of pearls woven around the strands. The sleeves of the dress just barely covered her shoulders, and her olive skin looked soft and almost luminous.

Traditionally the mother and father walked on either side of the bride, but she was alone. He knew his parents must have offered to walk with her, and she must have declined. He could understand why.

He attempted a cheerful expression, but she seemed so

miserable he found it hard to meet her eyes. He focused on a spot beyond her head as she made her quick descent down the aisle.

She stopped in front of him and did not smile. Her lips moved in a way that was meant to convey happiness, but her expression was something closer to terror. They turned to the priest.

"Let us give thanks to the ancestors who built our world," the priest said.

Cas bowed his head, fiddling with a string on the bottom of his jacket.

"We pray to Boda, with thanks for the body she created for us," the priest continued. "To Lelana for the fruitful land she bestowed on Lera. To Solia, for the soul that makes us human. And we pray for relief from the monstrous Ruined, who corrupted your gifts."

Out of the corner of his eye, Cas saw Mary's head lift slightly, and he glanced over at her. She was fidgeting, twisting her fingers around, and she quickly stopped when she caught Cas's eye.

The ceremony dragged on. Cas didn't know why the priest felt the need to drone on about love and marriage and sacrifice when he knew very well this was a treaty marriage. It was almost rude.

"And to seal this union," the priest finally said, signaling they were nearing the end, "we unite our souls with the elements."

Cas put out his hands, palms down, and Em did the same. The priest sprinkled a light dusting of dirt on their hands, followed by a splash of water.

"And we unite our souls with a kiss, to be bound until death.

May this union be blessed by the ancestors."

Cas turned to Mary. Her hands were shaking so violently it made her shoulders twitch. She took in a ragged breath, swallowing hard. He'd never made anyone tremble in fear before, and this was possibly the worst moment ever to experience it for the first time.

He leaned forward, and their eyes met briefly as she tilted her head up to his. He barely brushed his lips across hers, and the spectators burst into applause.

Cas slid his gaze to where Mary was seated at his right. She'd eaten her food, and she kept turning her wineglass around in her hands but never took a sip.

The room bustled with noise around them. Tables made a half circle around the edge of the Majestic Hall, and a dance floor stretched out in front of them, with the musicians at the other end. The wedding guests were a flurry of color around them—red and orange and green gowns spinning to the music, the men in mostly white or tan, with bursts of color in the forms of flowers on their lapels. No one wore blue, as that was reserved for Em's dress and the blue flower on Cas's gray jacket.

A man approached the head table to offer his congratulations, and Mary plastered a polite expression on her face. He was beginning to know it well—pursed lips, head tilted to the side like she was captivated by the conversation (she wasn't), and a sigh of relief as the person walked away.

Galo stood with the other guards against the wall to Cas's

right. Cas pushed out of his chair and stood.

"I'll be back," he said in the general direction of his parents, then quickly walked away before they could protest. He said a brief hello to the governor of the southern province, so he could at least say he was greeting guests if his parents asked.

Galo stepped away from the wall as soon as Cas approached. They walked a few steps from the rest of the guards, out of earshot, and Cas watched as the people in front of them began dancing to a lively song.

"I don't know who looks more miserable, you or your wife," Galo said, a hint of amusement in his voice.

Cas winced at the word *wife*. His father had a wife. All the advisers and governors had husbands or wives. The word didn't feel like something that should be part of Cas's life.

"Can you blame us? She just arrived two days ago." Cas scanned the room until he found Aren. The guard's gaze followed Mary, and it occurred to Cas that perhaps he was more than a guard or a friend.

"Have you gotten to know Aren at all?" he asked, trying to keep his voice casual.

"A little. He's clearly not in love with Mary, if that's what you're asking. He's already made an impression on a couple of female guards."

Cas shrugged, unwilling to admit that he cared if Mary was in love with someone else.

"He's a bit strange," Galo continued. "He's got six pins."

"So?"

"So it means he's killed sixty Ruined, but he's got the demeanor of a new hunter," Galo said. "The ones who can't handle it and come back after the first couple of kills and beg to be reassigned."

"What are the hunters like?" Cas asked, turning to him in interest. Galo had never spoken about meeting hunters. Cas couldn't imagine killing sixty people and then putting a reminder of it on his chest, but the Ruined weren't exactly *people*. Still, he wasn't sure he would be proud of it.

"The new ones are usually very much like Aren. Damaged. Terrified." Galo tilted his head toward Aren. "He jumps at loud noises and never takes off his weapon, even when we're drinking or exercising. He's on edge all the time, and he never brags about those pins, even when one of the guards pressed him to. The hunters with that many pins . . ." Galo shook his head, a sour expression crossing his face. "They aren't damaged. They usually enjoy hunting down the Ruined. They're confident, not scared."

Cas glanced at Aren again. "He could have stolen them. Put them on to try and impress us."

"It's likely," the guard said. "Don't put him on an important assignment until I can get to know him better. At the very least he's too traumatized to be in any kind of intense situation."

"I won't. Thank you." The word *traumatized* thumped in his brain, making him wonder for the first time how many hunters were currently being employed. Most came from Lera prisons, but there were some from Vallos as well. What would those people do, after they'd killed all the Ruined? Would they be expected to go back to their normal lives like nothing had happened?

"Mary looks very pretty tonight, don't you think?" Galo's words snapped Cas back to the present.

"Yes."

"Have you spoken to her much?" Galo asked slowly.

"No."

"It's—" Galo cut himself off.

Cas sighed, turning to his friend. "Free minute."

"I don't need it."

"Yes, you do. Say what you want to say. I won't get mad."

Galo lowered his voice when he spoke. "It's not her fault your parents made you marry her. No one from her kingdom came with her, except for one guard. It must be lonely, don't you think?"

Galo was right, of course, though Cas wasn't going to admit it. But maybe he should have gone by at least once to see Mary since she'd arrived. She probably thought he hated her.

He didn't think he hated her. He couldn't stir up a feeling about her either way, actually.

"I did try to be nice to her," he said. "I gave her the hint about Henry yesterday for the Union Battle."

Galo laughed. "I noticed she ignored that advice."

"Well, she clearly didn't need an easy win."

"She's practically as good as you with a sword."

"Let's not get carried away," Cas said.

"I said 'practically.'"

Cas shot him an amused look, then sighed. "I could have

tried harder. I should have gone to speak with her last night after the battle. It all just feels so awkward."

"I'm sure. But it will be more awkward if you never talk to her at all."

"Fine," he said, taking a step back and glancing at Mary. "But if she keeps refusing to smile at me, I'm going to stop trying."

"Maybe you should smile first."

"Free minute is over."

"Yes, Your Highness." Galo laughed and returned to his spot near the wall.

Cas headed back to the front of the room, trying to twist his face into an appropriate expression. There. He was smiling. Sort of.

"Would you like to dance?" he asked Mary, extending his hand to her. He was going to have to think of something to talk about while they danced, but at least it was a start.

"Oh yes!" his mother exclaimed before Mary could reply. She gestured at the musicians, and they stopped playing. "The traditional wedding dance."

"She didn't have time to learn it, Mother," Cas said. "We can just dance to something else."

"It's tradition! You can lead her, Cas."

"I really don't—"

"I can do it," Mary interrupted. Her gaze had gone hard, as if he'd insulted her. He hadn't meant to imply she couldn't do it; he was simply trying to spare her the embarrassment.

"Let's dance, then," he said, holding his hand out to her again.

She stood, her palm cool as she slipped it into his. She glanced at him, then at the room in front of them, where people had scattered off the dance floor. The musicians in back straightened in their chairs, bows poised across strings.

"I didn't know we'd be the only ones," she said as he led her to the center of the room.

"Regret this decision now?" he asked.

She bit her lip.

"You'll be fine." He grasped her right hand firmly in his left and placed his other on the center of her back. "I'm going backward and you're coming forward first," he said quietly. "Put your hand on my shoulder."

Her gaze stayed steady with his as she followed his instructions. He hadn't noticed that her dark eyes were flecked with gold, and now that he was close enough to see it, he didn't want to look away.

The music started, and he took a step, putting light pressure on her back. She came with him, her skirt swishing around her feet.

"Side," he said quietly. "Back, back."

She took to the steps quickly, letting him push and tug her around the dance floor. He straightened their arms, bringing his body against hers for a brief moment.

"Spin," he said, lifting their hands. She did a quick spin. When she placed her hand on his shoulder again, her eyes blazed with a fire that made him want to pull her closer.

He moved faster, quietly giving her some of the steps under his breath. He realized too late she was going the wrong way, and instead of letting her crash right into him, he tightened the arm around her waist and whisked her off the ground. He spun around, placing her on the ground again, and the people around them all clapped like it had been planned.

She gave him a grateful smile, her steps more confident as they continued dancing.

"I noticed you ignored my suggestion yesterday," he said softly. "For the Union Battle."

"I thought it might be a trap."

"A trap?"

"Yes. Like part of the tradition was trying to steer me to the easy choice, to see if I took it."

He laughed softly. "You're not terribly trusting, are you?"

"No."

He moved his hand from her back as he spun her, then returned it. He wasn't sure what to say to that.

"It wasn't a trap, then?" she asked.

"Of course not." He stole a quick glance at his parents. "My father would be furious if he knew I helped you. It's not allowed."

"Oh."

"You clearly didn't need any help, though."

"No." Her fingers curled around his shoulder. "Thank you, though."

"You're welcome." He looked down at her to find her lips slowly curving up. It was the first genuine smile he'd seen from her, and by far his favorite. That smile held secrets he desperately wanted to know.

She nodded at the musicians, and then the crowd as the song ended. They burst into applause, his mother beaming as she stood and clapped.

Cas offered Mary his arm, and she took it. A piece of hair had fallen loose and brushed against her shoulder, and he was struck by the sudden urge to push it behind her ear.

She cocked her head, her gaze on something in front of them. She took in a sharp breath.

Cas turned just in time to see the blade as it sank into his flesh.

SIX

EM'S FIRST THOUGHT was *What luck!*

This man with a sword was going to kill Prince Casimir, and she didn't have to do a thing but stand there and watch. She wouldn't even have to worry about the wedding night.

Her second thought, however, was for her plan. If Cas died, she would be sent back to Vallos, and Jovita would be named as the next heir. She would accomplish nothing if Cas died tonight.

The man pulled his sword out of Cas's left shoulder as screams ripped through the ballroom. Cas stumbled backward, his arm slipping out of hers. The man aimed his sword straight for Cas's heart. The prince was unarmed and blinking as if in a daze, blood dripping from his fingertips. He clearly wasn't used to being attacked.

The situation was this: one man with a sword, at least twenty members of the guard already running toward them, and—most importantly—her. Easy.

Em lunged for the man. She was plenty used to being attacked. This felt like home.

She launched her foot into the man's knee seconds before his blade could find its mark. He stumbled, his sword lurching to the side and missing Cas entirely. He spun toward her and she slammed her fist into his face, using her other hand to wrench the sword out of his hand.

He dove for her, but three members of the guard were behind him suddenly, pulling him back. Aren was one of them, and he gave Em a wide-eyed look that was either approval or confusion.

"Cas! Cas!" the queen screeched as she flew past Em. Cas was on his knees, his hand to his shoulder. His gray coat hid most of the blood, but a small pool had collected on the floor as it dripped down his arm. He'd gone pale.

Hands wrapped around Em's arms, holding tighter when she tried to jerk away.

"We need to take you to safety, Your Highness," a guard said, pulling on her arms. Two others closed in around her.

She glanced over her shoulder at Cas as they dragged her away, but people swarmed around the prince, hiding him from view.

Please don't die, she prayed. *Not yet.*

The guards delivered her to her room, closing and locking the door behind them. All three stood stiffly in front of the door, hands clasped behind their backs.

Pain shot through the hand she'd used to punch the man, but she ignored it. "I want to go see if Cas is all right."

The tallest guard shook his head. "I'm sorry, Your Highness. Procedure dictates that we keep you here until they've made sure the castle is safe."

"Does this happen often?" she asked, surprised. She'd been under the impression that Lera was the safest of the four kingdoms. They'd beaten everyone else down to make sure of it.

"We have procedures outlined for all possible situations," the guard said.

That wasn't an answer, which was interesting.

"Do you know who that was?" she asked. "Why did he want to kill Cas?"

"I'm sorry, Your Highness, I wouldn't know. He'll be questioned soon."

Em walked to her bed, hopping onto the mattress as she frowned in thought. She didn't know who would want to kill the prince. Well, besides her.

Long minutes ticked by, and Em moved from the bed to the window, and back again. It was at least an hour before the door finally opened.

Jovita stood on the other side of the door. Em jumped up from the bed and rushed to her.

"Is he alive?" Em asked.

"He's fine," Jovita said. "It's just his shoulder."

Em breathed a sigh of relief, which was echoed by all three guards.

"He'd like to see you," Jovita said, placing her back against the open door and beckoning at Em with two fingers.

He surely didn't want to continue with the wedding night after getting stabbed, did he? Em swallowed as she walked out the door and started down the hallway with Jovita and two guards. Maybe his wounds weren't very serious after all. There had been a lot of blood, but Em had suffered injuries that bled profusely but hadn't slowed her down.

"We should have a discussion soon about what to do in case of an emergency," Jovita said. "We have a meeting spot in case the castle is taken or unsafe."

"Where is that?" Em asked.

"Fort Victorra, in the Southern Mountains. Do you know it?"

"I do. It's near the Vallos border."

"Good. I'll give you a map later, just in case. All members of the royal family get one."

Five guards were outside Cas's rooms. Jovita led Em past them and through a dark office full of books. The door to Cas's bedroom was ajar, light streaming out through the crack.

"You should rest, Cas," the queen said from the other side of the door.

"I will, Mother." Then, in a softer voice: "I'm fine."

Jovita knocked and pushed the door open. The room was even bigger than Em's, with an impressive dresser and ornate mirror on one side of the room, and two big plushy chairs on the other, in front of a massive window currently obscured by deep-blue curtains. Cas lay on the big bed in the center of the room, shirtless, with a white bandage covering his left shoulder. He was still pale, but he smiled as she walked into the room.

The queen turned, and Em found herself crushed against the woman. She held Em so tightly it was difficult to breathe.

"Thank you," the queen whispered.

Em resisted the urge to roll her eyes as she extracted herself from the queen's embrace. The king stood next to his wife, his face full of gratitude. Em quickly crossed her arms over her chest so he wouldn't get any ideas about hugging her too.

"May we have a minute?" Cas asked.

The queen wiped at her cheeks. "We'll be right outside."

The king put a hand on Em's shoulder as he passed her.

"We owe you a debt of gratitude," he said softly.

Em tried not to appear too pleased. She couldn't have found a better way to endear herself to the king and queen than if she had planned this herself.

The door closed with a quiet thud as they left, and she clasped her hands in front of her, suddenly nervous. An elaborate jeweled sword hung on the wall not three steps away, and another one, sheathed and ready to be grabbed, sat on the dresser in the corner. Five seconds to kill the prince. If she hadn't just saved his life, she might have been tempted.

Cas was still smiling at her, and he gestured with his good hand. "Come here?"

He said it as a question, and she nodded in agreement as she stepped forward. She was tempted to stop in the middle of the room, but that seemed awkward, so she walked all the way to his bed and stood next to it.

She'd never seen a boy shirtless in his bed before. She and Damian had shared a tent many times, but that was different. They were both fully clothed, in the dirt, and usually Aren was there as well. This felt more intimate. Her heart pounded in her ears, and she wiped a sweaty palm against her dress.

"I just wanted to say thank you." Cas kept his gaze steady with hers, and she found it hard to look away. In a certain light his eyes were blue, in others they seemed a bit green. Either way, they were clear and striking.

"You're welcome."

"It's really above and beyond the call of duty to save my life on our wedding day."

"It was nothing."

One side of his mouth quirked up, his eyebrow rising with it. He was amused, but also . . . intrigued? He was looking at her as if he liked her. She didn't think she wanted him to like her.

But she had to admit that it would be helpful if he did. She couldn't ignore him and expect to be given inside information about Olivia's location and Lera's defenses.

She took a tiny step closer to the bed. "Are you in pain?"

"A little. It's subsiding." He glanced at the bandage. "The doctor gave me something. He said it would make me drowsy, so don't be alarmed if I suddenly pass out."

She tried not to let her body sigh with relief. If he was going to pass out, then there would be no expectation of her climbing into bed with him. She had another day or two until she had to face that particular challenge.

"Is it common for people to attack you?" she asked.

"This would be a first." He gave her a reassuring smile. "Lera is usually very safe. Especially the castle. You don't need to worry."

"I wasn't worried. I won."

He laughed, his eyes twinkling with amusement. "You did. It was impressive, actually."

"I've been attacked more times than I can count." She said it almost smugly.

Cas's smile faded. "I guess you have. The Ruined are all over Vallos, aren't they?"

"They were. There are less now."

"And they attacked often?"

Anger swirled in her gut as his features dropped in sympathy. Sympathy because she had to deal with those awful, evil Ruined.

"They were being hunted down and murdered, so yes, they defended themselves often." The words tumbled out of her mouth before she could stop them. She didn't care. She'd say them again, just to watch that stupid baffled expression cross his face.

"Do you—" He sat up straighter, wincing in pain.

"I should let you rest," she said quickly, before he could finish that sentence. The last thing she wanted to do was talk about the Ruined with the prince. It was unlikely she'd be able to keep her temper in check.

She took a step away from the bed and he reached out, catching her hand in his. He wore a thoughtful expression, his eyes soft and completely unlike his father's. "I'd like to hear about your experiences with the Ruined sometime. If you don't mind talking about it."

"Sure," she lied, hoping he would forget that request.

He rubbed his thumb across her fingers. She noticed for the first time that red and purple had bloomed across her knuckles, where she'd punched the man.

"Do you need the doctor to look at your hand?" He loosened his grip, as if he was afraid he was hurting her.

"No, it's fine," she said. "Just a bruise."

He slowly released her. She ducked her head as she walked to the door, but she couldn't resist glancing back at him before she left. Light flickered off his bare chest from the lantern next to his bed, and he tossed a piece of dark hair out of his eyes.

"Good night," he said.

She grasped the knob, mumbling a good-night as she wrenched the door open and walked out of his room.

SEVEN

CAS QUICKLY TURNED his head at the sound of footsteps approaching his door. He'd been alone most of the morning, and his first thought—or hope—was that it was Mary. He shifted against his pillows, running a hand through his hair.

The door opened to reveal Galo, and Cas tried to convince himself he wasn't disappointed.

"Your Highness," Galo said as he stepped into the room.

"Are we being formal this morning?"

"Seems appropriate, considering I let you get stabbed last night." There was an edge to Galo's voice, and he wouldn't quite meet Cas's eyes.

"Almost every member of the guard was in that room. I'm not sure we can hold you personally responsible," he said lightly, but Galo didn't crack a smile. "Did my father yell?"

"And your mother. And Jovita. They fired the guards at the door, the ones who let the man slip in."

Cas leaned back with a sigh, pain rippling through his shoulder. "Do they know who he was?"

"I haven't heard. The king is with him now." Galo rubbed a hand over the scruff on his jaw. "I need to apologize for—"

"No, you don't," Cas interrupted. "I don't want guards hovering at my side all hours of the day. You can't protect me all the time."

"That is actually our job. Protecting you all the time. Though it appears Mary is more than willing to pick up the slack."

"Yes, she is," Cas murmured, the image of her fist connecting with that man's face flashing through his brain. Years of battling the Ruined had made her an excellent fighter.

"But I do need to apologize on behalf of your entire guard," Galo said. "We wouldn't blame you if you replaced all of us."

"You know I'm not going to do that," Cas said.

"It wouldn't be the worst idea." Jovita appeared in the doorway. She jerked her head, indicating that Galo should leave, and the guard quickly exited the room.

She stepped inside, closing the door behind her. "How's the shoulder?"

"Fine. It's not that bad of an injury, but the doctor insisted I stay in bed today."

"I'm glad it wasn't serious."

Cas snorted. "Sure you are."

Jovita gave him an annoyed look, but a smile tugged at her mouth as she plopped down in the chair near the window. "I would be very sad if anything happened to you, Cas."

"I'm sure. You'd be devastated all the way to the throne."

Jovita sat sideways in the chair, her long, dark braid dangling off the armrest as she tilted her head back. "You've caught me. It was me who hired that man to try to kill you at your wedding. I'm horribly jealous of you."

"I knew it. Though I always thought you'd go with poison."

"Much more theatrical this way." She turned her head, grinning at him. "I've come with official news, though," she said, swinging her legs around and sitting straight in the chair. "The man who stabbed you talked. He was a hunter."

Cas's eyebrows lifted. "A hunter? Of the Ruined?"

"Yes."

"What did he want with me?"

"A small group of hunters have organized against the king. They've been demanding changes to the hunter policies for a while. Mainly that we make it a voluntary position."

"Would people actually volunteer to hunt down and kill Ruined?"

"Not many, which is why the position is used as a punishment instead of prison." She rubbed a few fingers across her chin. "What criminals want is irrelevant. We need hunters. The king had heard rumblings about them organizing, but clearly we need to start taking them more seriously. He hasn't given up any others yet, but he must have had help. We'll find them. In the meantime, we still have plenty of hunters making multiple Ruined kills every day."

They were being hunted down and murdered, so yes, they defended themselves often. Mary's words ran through his brain for the hundredth time since she'd said them. He'd never heard anyone even come close to defending the Ruined. No one used the word *murdered.* They were *eliminated* or *killed* or *disposed of.* Mary's word hung in the air, taunting him.

"Do you ever wonder whether it was the right decision, to kill all the Ruined?" he asked slowly.

Jovita's eyebrows shot almost to her hairline. "No."

"Are they really all bad? Every single one of them?"

"Yes, every single one of them," Jovita said, a hint of exasperation in her tone. She'd only been an adviser to the king for a year, but she always acted like she knew more than Cas. "The Ruined ruled over us for centuries without an ounce of compassion. We're returning the favor."

"True," Cas said quietly. He hadn't been alive to see the days when the Ruined enslaved humans and killed them for sport, and neither had his father. His grandfather had driven them out of Lera, but the Ruined had lost their hold on humans years before, after their powers weakened. Punishment from the ancestors for misuse of them, his grandfather used to tell him.

The ancestors had nothing to do with the Ruined losing their power, Cas's father had said with a roll of his eyes. He was never the type of man to believe in things he couldn't see. *The Ruined will rise again. Unless we stop them.*

The Ruined will rise again used to send a chill down Cas's spine. Now he felt nothing but the weight of those lost lives. For all the Ruined's power, they couldn't rise from the dead.

Jovita stood. "The warriors from Olso arrive in two days. Will you be well enough to attend the dinner?"

"I'm sure I will be. I'm not going to miss the warriors' first visit to Lera in two generations."

"Good. Try not to get stabbed at that event too. We don't want the warriors thinking we need someone from *Vallos* to save our prince." She said *Vallos* as if it were distasteful, but a smile crept onto her face.

"The horror. Almost as embarrassing as getting beaten by their princess in the Union Battle."

She glared at him, and he laughed as he sank down farther into his pillows.

"I wasn't planning to poison you before, but now I definitely am," she said as she threw open the door. "Watch your back, Prince Casimir."

He grinned at her. "I have Mary to do that for me."

"Why is it always sunny?" Aren looked up at the sky in disgust, shielding his face with his hand. "Even their weather is mocking me."

Em followed his gaze to the clear blue sky. The air was fresh and cool, the birds soaring in the direction of the ocean. The castle gardens bloomed with red, yellow, and pink flowers, and various citrus fruits hung from trees. It really was disgustingly beautiful in Lera.

"The ancestors blessed them," she said with a mock-serious expression.

Aren rolled his eyes. "If I have to hear that one more time, I'm going to kill someone. Don't be surprised if you see one of their heads just suddenly separate from their body."

She glanced over her shoulder, at the empty path behind them. "Say that a little louder. I don't think they heard you on the other side of the gardens."

"Sorry." He lowered his voice. "My mother used to tell me the ancestors had blessed me. I don't like hearing it out of their mouths."

"I know," Em said softly.

"Maybe the ancestors didn't bless anyone. Maybe they never even existed," Aren said, his voice wobbling. His mother had been the castle priest, and his words weighed heavy on Em's heart. He never would have dreamed of saying those words a year ago.

She reached over and squeezed his hand briefly. He squeezed it back.

The castle wall came into view as they reached the edge of the gardens. A wide swath of grass stretched between the wall and the gardens, making sure that anyone who jumped it would be in plain view of the guards.

"There's one guard in that tower," Em said without looking back at it. The tower was on the east side of the castle, stretching higher than the rest of the building. A perfect spot to watch the entire wall.

"Maybe two," Aren said. "And did you see that watch post

when we came in? From where it's positioned, the guard would also have an excellent view of the entire castle grounds."

"I couldn't see anything in that stupid carriage."

"It's in the trees, not far from the main castle gate."

"Find out how those shifts are assigned. I want to know if it's always the same few people, or if they rotate."

"Got it."

She touched the wall. Stone. It was very tall, but there was a tree near the wall ahead that could easily be climbed, though it would be quite a jump to the other side.

"Guards posted on the other side of the wall?" she whispered.

"Yes. Not a popular position. Very boring, apparently. And you have to stand the whole time."

"Find out how many and where."

"Already on it."

"A Ruined could take this wall down, right?" she asked. "At least a piece of it?"

"Damian could take down a large chunk of it at full strength."

"Good."

They continued walking, Em making a note of how long it took to walk the entire perimeter. If a hasty escape was necessary, the wall would pose a significant problem.

"How was the prince last night? You saw him, didn't you?" Aren asked.

"Fine. It's just a shoulder injury." She blew out a breath of air. "He wants to talk to me about the Ruined."

"What? How did that come up?"

"It's my fault. I can't keep my mouth shut. I may have said they were murdering us."

"Mary would have hated the Ruined, Em. They murdered her parents."

"So? No one here ever met her. They don't know that for sure."

"Was he mad? Was it like, 'We'll discuss this later, peasant. Now leave me to my murdering'?" He lowered his voice in an impression of Cas and grinned.

"No. It was more like he was intrigued. Like he was willing to talk about it," she said, and Aren gave her a baffled look. "I know! I never considered the possibility that I could actually talk sense into him."

"It's not a possibility," Aren said. "Even if Cas is willing to listen to you and the king died tomorrow, it wouldn't change anything. The king's advisers support the Ruined policies. Besides, he's what . . . seventeen?"

"Yeah."

"He's been able to take the throne for two years. He was in those meetings when they decided. If he had something to say, he would have done it already."

"True. Sympathy doesn't mean much if you don't take action." She shuddered as the image of a shirtless Cas ran through her head. She didn't like him in her head.

"Have you heard anything about Olivia yet?" Aren asked.

"No. I'm waiting for a natural way to slide it into conversation. I don't want them getting suspicious. So far all anyone will talk to me about is dresses and the wedding. They haven't even bothered to tell me the Olso warriors are coming. I've been practicing my surprised face." She lifted her eyebrows, parting her lips dramatically. "How is that?"

"Terrible. Don't do that."

"Maybe Cas will remember to tell me today, since they're supposed to arrive very soon. He'd barely spoken to me before yesterday, so I guess there wasn't much opportunity." She scrunched up her face. "Now I think he likes me."

"That was the point, wasn't it?"

"I guess."

He rubbed his hand across the back of his neck. "We never talked about . . . uh . . . the sex part."

"And we will continue to not talk about it."

"Are you going to ask him to wait? I don't think that's unreasonable. You just met, after all."

"Aren, we're not talking about it."

"Right. Sorry." He slid his hands in his pockets, taking a few steps away from her. "I have to get back. I told them I was just checking in with you, so they'll expect me back soon." He grinned. "Plus, we shouldn't be seen together too often. People will think we're having sex."

Em wrinkled her nose, trying to keep a smile off her face. "Gross."

"The feeling is mutual."

EIGHT

PEOPLE IN THE castle had started addressing Em as "Your Royal Highness" or "Princess of Lera." She cringed inwardly every time.

The queen said she was going to start training Em in her "royal duties," though for the last two days Em had been mostly alone, memorizing the castle grounds and searching for weaknesses. She ate meals by herself, since the king and queen had mostly disappeared after Cas's stabbing. They were probably dealing with that hunter who had decided to kill the royal family instead of the Ruined.

Cas never sent for her, so she didn't visit him. The guards reported that he was healing well. Em was glad for the break from him. Since he didn't expect her to join him in his bed, she was free to wander the castle at night, slipping into rooms and sifting through drawers to search for information about Olivia's location.

Jovita finally remembered to let Em in on the fact that the Olso warriors were coming to Lera for the summer, and Em put on her best surprised face when she heard the news. She was given a stunning light-pink dress to wear for the welcome dinner.

She'd already amassed a good selection of dresses, and Davina informed her she'd have many opportunities to wear them. It seemed the only thing the people of Lera liked more than fighting was partying.

Tonight's dress had a whole parade of buttons in back, but dipped down very low in front, showing a generous amount of cleavage. Most of the dresses that had been sent didn't exactly cover a lot of flesh, and she couldn't help but think the queen had done it on purpose, to make a conservative girl from Vallos uncomfortable.

Em pushed back her shoulders with a smile. Good thing she wasn't from Vallos.

Cas arrived at her door after the sun had set. He wore black pants, a white collared shirt, and a black coat with silver buttons down the middle. The coat hung open unbuttoned. He was a bit disheveled, like he'd run around the castle a few times before coming to see her. It would have been cute, had she not been determined to hate him.

"Good evening," he said as she stepped out of the room. She was suddenly unsure what to do with her hands.

"Hello," she murmured, avoiding his gaze. He offered her his good arm, and she took it and let him steer her down the hallway.

"Are you feeling all right?" she asked, stealing a glance at him. The deep black color of his coat made his eyes stand out even more than usual. It was hard not to stare.

"I am, thank you. A little sore still, but it's healing fine."

"Glad to hear it," she lied. Just how "fine" was he? Ready to make up for the wedding night "fine"? She shuddered and let her fingers brush against the rope tieback on the curtains as they passed them.

"Jovita told you about the warriors?" he asked.

"She did. I was surprised. I thought relations between Olso and Lera were tense."

"They have been for a long time. But the warriors reached out recently, wanting to come in person to discuss a few treaties. Said they wanted to keep the peace."

"That's wonderful," she said, suppressing a smile. Not a hint of suspicion in Cas's tone. He really thought the warriors were there to bow down at Lera's feet, like everyone else.

"Have you ever met a warrior?" he asked.

She had. And not just the ones she'd negotiated with recently. Many citizens of Olso had come through Ruina, since their kings and queens always seemed more intrigued by the Ruined than scared. Em's mother had admired the way warriors dedicated their lives to training for battle, and had invited many to stay as guests in the castle.

Cas was watching her, waiting for her answer. Would Mary

have met any warriors? It seemed unlikely. Olso looked down on Vallos.

"Not that I recall," she said carefully.

They walked to the main dining room, the sounds of laughter and chatter filling the air as they approached the double doors. A staff member opened them, and Cas and Em stepped inside.

Several long rows of tables ran down the center of the room, most of them already full. Large bowls of bread and fruit sat in the middle of every table, and staff members scurried about, refilling wineglasses.

There were at least a hundred people, maybe more. Most of the wedding guests were staying in the castle for weeks, exactly as the warriors had said they would. To properly take down Lera, she needed to destroy many of their leaders, and a good number of them sat in this room. The governors of the six provinces reported directly to the king, and five of them were present. There were also a few captains, the Lerans responsible for managing safety and soldiers in their area. The queen had informed Em that judges, the lowest rank in Lera, had mostly stayed behind to manage their provinces in the absence of the governor or captain. They weren't terribly important anyway.

"Prince Casimir and Princess Mary," a voice announced.

Everyone in the room quickly stood, and Em scanned the crowd, looking for the warriors.

"Please be seated," Cas said. Everyone obeyed and took their seats again.

Three people in white-and-red uniforms stayed standing for

a beat longer than everyone else. The warriors. Two men and one woman. In fact, Em knew the girl. She had spent several days in the Ruina castle three years ago with her mother and father, a powerful Olso family.

Iria. That was her name.

A smirk crossed Iria's face, and Em resisted the urge to roll her eyes. Iria had spent most of her time in the Ruina castle challenging Em to "duels" ("To the death!" she'd always yell, and then giggle), and the rest of the time antagonizing Em and Olivia at every turn.

Of course King Lucio had sent Iria. She had probably requested to come, because she knew it would annoy Em.

She took a deep breath and glanced at Cas. He was staring at her.

"Are you all right?" he asked, his eyebrows furrowing.

"I'm fine." She cleared her throat. "Should we sit?"

Cas steered her toward the table at the front of the room, where Jovita and some of the governors were already seated. Em noticed the warriors were not seated with the royal family, which seemed like an intentional slight.

She and Cas sat as a member of the staff brought the warriors to meet them. Em leaned forward in her chair, plastering a smile on her face.

"Koldo Herrerro," the staff member said, and the young bright-eyed warrior smiled at them.

"Benito Lodo." The man with a dark beard nodded.

"Iria Ubino."

Iria stepped forward. Her long, wavy dark hair was tied back in a braid that fell over her shoulder as she bowed her head in the traditional Lera greeting. Her dark eyes were trained only on Em as she straightened, and Cas looked between them.

"Have you met before?" he asked, loud enough for the warriors to hear.

One side of Iria's mouth turned up, and Em hoped the warrior knew she was imagining strangling her. "I don't think so."

Iria waited a long time before speaking. Em wished Iria would hide her delight at torturing her a bit better.

"Apologies," Iria finally said. "You look very much like someone I used to know, Your Highness."

Em hoped her face was currently in some kind of pleasant expression and didn't give away the fact that she was barely restraining herself from kicking Iria in the gut.

Cas lightly touched her hand, his fingers curling around hers, and Em jumped in surprise. Iria's amusement intensified as she watched them.

"Please have a seat," Cas said.

The warriors walked back to their seats, Iria throwing another glance at Em over her shoulder. Cas leaned closer to Em, moving his hand away from hers.

"She was trying to throw you off balance," he said rather perceptively. "Don't let her."

It was excellent advice, though entirely misguided given the circumstances.

The servants filled her plate with food, and the hall buzzed with laughter and chatter. Em forced her food down so Cas wouldn't become concerned.

After they'd finished eating and the musicians had started playing, the king and queen finally entered the hall. The festivities stopped for a moment, and Em watched as they breezed by the warriors without saying hello. All three of them stared at the queen, hard expressions on their faces. Fabiana must have been the most notorious traitor in Olso, and she certainly wasn't doing anything to smooth things over now.

Em glanced at Cas as the music started again. She leaned into him, until her lips were close to his ear. "Why were they late?"

He shook his head slightly. "I don't know."

"It insulted the warriors," she said. "Look at their faces."

Cas casually glanced over at the warriors, then back to Em. "I think that everything insults them. They're always mad about something."

"And your parents made sure they'd be angry about this."

He lifted an eyebrow. "You think so?"

"Yes." Typical Lera strategy. They were always more concerned with making sure everyone knew how much better they were than with actually showing a little respect.

"I'll go say hello," she said. "Make them feel welcome."

"I got the impression you were scared of them," he said. "You were staring at Iria as if she was going to jump across the table with a sword and stab you."

Em's face twisted in a way that made Cas laugh. "I am not scared!"

"A little fear of the warriors is probably good sense."

"I'm not scared," she repeated firmly. "What's she going to do, stab me in front of everyone?"

"It's unlikely."

"That wasn't very comforting."

His eyes were bright with amusement. "It was meant to be honest, not comforting. I've recently been stabbed at my own wedding, let's not forget."

"True."

He glanced over at the Olso warriors. "Let's ask them to come over here."

"No, it would look better if I went to them. It's a sign of respect."

He paused for a moment. "All right. I'll come with you."

She couldn't protest that, not without giving away the fact that she wanted to talk to them alone. She stood, and Cas did the same, leaning over to say something to his father. The king frowned, but didn't protest.

The room quieted as they walked. The Olso warriors turned, then stood as they approached. Surprise crossed the men's faces as Cas and Em walked around the table and sat down on the bench across from them. Iria still wore her smug expression, which Em decided to pretend she hadn't noticed.

"How was the food?" Cas asked, gesturing to their empty plates.

"Very good, Your Highness, thank you," Koldo said.

"They'll be coming around with more, if you're still hungry,"

Cas said. "And dessert soon. I recommend the fig tarts. They're delicious."

Koldo perked up, his eyes scanning the room for the treats. Benito didn't look at all impressed at the idea of dessert.

"I will be sure to get one," Iria said. She fixed her gaze on Cas. "Congratulations on your marriage."

"Thank you."

"How wonderful that Lera and Vallos could finally be united." Iria turned her smile from Cas to Em.

"Have you been?" Cas asked. "To Vallos?"

"I have," Iria said. "A bit dreary, compared to here. Though not nearly as grim as Ruina."

Em forced her expression to stay neutral. "I've never been to Ruina, but I'm sure you're right."

"Your Highness," Iria said, glancing at Cas. "Do you mind if I dance with your wife?"

"If she would like," he replied.

"I would love to," Em said, lifting her skirts as she stood. She looped her arm through the girl's and walked with her to the dance floor.

Iria put a light hand on her back and Em decided to let her lead. No need to antagonize her.

"Is it entirely necessary to have that look on your face?" Em asked through clenched teeth as they began to dance.

"What look?"

"Like you've figured something out and are delighted about it. You're here to help me, remember?"

Iria chuckled. "I'm sorry. I'm just so amused. Emelina Flores as the princess of Lera. It's ridiculous." Her eyes slid to Cas, and Em glanced over as well. He was talking to the two other warriors, but he had one eye on them. "Though he seems thoroughly convinced."

"Why wouldn't he be? I told the warriors I could do it."

"So you did. I bet against you. Lost a good bit of money, actually."

"What a shame," Em said drily. She looked at Benito and Koldo. "Do they both know about me?"

"Of course. They can be trusted."

"I'll decide that. You didn't tell anyone else I'm here, did you?"

"No. Not even your own people. It's strange to keep the Ruined in the dark about this plan, if you want to know my opinion."

"I don't. The less people know, the better." The Ruined wouldn't have faith in Em or her plan anyway. The looks on their faces would be that much better once they realized she'd succeeded.

"I heard you saved your prince from death on your wedding day. That was a stroke of luck, wasn't it?"

"Yes, it was." Em regarded Iria suspiciously. "Wasn't it?"

"We had nothing to do with it. But we're trying to find those hunters now, to see how organized the movement is. They may be helpful."

"Do you have any news?"

"I saw Damian briefly before I left Olso. He's helping the Ruined cross the border. We've succeeded in getting several through, safe and sound. They were on their way to see King Lucio when I left."

"Why do they need to see the king?" Em asked.

"He's very friendly, our king."

She wasn't going to get a straight answer about that, so Em filed it away to ask Damian about later. She didn't trust the Olso king in the slightest. He'd agreed to help her because he wanted to seize control of Lera, but had done nothing to help the Ruined when they were being hunted and executed.

"Damian gave me a note to pass along to you," Iria said.

"Not now," she said, even though she desperately wanted to read it. "I don't want them seeing you give me anything."

"Fine. Would you stop squeezing my hand like that?" Iria asked. "I'm going to need it later."

"Sorry," Em muttered, loosening her grip. Breaking Iria's hand would make a nice distraction, though. Em could break the hand, dart around Iria, and put her in a chokehold. Em was taller than the warrior, so she had a pretty good chance of being able to maintain the hold.

Em beat down the urge. The warriors were her partners. She didn't need to kill them to keep herself safe.

"There's no chance of you doing something stupid like killing the king too early, right?" Iria said, her expression growing serious. "I remember you having a bit of a temper."

"I'm perfectly fine," Em said. "We shouldn't talk about this here. Come to my room tomorrow morning. Bring the note. I'll have Aren come as well."

"Fine. But if I'm going to be stopping by your room, you'll need to tell Cas that we got along wonderfully. Tell him we're instant friends."

Em rolled her eyes. "What should I say we talked about that made us such fast friends?"

"We were talking about Vallos, and how sad you were to leave."

"Agreed. And I will say that you mentioned how much you love your home, and you were nervous about how the visit here would go, considering the tense relations between Lera and Olso."

"I'm not nervous." Iria had a trail of freckles across the bridge of her nose, and they moved as she wrinkled it.

"Well, now you are. You like me. You've decided to confide in me. That's what I'll tell him."

"I don't actually like you, just so you know."

"I'm heartbroken," Em said.

"I do admire this, though," Iria said, gesturing to Em. "I didn't think you had it in you, honestly. You seemed a bit whiny when I met you. Sulky."

The song ended, and Em stepped back and dropped Iria's hand. The warrior wasn't wrong, but Em certainly wasn't going to admit that to her. Three years ago, when they'd met, Em had been bitter about her lack of power and jealous of Olivia's. "Whiny" was probably putting it nicely.

"Things have changed," Em said.

Something like sympathy flashed across Iria's face. "I will keep an ear out for news about Olivia," she said softly.

"Thank you." Em turned on her heel. The last thing she wanted was sympathy.

NINE

CAS LOOKED AT Mary curiously as she walked off the dance floor and away from Iria. The warrior was smiling, like Mary had put her at ease. Not an easy feat.

They walked back to his parents and sat next to them for the remainder of the evening. When the king and queen stood to leave, Cas did as well, extending his arm to Mary. She took it as they walked through the room and out the door. The sounds of the party became muffled as the door shut behind them.

His father grinned at Cas and Mary. "Finally time for the wedding night, I presume?"

Cas stiffened as his mother gave her husband a poke in the ribs. The king just chuckled and slapped Cas on the shoulder. He wanted to strangle his father.

Cas glanced at Mary, but her gaze was downcast, her cheeks pink. He had no idea what to say that would make the moment any less awkward, so he said nothing at all as he turned and walked in the direction of her rooms. She followed him silently.

They reached her door and he pushed it open and stepped back, letting her enter first. The skirt of her dress brushed across his legs as she walked past him.

He stepped inside and closed the door behind him. It was deathly quiet, and the wooden floor creaked as Mary walked across it. She smoothed a hand over the skirt of her dress. Her hands shook, and her chest moved up and down too quickly, like she was on the verge of panicking.

"Would you rather not do this?" he asked softly.

Her eyes met his briefly, her cheeks turning a deeper shade of red. "I . . ."

He waited, but she didn't finish the sentence. Her calm composure was crumbling right in front of him. Her hands shook harder, and she swallowed as if she was about to be ill.

"I would never make you do anything you don't want to," he finally said. "We've only just met each other. I understand if you want to wait."

A sigh rolled through her body, and she nodded so enthusiastically he almost laughed. He'd never had sex with anyone, and doing it for the first time with a girl who looked as if she might vomit sounded miserable.

"May I ask a favor, though?" he asked. "Do you mind if I stay in here for a little while? I'd like my parents to think we consummated the marriage. We'll never hear the end of it otherwise." He could only imagine the comments from his father. He'd never live it down.

"Of course," she said. "That's a good idea, actually." She gestured to the chair in the corner of the room, and he shrugged out of his coat as he walked over. He draped it on the back of the chair and sat down. She perched on the edge of the bed, rubbing her thumb over the necklace she always wore.

"You seemed to get along very well with that warrior. Iria," he said, and she nodded. "What did you talk about?"

"Vallos. Her journey here. She's nervous about how negotiations will go."

"I don't think Olso warriors get nervous," he said with a laugh.

"Anxious, then. Not everyone is as tough as they appear, you know."

"And not everyone is as weak as they pretend." He sat back and cracked a knuckle.

"Are you referring to me?" she asked quickly.

"No, actually. It's something my mother always says."

"Oh."

"Were you pretending to be weak?" he asked. "Because I'd hate to see you at full strength."

Mary laughed loudly, without a hint of self-consciousness. She let go of something deep inside of her when she laughed.

"No," she said. "I certainly have never had to pretend to be weak. But your mother is right. There's a benefit to being underestimated."

"I suppose there is. My father underestimated you at the Union Battle, that's for sure. He didn't even hide his surprise well."

"Your father thinks there is no one greater than himself," she muttered, then seemed to immediately realize what she had just said. She took in a sharp breath, her gaze snapping to his. "I'm sorry, I didn't—I didn't—"

He burst out laughing. "Do you not like my father? Everyone loves my father."

"Um . . ." She seemed to be searching for the right lie.

"You can tell me the truth," he said, resting his elbows on his thighs and leaning forward. "We can have some secrets just between us."

She hesitated, then finally said, "No," barely above a whisper. "I'm not fond of him."

"Why not?" he asked.

"It's like he's always putting on a show."

"How do you mean?"

"He's always smiling. And being friendly." She wrinkled her nose, her lips turning downward in the most hilarious expression he'd ever seen. It was like she was both disgusted and annoyed.

Cas rested his chin in his hand, thoroughly amused. "I hate it when people are friendly. It's terrible."

"No, I mean . . ." She laughed. "It doesn't feel genuine. It feels like an act. Like it's hard to tell who he really is?"

"Ah."

"Does that make sense?"

"Perfect sense." He held her gaze, a warm feeling invading his chest. Perhaps it was wrong to be delighted that she didn't worship his father like the rest of the world. But he couldn't help it.

"And your parents?" he asked softly.

Something in her expression shifted. "What about them?"

"What were they like?"

She grasped her necklace, thinking for a moment before answering. "My father was quiet. Everyone listened when he talked, because he didn't do it very often." She smiled, though it didn't reach her eyes. "My mother was the exact opposite. My father used to say that she needed an audience, which was why she married him. He was always her audience."

"Sounds like your mother and my father would have gotten along."

Mary tilted her head, pressing her lips together. "In a way, I think they would have. But my mother . . . she had a certain darkness to her. She could go from happy to furious very quickly. Your father seems to have a better handle on his emotions than my mother did."

A long silence followed her words. "I'm sorry," he finally said. "That they're gone."

"Thank you," she said, without much feeling, like she'd given that response a thousand times. She was silent for several seconds, staring at him like she was mustering up the courage to ask something. "Why did you want to talk about the Ruined?" she asked.

"I'm curious. People don't talk about them much here."

"Your father is engaged in a war with them."

"There are no Ruined in Lera. It's easy to pretend they don't exist."

"Not even Olivia Flores?" she asked. "Your father took her prisoner, didn't he?"

"I don't think she's in Lera. If she is, she's far away."

"You don't know where?"

He shook his head. "She was moved recently."

Mary twisted her lips around, looking at the wall past him.

"You disagree?" he asked. "With keeping her prisoner?"

She looked at him sharply. "I didn't say that."

Her tone held more fervor than he was expecting. "Do you agree then?"

"No."

He waited, laughing when she didn't offer anything more. "Is there another option?"

"He could have not taken her prisoner at all."

Cas lifted his eyebrows. "My father hasn't talked about her much, but I got the impression she wasn't so much a prisoner as a guest."

Mary let out a loud laugh. "A guest!"

"I . . . that's the impression I got. That she's helping and healing."

"A Ruined. Helping you!" She threw her head back like it was the funniest thing she'd ever heard. "After you killed her mother and declared war on her people!"

"I . . . it sounds stupid when you put it like that."

"It sure does, Cas."

Her tone held a tone of condescension, and he laughed despite his embarrassment. "Perhaps I didn't think that through."

"Perhaps not. Olivia Flores is a prisoner, not a guest." Her amusement faded, her eyes locked on his. "You should ask your father about her. Find out the truth."

"I will." He was suddenly embarrassed that he'd never inquired about Olivia before. How old was she? Fourteen? Fifteen? What exactly was his father doing with her?

There didn't seem to be much to say after that, so they sat in silence for several long minutes, until he decided he had probably stayed long enough. He stood and headed for the door. "I should go. I'll see you tomorrow."

"Cas."

He paused with his hand on the doorknob, his heart skipping around his chest. Had she changed her mind? Did she want him to stay? He turned back to her.

She stood, gesturing to her pink dress. "I can't get it off myself. I'll have to call my maids in to help me unbutton it, and if you'd like them to think we consummated . . ." She trailed off, clasping her hands in front of her.

"Oh. Of course." He hadn't even thought of that.

She turned around, revealing an impossibly long row of tiny buttons down the back of the dress. He stepped closer to her, grasping the top one, behind her neck.

"Are all these buttons really necessary?"

"I wouldn't know. Your mother sent the dress and told me to wear it tonight."

"Of course she did." He moved on to the second button.

Mary lightly grabbed the edge of the skirt, the fabric rustling as it moved. "It's beautiful. Your mother has excellent taste."

"I suspect she told you that herself."

She laughed softly, and Cas could feel her body rise and fall beneath his fingers. "She did."

He moved down the row of buttons, slowly freeing each one. As the material parted, it began to reveal the bare flesh of her back, and he found it hard not to look. Her smooth olive skin practically glowed, and he was almost tempted to run his fingers down her spine.

The left shoulder of the dress slipped down, and she quickly crossed her arms over her chest, holding it in place.

The buttons ended below her waist, and he swallowed as he undid the last ones. His palms were sweaty and his insides had started dancing in a way he didn't particularly like.

"Thank you," she said softly, without turning around.

"You're welcome." He forced his gaze away from the open dress, revealing a part of a woman he had never given a second thought to. Now he thought he might like to see that every day.

He strode to the door, grabbing his coat off the chair. He didn't look at Mary for fear of his face giving away his feelings. "Good night."

TEN

EM FOUND AREN waiting in the hall the next morning, and she gestured for him to follow her into the sitting room. He peeked around the corner like he expected someone else to be there. When he found it empty, he stepped inside.

"Everything . . . all right?" he asked slowly.

"Fine. How are you?"

He lifted one shoulder in response.

"I asked Cas about Olivia last night. He doesn't know where she is, but I think I convinced him to ask his father about her."

"He wasn't suspicious?" Aren asked.

"Didn't seem to be."

A knock sounded on the door, and Em opened it to find Iria.

The warrior wore all black today, her wavy hair loose around her shoulders.

"Aren," Iria said, nodding at him as she walked inside. "Nice to see you again."

Em shut the door. "Let's be quick. We don't have much time before our meeting with the king."

Iria reached into her pocket, producing a crumpled envelope. She held it out to Em. "For you."

The outside of the envelope was blank, but Damian wasn't stupid enough to write her name on a letter and send it to the castle. It had been hastily sealed with a splatter of glue, and she ripped it open, turning away from Aren and Iria. Her name wasn't on the inside either.

Made it back safely—passengers are gone. Everyone here is excited about the next step, and I wish I could tell them where you are and what you're doing. But I understand the need for secrecy. Thank you for trusting me. I know it probably wasn't easy, after everything.

I'm preparing for a trip. Several have already gone safely.

I think about you every day. I hope everyone is being kind to you.

I know you can do this. I never doubted you, not for a second.

She blinked back tears before turning to Iria and Aren. "He got rid of the bodies. He said several Ruined have already made it across the border into Olso safely."

Iria leaned against the back of a chair, bracing her hands against it. "That's right. We've sent a good number of warriors to the border to help them cross over into Olso, as promised. There are a decent number of hunters on the Ruina side, but hopefully they won't be a problem. I'll let you know as soon as I hear a report."

"And then they're going to see your king?" Em prompted.

"Why?" Aren asked, his brows knitting together.

Iria threw her hands up. "The two of you, honestly. So suspicious all the time. He just wants to meet everyone for himself. See what they can do. We're bringing them to Olso to join our army. We need to understand what we have at our disposal."

"At your *disposal*," Aren repeated with an eye roll.

"Ruined have never partnered with anyone before! We need to figure out how to integrate you into our battle plan," Iria said. "May I remind you that we are the ones helping you?"

"Yes, please remind me." Aren's voice turned cold. "Remind me how you all sat back while they rounded us up and killed us. And remind me how I should be grateful now that you've decided to step in with no apology, no explanation, no *understanding* of why Em and I might be a bit suspicious of everyone. Remind me why I should just forget all that and move on, because you've decided we're useful."

Pink appeared on Iria's cheeks. Em gave Aren a small, sympathetic smile, and he lifted one shoulder as if to say *sorry*. She shrugged, a *don't apologize to me* shrug. They didn't need words to communicate about this, didn't need to be sorry for losing their grip on the anger for a moment. They'd been friends before, but they were bonded together now, bonded by a rage even Damian didn't understand. He'd reacted with sadness; Em and Aren had clawed their way through the wrath and come out the other side together.

"What happens after they see the king?" Em asked, resisting the urge to let Iria suffer a few seconds more.

She cleared her throat, obviously still uncomfortable. "They'll be taken to a ship. We have several that will be headed this way in preparation for the attack." She turned to Em. "We'll need you to find out what their defenses are on the shoreline near the castle. They have people on watch, and if you can tell us where, we want to put a Ruined on each person. Cloud their minds so they don't even see the ships coming until it's too late."

"I like that plan," Em said. "I'll work on it."

"And if we're going to partner, we need to know about the Ruined's weaknesses. We've gotten word about a flower called Weakling? Apparently some hunters are carrying it?"

Em and Aren exchanged a look. Weakling, named because it made a Ruined weak (or dead, if exposed long enough), had been a closely guarded secret for generations. The blue flower grew in Ruina, and her mother had taken her and Olivia to a small patch of it once. She still remembered the disappointment in her mother's eyes when Em stuck her nose between the petals, took a deep breath, and nothing happened. Her mother said Em's immunity was a strength, but she hadn't meant it. Her immunity meant she was doomed to be useless forever.

Her mother had spent a lot of time burning every field where the Weakling flower grew, like every king or queen before her. It always grew back, a constant plague that could never be fully erased.

"The hunters say that a Ruined can't use magic on them if they have the flower on their body," Iria continued. "Is that true?"

Aren rubbed the back of his neck. "Somewhat. Depends on how powerful the Ruined is. And it may not protect the whole body from someone like me. If you have it on your chest, I may still be able to control your legs."

"Interesting," Iria murmured. "And it harms you?"

"It closes the throat, so we can't breathe. And if it comes in contact with the skin, it can cause the skin to split open at the Ruined marks." Aren peered at his arms, searching for his Ruined marks. He'd had many, evidence of the impressive power that ran through his veins.

Only charred flesh stared back at him, and he twisted his face into a blank expression.

"Would it still have that effect on you?" Iria asked quietly.

"The marks are still there, you just can't see them anymore. And more will appear eventually. Hopefully not anytime soon." His gaze hardened. "But I know the hunters have been testing out Weakling on some of the Ruined, so I suspect you already knew what it did."

"We only wanted to know in order to protect you," Iria said.

She was right, of course. The Ruined's numbers were so

diminished that partnering with the warriors was the only option. The Ruined needed their help, and their protection.

"Anyway." Iria cleared her throat. "Find out where the royal family goes in case of an emergency. If any of them escape, we want to know where they'll be headed."

"They've already told me." Em crossed the room and opened a dresser drawer. She pushed aside a dagger and pulled out a map. She held it out to Iria. "The day after Cas was attacked, Jovita gave this to me. She said there's a small fortress in the Vallos Mountains—they call them the Southern Mountains here—and in case of an emergency, I can always go there. It's called Fort Victorra."

"I know that place," Iria murmured, twisting a lock of hair around her finger as she examined the map.

"I don't think the location is much of a secret, but you shouldn't be found with that map." Em held her hand out for it, and Iria took one last look before giving it back. Em returned it to the drawer, putting the knife back in its place.

"My parents argued for immediate action. They wanted to go in and help as soon as we heard the king killed Wenda and took Olivia." Iria lowered her voice. "For what it's worth."

"Not worth much now, considering that didn't happen and most of the Ruined are dead," Aren said, striding toward the door. "I have to get to training. Careful with that one guard, Galo. He's friends with the prince, and rumor has it he reports everything back to Cas."

"Is he captain of the prince's guard?"

"No, that's Julio. But Galo is the one who knows everything."

"Good to know," Em said.

"I'll get you the guard's schedules and rotations soon. I'm still working them out."

"Thank you," Iria said. Aren walked out the door, pulling it closed behind him. Iria stared at the spot where he'd been.

"He's not the same as he was," Em said.

"I barely knew him before. He only spoke to me to tease me when I visited the castle."

He'd probably been flirting with her—Aren was a terrible flirt when he was younger—but Em decided not to point that out.

She gestured for Iria to follow as she walked to the door and headed out into the hallway. "I'll keep you updated," she said quietly.

Iria nodded at something behind Em. "Your Highness."

Em turned to see Cas coming down the hallway. He wore dark pants and a gray shirt that had several buttons undone, and he tossed a piece of hair out of his eyes as he approached.

She really wished he wouldn't do that thing with his hair.

"Hello, Iria," he said.

"I'll leave you two alone," the warrior said. "I need to find Koldo and Benito before the meeting."

Cas watched Iria go, then turned to Em. "Good morning."

He was smiling. He should definitely stop smiling. "Good morning."

"I thought we could walk to the meeting together. My father

is always late, so we can entertain the warriors until he gets there." Cas offered his arm, and she took it.

"Is this an appropriate outfit?" she asked, gesturing down to the loose black dress. It was short-sleeved and casual, with a long, simple skirt that moved around her legs when she walked. "I didn't know if there was a certain type of dress for your meetings. Your mother didn't give me any instructions."

"No, there's not. The meetings are casual." He paused, then cleared his throat. "You look very nice."

"Thank you." Em stole a quick glance at him. She wasn't sure what to make of last night. He hadn't even seemed angry that she didn't want to consummate the marriage. Maybe he didn't want to have sex with her either.

The thought should have been more comforting than it was.

They walked to the Ocean Room, and when Cas opened the door, she understood why the king took meetings there. The space was huge, easily bigger than all her rooms combined. The floor-to-ceiling windows on the east wall showed off an impressive view of the ocean in the distance, and the deep-blue curtains were all open.

Several chairs and couches surrounded the fireplace, and the white carpet spread throughout the room was immaculate. A long wooden table with chairs on either side was in the middle of the room, and a generous spread of fruit and pastries sat in the center.

Besides two staff members, they were the first ones there, and Em took a seat next to Cas. The servants poured them tea and piled their plates with food. Em reached for a pastry covered in sugar, noting that there were no knives on the table. Her chair was made of wood, though, and could easily be broken. The king would probably sit at the end of the table, and she could smash the chair over one of his advisers' heads, and then use a sharp edge to cut the king's throat or maybe jam it into his chest.

"Feel free to speak up at this meeting, if you want," Cas said. "I didn't ask enough questions or talk when I first started attending, and everyone took it to mean I was bored and uninterested."

She ran a napkin over her mouth. "Were you?"

"No. I just thought it was best to listen first. Get all the facts before forming an opinion." He laughed. "My father is more of the type to form an opinion and then ignore facts later, so I don't think he quite understood."

She barely suppressed the urge to roll her eyes at the mention of his father. She stuffed the rest of the pastry into her mouth instead.

The warriors entered and took the seats across from Cas and Em. The staff served them food and tea as well, but the warriors all just sat there, regarding the provisions suspiciously.

Koldo's full red cheeks made him appear younger than the other two, and he glanced at Iria and Benito, as if asking for permission to eat. Benito frowned at him.

"We didn't poison it," Cas said with a laugh, then took a sip of his tea. "If we were going to kill you, we would come up with something much better than poison."

The warriors chuckled. "Perhaps we just don't like the food here, Your Highness," Iria said.

"Sure you don't," Cas said with a grin. He took a big bite of a meat pie on his plate. There was really no arguing that Lera had delicious food down to a perfect science.

"We don't usually eat at meetings in Olso," Benito said, but he reached for his tea, his huge hand engulfing the cup. Koldo's eyes brightened, and he reached for a pastry.

The queen and Jovita entered the room, followed by four of the king's advisers. They all took their seats, Jovita sliding into the chair next to Iria. The advisers sat down next to Em, opposite the warriors.

Em leaned closer to Cas, speaking in a whisper. "Is Jovita usually in these meetings?"

He nodded. "She's being groomed to take over her late mother's advisory spot. She's only begun attending in the last year or so."

The king strolled into the room, his usual big smile plastered on his face. The Olso warriors stood for him, and Em begrudgingly got to her feet with Cas.

"Good morning," he said as he pulled his chair out and sat down. Chairs scraped against the floor as everyone else sat. "How was your first night in the castle?"

"Very nice, Your Majesty," Benito said.

"You should visit the shore while you're here," the king said, sweeping his arm out to the window, in case they'd missed the view. "It's lovely, you know."

The warriors nodded without reply. Em suspected they would rather stab themselves in the eye than frolic on Lera's beaches. She couldn't blame them.

"Let's get started right away," the king said. "You're here because your trade agreements with Vallos are no longer valid, since we control the country now. So tell me what you want."

Iria slid a piece of paper across the table. "Those were our terms with Vallos. We'd request the same from you."

The king frowned at the paper for a moment, then pushed it aside. Cas nudged it closer to him, and Em noticed him stealing a glance. The terms were most likely purposefully terrible, since the warriors had no intention of signing any new trade agreements. It was simply a distraction, so they could remain in Lera to plot the attack.

"No," the king said.

"Do you have terms you'd prefer?" Koldo asked.

"No. That's your job. Come up with something better."

"We will send word to our king and draft new terms," Iria said. "Should we move on? We'd like to discuss the port of Olso."

The king folded his hands together and rested them on his stomach as he leaned back in his chair. "Yes?"

"The clause in the peace treaty that gave you the port expired five years ago," Iria said. "Yet Lera ships are still there."

"The clause expired only if Lera was satisfied that Olso didn't pose a threat to any of the other kingdoms," the king said.

"We don't," Koldo said.

"No?" the king asked. "I've just received word from my hunters that the Ruined were spotted trying to enter Olso."

Em's breath caught in her throat, and she looked at Iria, trying to keep her expression neutral. The warrior's face showed genuine surprise. Koldo and Benito wore matching expressions.

"When did you hear this, Your Majesty?" she asked.

"Just yesterday."

"I don't know anything about that, but we can't control what the Ruined try to do, Your Majesty," she said.

"I have other reports saying that warriors have been spotted in Vallos as well. What would warriors be doing in Vallos?"

"Enjoying the countryside?" Iria guessed, twisting a lock of hair around her finger. Em pressed her lips together to keep from laughing.

The king narrowed his eyes. "Many of the Ruined are currently in Vallos."

"As is the entire population of Vallos. We are allowed to visit Vallos, Your Majesty," Iria said. "Their entry laws are far more relaxed than yours."

"That will be changing."

"I'm sure," Iria said.

"Partnering with the Ruined is an act of war," the king said.

"Understood. But like I said, I don't know anything about that. And regardless, that clause is five years expired. We've been patient, and we ask that you honor your agreements."

"It's not happening."

"Why not?" Cas asked.

All heads swiveled to him, matching expressions of surprise on the faces of every adviser. The queen's eyes widened, and she put a hand on Jovita's arm, like she was afraid the girl would jump in with her own questions. Jovita merely raised an eyebrow.

"Casimir!" his father exclaimed.

"I wasn't agreeing with them, I was asking a question," he said. "Why do we still control that port?"

"Because of the clause in the treaty," the king said.

"Is it true the treaty said we'd return the port to them five years ago if they hadn't shown violence against other kingdoms?"

The king paused for a moment. "I would need to see a copy to be sure."

Em barely held back a snort. It was smart of him not to admit to that, even if it was true.

"I'd like to think we honor our word," Cas said.

His father rose suddenly, shooting his son a look so full of venom that even Em was tempted to crawl under the table. To Cas's credit, he just stared back at his father.

"We will continue this discussion another time," the king said. He glared at the warriors. "I've ordered any Ruined attempting to sneak into Olso captured and brought to me for questioning. If you're lying about helping them, I *will* find out."

Em gripped her hands together so tightly it almost hurt. It wasn't unexpected that the hunters had noticed the Ruined moving into Olso. She had hoped they would have more time before the king became suspicious, but that was all he had. Suspicions.

The king walked out of the room, and the advisers followed suit. The queen and Jovita stood behind Cas's chair until he finally noticed and stood as well.

The queen leaned over and said something to Cas as Em followed them out of the room. He shrugged, which was apparently not the answer his mother wanted. She marched away, her skirts swishing around her feet.

Jovita lingered, and Cas gestured for Em to follow them. She obediently walked down the hallway and into the library. Jovita pushed the door closed behind them.

"What are you doing?" Jovita had a way of speaking that was both furious and quiet and calm.

"What do you mean?" Cas asked, plopping down in a chair and stretching his long legs out in front of him.

Jovita glanced to where Em stood by the door, as if just noticing she was still with them. Jovita hesitated, but Cas looked at her expectantly.

"Defying your father in front of the warriors is inappropriate. And not helpful."

"I wasn't defying him. I asked a question."

"It was an inappropriate question," Jovita said, planting her hands on her hips. Em edged around her and sat down in a chair across from Cas.

"It was not," Cas said. "What is the point of making treaties if you're not going to honor them?"

Jovita sighed like Cas was an idiot. "You just don't understand, Cas."

Cas imitated her sigh. "Neither do you, Jovita."

Em choked back a laugh, brushing her fingers across her mouth. Cas caught her smile and his lips turned up as well.

Jovita rolled her eyes. "Gross. I don't need to see your budding romance right now."

"Jovita," Cas said in a warning tone.

"Your father is going to throw you out of the meetings if you disagree with him."

"I've been in those meetings longer than you. I'm allowed to start asking questions."

Jovita walked to the door. "You may have been in them longer, but at least I know when to keep my mouth shut and obey."

Cas pulled on his knuckle, turning away from Jovita. She left the room, letting the door shut behind her.

A long silence settled after Jovita left, and Em watched as Cas stared at the floor.

"It was a fair question," she finally said.

"You don't have to agree with me just because we're married," he said with a hint of amusement.

"Trust me, there's no danger of that."

He cocked his head, studying her for a moment. "How do you feel about a little adventure?"

"I'm for it."

"It's kind of dangerous. And my parents will be furious if they find out."

"Then I'm definitely for it."

He hopped up. "Good. Change into pants. Something discreet."

ELEVEN

EM WAITED FOR Cas outside the door to the staff kitchen, as he'd instructed her. She'd changed into black pants and a loose green shirt. She rolled up the sleeves as she waited.

Cas rounded the corner with a guard, the young dark-haired one who was always at his side. The guard smiled at Em, revealing a tiny gap between his two front teeth. His square jaw, wide nose, and green eyes all worked together to make an unexpectedly handsome face.

"Mary, have you officially met Galo?" Cas asked.

"I don't think so. Nice to meet you, Galo."

He tilted his head forward. "You too, Your Highness."

Cas pushed open the door behind Em, and she followed him into the kitchen, with Galo trailing behind her. The first room was where the staff ate, with a door off to the side that led to a bustling area where they prepared the food. A few small tables were scattered around the room, and a boy sat at one, polishing a pile of forks.

The boy had a small scar above his left eyebrow, and he couldn't have been more than thirteen or fourteen, though he was already quite tall and broad. Em's mother hadn't allowed children under the age of sixteen to work in the kitchens, or anywhere remotely dangerous in the castle.

Cas led them outside into the sunlight. They headed through the gardens, Cas glancing back at the castle once like he was checking to make sure they weren't followed. Em got the impression they were sneaking out, and she was eager to see how Cas was going to do it. If there was a way to get out undetected, there was a way to get in.

They made it to the back wall, and Cas walked to the tree Em had already pegged as a good escape route. He grabbed a thick, low branch and hoisted himself up. He climbed until he could step onto the wall.

"When you're king, perhaps you can use the gate?" Galo called to him. He still stood on the ground with Em.

"Not if my mother is still alive," Cas said. He looked down at her. "Coming up?"

"I'd be happy to help you," Galo said.

She snorted. "Thanks, but I'm fine." She grabbed the branch and climbed up, easily hoisting herself onto the wall. Cas was peering over, and she followed his gaze to the other side. A guard lifted his hand.

"Hello, Roberto," Cas said.

The guard's mustache quirked up. "Hello, Your Highness." He reached for the rope near his feet and tossed it to Cas.

Cas passed the rope to Galo, who had just climbed the tree. Galo tied it to the trunk and waved that it was ready. Cas grasped the rope with both hands.

He braced his feet against the wall as he climbed down. She noticed that he winced as he descended, favoring his right side. The left shoulder was still sore from the attack. She tucked that into the back of her mind, in case she needed to use it against him later.

Em grabbed the rope when he was on the ground and began her own descent. Galo followed, his boots hitting the ground with a thud. He straightened and grinned at the older guard standing by the wall.

"Usual warning," Roberto barked at Galo.

"Yes, I know," Galo said. "Endless shame and a lifetime of misery if anything happens to Prince Casimir." He took a quick glance at Em. "Or Princess Mary."

"I'll also remind you that an attempt was just made on Prince Casimir's life," Roberto said.

"I'll be fine," Cas said. He gestured at Em. "I brought her."

Em barely managed to hold back a laugh. That was her. Protector of the prince of Lera.

Roberto pointed out at the city. "Go ahead, then. If you're not back by sundown, I'll alert the king that you left."

When Cas turned away, Roberto grabbed Galo by the arm and said something Em couldn't hear. Galo nodded, his expression more serious when the guard let him go.

Em traipsed down the hill behind Cas. It was clear and sunny, the ocean breeze rustling the leaves of nearby trees. Green grass dotted with a few trees spread out in front of them, and Cas headed to a thin dirt path.

"Did you see Royal City when you came in?" Cas asked, slowing so he was walking beside her. Galo walked on his other side, scanning the area around them. She'd never seen this guard in action, but she liked the way he didn't keep his hand poised over his sword. She could easily take it from him, if she caught him by surprise.

"No," she said. "The royal escorts took us around the city."

The dirt path rounded a corner, and the sounds of people talking and hooves clomping filled the air. They were suddenly in the center of Royal City, with people streaming in and out of shops and making their way through the streets.

Em watched a father and daughter walk across the street with bags full of food in their arms. She could see a food market, a clothing store, and a feed store just in her immediate area. Carts lined the street, with men and women selling jewelry, trinkets, and sweet-smelling breads.

There was nowhere like this in Ruina. Even before King Salomir destroyed their cities, they weren't like this. A city was maybe made up of three shops, and it wasn't unusual to find the food market had run out of everything except dried beans. She'd never even considered sneaking out to visit Ruina cities by herself.

Cas jerked his head, indicating that she should follow him. He had his hands in his pockets, his thin white shirt flapping with the wind against his chest. He didn't look much like a prince to the unsuspecting public, but the people of Royal City must have known him.

"Does anyone ever recognize you?" she asked, glancing around at the people walking past.

"No. Sometimes I get a few looks, but no one expects me to just be wandering around the city by myself, so they don't notice." He stopped at a cart with an umbrella over it. "Three, please."

The man reached into the cart with a pair of tongs and pulled out three steaming buns. He put each one in a separate paper bag, holding his open hand out to Cas without giving him much of a glance. Cas dropped a few coins in his hand and took the bags.

"Cheese bread," he said, handing one bag to her, and another to Galo. "Every time you come to the city, you buy one. It's a rule."

She opened the bag and peeked inside, the smell of fresh bread wafting through the air. She grabbed the bun and took a small bite. It was soft and chewy, with a hint of cheese flavor, and she took a second, bigger bite.

"It's delicious," she said.

"I'm glad you like it. The marriage might not have worked out if you didn't." The edges of Cas's mouth twitched.

"How tragic. The union between Lera and Vallos destroyed over cheese bread."

Cas laughed, revealing the dimple on his left cheek. His eyes sparkled in the sun, and it was easy for Em to forget for a moment that he was the prince of Lera. He was more relaxed than she'd ever seen, like the castle sucked half his energy away.

"Cas takes his food very seriously," Galo said. The prince didn't blink at being called "Cas" by a guard.

"I don't blame you," she said. She took another bite of her bun.

They finished their bread and Cas led them down the street. Em realized they hadn't even been in the busiest part of town, as the crowds and stores increased the closer they got to the shore. Something must have made Galo nervous, because he said something to Cas, and they cut across to a less populated street, lined with small homes and apartments.

The ocean came into view, and Cas looked both ways before crossing the wide street dividing the city from the beach. Em followed him, stepping one boot into the sand, then the other.

The beaches of Vallos and Ruina were rocky and often chilly. She'd never seen one with white sand stretching out as far as she could see in either direction, the ocean glittering in the sun. Several ships were docked at the harbor in the distance, their sails flapping in the wind.

A few groups of people dotted the sand, many dressed in strange outfits. The men wore loose, short pants, with sleeveless shirts. The women wore something like very small dresses. The hems barely reached mid-thigh, and their arms were totally bare. Em's mother had been a fan of flesh-baring fashion—Em remembered a dress with a neckline that went all the way down to her belly button—but this would have gotten an eyebrow raise even from Wenda Flores. Then she would have immediately demanded one of her own.

Cas took off his shoes and socks and left them in the sand like he didn't care if someone came along and took them, so she did the same. Galo left his on, hanging back as they headed closer to the ocean. They walked until the cool water rushed over their feet, and Em curled her toes around the sand.

"Can I ask you a question?" Cas asked.

"Sure."

"Why didn't you bring anyone with you? Friends or maids or guards? If I were leaving my home, I'd want to bring as many people with me as possible."

"There aren't that many people left," she said, squinting out at the ocean. "My parents are gone. A lot of people I knew were killed after the attacks on the Ruined began."

"And your parents never had any children besides you, did they?"

"No," she lied, a sharp pain stabbing through her chest as she thought of Olivia. "My mother wanted to have more, but she couldn't. I would have had ten brothers and sisters, if it was up to her."

"Was it lonely?" he asked.

"Sometimes. It was tough, not having anyone around who really understood what my life was like. You know what I mean?" She looked to him for confirmation, and he nodded. "But my mother brought other children our—my—age into the castle, so there was always someone around to play with. Two boys became very good friends. Aren is one of them, actually."

"Just friends?"

She glanced at him. His voice seemed intentionally flippant, and she wondered for the first time if he was jealous of Aren.

"Yes, just friends," she said honestly. "He's like my brother."

"Ah."

"You don't think I would bring a boy I was in love with to watch me marry someone else, do you?" she asked with a laugh.

He shrugged, his expression a bit sheepish at having been caught. "I guess not."

"We did try to kiss once. We were thirteen. Neither of us could stop laughing long enough to actually do it."

"Did you have someone you left behind?" Cas asked. "Someone you loved, I mean."

She lifted her eyebrows. "Are you sure you want to know that?"

"Sure. You can tell me the truth."

"Not really." Damian's face flashed in front of her eyes. "I had a friend who would have liked to be more, but it never became anything. My mother was very disappointed in me, I think."

"Why? She liked him?"

"Everyone liked him. He came from a powerful family, but he was still everyone's best friend. The kind of guy who never forgot a name. Always made everyone feel special. It would have been a good match, but my mother didn't force me."

She didn't know why she'd blurted out that story about

Damian, but Cas's expression brightened as she told it. She might be inclined to tell him all her stories, if he was going to look at her like that.

She took a tiny step away from him. It was easier to think when he wasn't close enough to touch, and she needed to use this opportunity to get information about Lera's defenses.

She pointed to a tall, round tower in the distance, at the edge of the coastline. "Is that your coastal defense?"

He nodded. "Those towers are scattered up and down the coast, though we have three just in this area."

"Have you had any threats since the last war with Olso?" she asked.

"No. An Olso ship was spotted several years ago, but when they contacted the crew, they claimed it was off course. It turned around when the guard in the tower fired a warning. Once the warning is fired, troops immediately come down from the castle and surrounding areas. By the time the ship arrives, an army is ready for them."

She pointed to the ships in the harbor. "Where are they coming from?"

"Vallos and Ruina."

"Do you have a lot of ships from Ruina?" she asked.

"We have people there, working the coal mines. The criminals who aren't suited to be hunters are sent there to work."

"The hunters are criminals?" she asked.

"Yes. We didn't have enough volunteers, so my father sent most of the prison population."

"Were they given a choice?"

"No. And my father used the entire prison population, even petty thieves and people who would have served only a few months. He promises everyone a pardon, but with no end date for their service. Just offers them money for each Ruined kill and sends them out."

She had no room inside of her to feel compassion for the hunters, but maybe she understood them for the first time. Maybe they were as trapped by their circumstances as she was.

"No wonder they want to kill you." She glanced over her shoulder. They were alone except for Galo, standing a few paces away. "Come to think of it, I should have brought my sword. There are probably a few people nearby who want to kill you."

"Oh, at least a few?" He looked like he was trying not to smile.

"I'm sure. They might try to kill me simply for standing next to you. Perhaps you could keep a larger distance between us?" She scooted away from him, a grin spreading across her face almost against her will.

He laughed. "I think I'd actually prefer to have you close by."

He extended his hand to her, and her breath hitched in her throat as she realized she wanted to take it.

"Walk?" he asked.

She slipped her hand into his, and when he laced their fingers together, her entire traitor body flushed. She ducked her head, pretending not to notice the bursts of happiness exploding in her chest.

TWELVE

CAS WOKE TO someone shoving his shoulder, and he rolled over, squinting in the sudden light. His father stood next to his bed, holding a lantern in the pitch-black room.

"Get up," the king said. "I want you to see this." Light flickered off his face, and Cas could see his father's mouth pulled into a thin, grim line.

Cas hurried out of bed and didn't question his father.

He pulled on pants and his boots and followed the king out of the room. The castle was quiet as they headed quickly down the hallway to the stairs.

Several guards waited at the main door, including Galo. They formed a circle around the king and the prince as they strode out the door and into the cool night air.

Cas glanced at his father's tense face. They hadn't spoken since the meeting with the warriors last week, but he got the feeling the serious expression the king was wearing didn't have much to do with Cas.

They walked so quickly they were practically jogging. They passed the front gate, where horses waited, and Cas jumped onto one. He followed his father to the east, away from Royal City, the horses at a trot.

They rode for only a few minutes before the glow of several torches lit up the night sky. The king slowed, then stopped and dismounted his horse. Cas and the guards did the same.

His father motioned for him to come closer, and Cas fell into step beside him as they headed in the direction of the torches. A large group of guards surrounded something Cas couldn't see yet. Four men dressed in black-and-gray hunter uniforms stood with the guards.

"We've caught one of them," the king said. "One of the Ruined trying sneak into Olso."

Cas took in a sharp breath and turned his attention back to the circle of guards, hoping to catch a glimpse. He'd never seen a Ruined before.

"We're bringing him to the castle for questioning, but not while he's at full strength. It's not safe. I want you to see what they're capable of."

"How will you weaken him?" Cas asked.

"A Ruined can only use so much power before it starts to wane. The more power you bring out, the weaker they get."

Cas suddenly wished he'd brought his sword. It had been stupid to run out of his room without grabbing his sword first. His father had one at his hip.

The circle of guards parted as they approached, revealing a young man in the middle. He sat in the dirt, his hands tied behind his back. He was dressed in all black, with spots of dust on his pants and shirt. He had a small cut under one eye, but he was otherwise unharmed. His arms were covered in an intricate web of marks, and Cas squinted to see them better. He'd always assumed the Ruined marks were ugly. But this Ruined's were a shade lighter than his olive skin, a series of thin lines that wrapped around his flesh like a complicated series of vines. They were more art than ugly.

"He hasn't spoken, Your Majesty," one of the guards said to the king.

The Ruined straightened, and he looked from the king to the prince. He stayed focused on Cas, his eyebrows furrowing.

The Ruined was staring at him like he was considering the best way to murder him. Now Cas really wished he had a sword.

"He will," the king said. "But that's not my concern at the moment." He frowned at Cas. "Plant your feet. Watch the trees."

Anticipation and fear fluttered in Cas's chest. He nodded solemnly. The Ruined was still staring at him. He pretended not to notice. Galo stepped next to him, sword drawn.

"Up," a guard said to the Ruined, kicking him in the side. The Ruined glared at him, slowly getting to his feet. He was young. Maybe the same age as Cas.

The guard delivered a punch straight into the Ruined's stomach, and the gasp echoed through the trees. The wind blew Cas's hair into his eyes, and he pushed it away as the guard punched the man across the face.

"What is he doing?" Cas asked his father quietly.

"Making him angry."

The Ruined stumbled backward, hitting the ground with a thump. Another guard hauled him to his feet, shoving him back to the center of the circle.

Another gust of wind blew across Cas's face, this one stronger than the last. A hunter stepped forward, pulling a dagger off his belt. He held his hand up to the guard, indicating that he should stop.

"You have to work harder with this one. He has pretty good control." The hunter grabbed the Ruined by the arm, cutting off his ropes with a quick slice of the knife. He pulled one hand behind the Ruined's back.

The hunter sliced off one of the Ruined's fingers.

A scream tore through the night, and Cas's entire body went cold. Blood dripped from the Ruined's hand, his face twisted in pain.

The ground started to shake.

Cas stumbled, throwing his arms out to steady himself. A long crack ripped through the dirt right in between his legs, and he quickly jumped to one side. A guard had his arm, keeping him steady as the ground rumbled.

"Heads up!" someone yelled, and Cas spun around to see

the tree just next to the Ruined tilting dangerously to the left. A few hunters scrambled out of the way as the roots ripped out of the dirt. The trunk slammed to the ground, narrowly missing a guard. Two more trees quickly followed.

The Ruined tried to make a run for it, but a guard grabbed him from behind. Another one punched him across the face. Dirt lifted off the ground as if caught in an invisible wind. The Ruined glared as he tossed it in the faces of a few guards.

Cas whirled around, shaking off the guard who still had his arm. His father stood in front of him. Behind him, Cas heard a loud smack, then a grunt from the Ruined. The ground rumbled again, though not nearly as powerfully as the first time.

"Imagine if you were alone with him," the king said. He gestured at a fallen tree. "Look what he's capable of."

Look what he did because you tortured him. The thought hit him so forcefully he felt sick.

"Who is he?" Cas asked quietly. He wanted his father to tell him that this was one of the worst Ruined. Explain how he'd killed innocent people. Maybe he'd been with the group that murdered Mary's parents.

"You heard them," the king said, gesturing at the guards. "He hasn't spoken. We'll find out who he is and why he was crossing into Olso soon enough, though."

Dread filled Cas's chest, and he dropped his gaze from his father's.

Was this what the hunters did in Ruina and Vallos? They hunted down Ruined and tortured them? Killed them?

Of course they did. Cas knew that. He'd known it since his father issued the order. But it felt different, seeing it in action.

His father took a step closer to him. "If Olso partnered with the Ruined, it could be devastating to us. Do you understand that, Casimir? The combination of Olso's military abilities with the Ruined's powers could destroy us."

"They said they didn't know the Ruined were coming into Olso," Cas said. "Do you think they were lying?"

"Yes." The king ran a hand over his beard. "Always assume everyone is lying. Don't trust anyone, except those closest to you. You have a tendency to see the good in people, and I admire that, but it will destroy you. I promise you it will."

Cas's head was starting to pound, and the screams from the Ruined were doing nothing to help it. The gusts of wind blowing across his face kept getting softer as they drained the man of his power.

"What will you do if he admits to working with the warriors?" Cas asked.

"We will plan an attack. We've defeated Olso before, and we can do it again. We just can't allow ourselves to be caught off guard."

Cas glanced over his shoulder at the Ruined. He was on the ground, his injured hand cradled against his chest. His eyes fluttered, a moan escaping his lips.

"I understand. But is this the best way?" He lowered his voice, unable to keep back the questions he'd often wanted to ask the past year. "Is killing the Ruined the only way?"

"When you think you've come up with a better plan, please share it. I'll be eager to hear it." The king walked back to his horse, gesturing to a few guards to follow him.

Laughter sounded from behind Cas, and he turned to find a hunter with his dagger poised over the Ruined's other hand. The Ruined had his eyes squeezed shut as he waited to lose another finger.

"Stop!" Cas yelled. The hunter jumped away, almost losing hold of the dagger. "He's had enough."

Every guard focused on something behind him, and Cas glanced over his shoulder to see his father atop his horse, watching him.

"You want him alive, correct?" Cas asked.

"I do, for now. You can handle his transport to the cell with the guards, since you're confident he's weak enough."

"I'd be happy to," Cas said. His father gave Cas a look that wasn't exactly disapproval, but maybe wasn't supportive either. He turned his horse toward the castle. Three guards followed him.

"How did you transport him to Lera?" Cas asked the nearest hunter.

"Wagon," the hunter said, pointing into the darkness. "It's not far that way."

"Put him in it and bring him to the castle. I assume he's going to the cells on the south lawn?" He doubted his father would let any Ruined step one foot inside the castle.

A guard nodded. "Those are our orders."

"I'll meet you there." Cas mounted his horse, and Galo and a few other guards rode with him back to the castle grounds. He left his horse at the gate and walked in the dark to the south lawn. Outdoor and sporting events were often held there, but there was a small underground prison at the far end of the property. It was used to house the more dangerous prisoners, the ones they didn't want sleeping beneath the castle.

The hunters brought the wagon straight onto the south lawn, and one of them had to practically hold the Ruined up as they pulled him out.

Galo grabbed the handle of the door in the ground and opened it. He hopped in first, and Cas followed him down the stairway into the underground cells. It was pitch-black, but the narrow space filled with light as Galo lit the first lantern.

There were five cells in a row to Cas's left, every one of them empty. A walkway ran between the cells and the wall, and two chairs sat at either end of the room, for the guards.

Several guards descended the stairs, and Cas moved to the far end of the area as the hunters dragged the Ruined down the steps. They thrust him into the first cell, not even the slightest bit gently. He hit the ground on his hands and knees, and Cas studied his dirty left hand, missing its pinkie finger.

"Can someone please bring something to clean his wound?" Cas asked. "And bandages?"

A hunter gave him a confused look.

"I don't know how long my father wants him alive," Cas said. "Do you want him to die of an infection?"

"Yes, Your Highness," a guard said, turning away.

"You can go," Cas said to the four hunters crowding around the cell. "Thank you."

They disappeared up the stairs, leaving just Galo and three other guards. Cas stepped to the open door of the cell, leaning against it.

"Perhaps we should close the door, Your Highness," a guard said.

"After his wound is cleaned." He held out his hand. "May I have a sword, though?"

A guard withdrew his blade from his belt and offered it to Cas. He took it and turned back to the Ruined. The Ruined straightened, scooting back to lean against the end of the small bed in the corner. One of his eyes was starting to swell shut, and he lifted his head to meet Cas's gaze.

"What's your name?" Cas asked.

The Ruined didn't reply.

"I'm Casimir. Prince of Lera." He waited for the Ruined to offer his name, but he remained silent. "How old are you?"

"A hundred and two." The Ruined smirked. "I've learned how to live forever and keep my good looks."

"Really?" Cas asked, feigning surprise. "My father would love to talk to you about that."

A snort came from one of the guards behind him, and the Ruined stared at Cas as if he wasn't sure if that was a joke.

"A name?" Cas asked again. "Just a first name, so I know what to call you."

"You can call me Ruined," he said, leaning his head against the bed. "I'm not ashamed of it."

Footsteps sounded on the stairs, and the guard who'd left reappeared with a bucket of water, a clean cloth, bandages, and a small silver tin. The guard hesitated, like he didn't want to enter the cell, and Galo held his hands out for the items.

"I'll do it." He grabbed everything from the guard and walked past Cas into the cell, placing the bucket and tin on the ground. He dipped the cloth in the water. "Hold out your hand."

The Ruined hesitated, peering at his bloodied fingers.

"It's going to hurt, but I'm not going to make it worse on purpose," Galo said.

The Ruined slowly put his hand out in front of him. He winced as Galo began wiping it down.

"This is berol root," Galo said as he scooped some of the black paste out of the tin with the cloth. "It will help the wound close without getting infected." He gently applied it over the stump where the Ruined's pinkie finger used to be.

"We wouldn't want me getting an infection before you kill me," the Ruined said through clenched teeth.

"If you tell my father what he needs to know, maybe we can come up with a way to spare your life," Cas said.

The Ruined let out a hollow laugh. "Like keeping me prisoner for the rest of my life? No thank you."

He wasn't wrong, so Cas said nothing. His father would never just release one of the Ruined, even if he'd done nothing wrong.

He rubbed a hand across his forehead, the full weight of those words settling in. *Even if he'd done nothing wrong.*

Galo wrapped the Ruined's hand in the bandage and stood, grabbing the remaining supplies. Cas stepped back and a guard closed the cell door.

"Two guards should stay down here with him," Cas said. "He should have water and three meals a day."

"Yes, Your Highness," the guards murmured.

Cas looked at the Ruined to find him staring, his eyebrows drawn together.

"I'll be down often to check on you," Cas said. "We don't mistreat our prisoners in Lera, Ruined or not." He glanced over his shoulder at the guards. "Please remind the other guards of that."

"I look forward to being treated well right up until you chop off my head, Casimir," the Ruined said, bringing his knees close to his chest and throwing his good arm over them.

Cas wanted to ask what the Ruined's life was like. Who he'd killed. If he'd kill everyone in the room, if given the chance. If he hated everyone who wasn't Ruined, and if he'd always felt that way, or if Cas's father had caused it.

But whatever he said to the Ruined right now was likely to get repeated all over the castle by the guards.

"People call me Cas," he said. "And I'd rather not call you Ruined. I'd prefer to use your name."

The Ruined's eyes flashed with anger and a tiny hint of interest. He held Cas's gaze almost to the point of discomfort, like he was testing the prince to see how much he really wanted to know.

"Damian," the Ruined finally said. "My name's Damian."

THIRTEEN

EM FLEW OUT of her room, the door slamming closed behind her. A maid looked down the hallway, startled. Em rushed past her and to the stairs.

They'd captured a Ruined. The news was all over the castle this morning, according to Davina. He was being held in a cell on the south lawn and was only being kept alive long enough to spill information to the king.

Her heart pounded as she reached the bottom of the stairs. It was very likely that she knew the man they had captured, since there weren't that many of them left. Would he leak the secret about their pact with Olso? And if he didn't talk, would she have to stand by and watch him die, or risk blowing her cover?

The castle was just starting to come alive for the morning,

and she edged around the corner to avoid the queen and several ladies walking across the foyer. She headed for the back of the castle, pushing open a door to the west wing. The guards' rooms were down this wing, and two of them straightened as she walked through the door.

"Have you seen Aren?" she asked.

"I'll get him for you, Your Highness," one of the guards said, jogging down the hallway. He knocked on a door, and Aren stuck his head out a few moments later. He stepped out of the room, buttoning his blue shirt as he walked. She could tell from his expression that he'd already heard.

She jerked her head, indicating that he should follow her. He trailed behind her through the castle and into the gardens. They walked through the flowers into the center of the tall hedges, away from any prying ears.

She took a quick glance around before facing Aren and lowering her voice so it was barely a whisper.

"Have you heard a name?" she asked. "Did he talk?"

"The guards I asked didn't know. And they don't want us going down there unless we're assigned a shift. I can volunteer for a shift, but I thought it was best to time it right."

She swallowed down a wave of panic. "If he tells them the Ruined are partnering with the warriors—"

"He won't," Aren interrupted.

"We don't even know who they have."

"That doesn't mean he would betray us. There's nothing the king could say or do that would make him want to talk. Would you talk, if it was you who were captured?"

She pushed her hands through her hair with a sigh. "Of course not. They would kill me as soon as they got the information."

"Exactly. Whoever this is knows that too. But don't go down there, just in case. We don't want him recognizing you and using it as leverage."

"What do you think our chances are of being able to rescue him?"

"Not good," Aren said, rubbing the back of his neck. "But maybe you can convince them not to execute him for a while. If you can stall them, he might have a chance."

"I can try."

"They're saying Cas was there last night."

"Good. I'll go find him. I'll let you know if I figure out who it is."

"Be careful," Aren warned. "Don't blow your cover for this. If we have to let one Ruined die . . ." He lifted his shoulders. "Then we have to let him die. It's unfortunate, but there are bigger things at stake here."

He stared at something behind her, and she turned to see Iria crossing the gardens, a grim expression on her face.

"You were supposed to protect them!" Em hissed as soon as Iria was near. "Why is there a Ruined in that cell?"

Iria tugged on a piece of hair, twisting it around her finger. "It's Damian."

Em's heart stopped beating. All the sounds of the garden faded away and were replaced by a loud buzzing noise in her ears, like a million bugs had descended around her head at once.

Damian would never talk. Even though he knew the biggest secret, Em's secret, he wouldn't give the king one shred of information.

But he would die.

"How do you know that?" Aren asked.

"Cas went down there. Got his name out of him. Koldo heard it from one of the guards."

"What?" Em practically yelled.

Iria's usual smug expression fell into a mask of annoyance. "Would you keep your voice down? Do you want them to throw you in that cell with him?"

Yes. She did. That was where she belonged, not married to the prince who had put Damian in that cell.

"How did Cas get it out of him?'" Em asked, lowering her voice. "Did they hurt him?"

"Yes. The king and Cas tortured him last night to weaken him, from what I understand."

Anger boiled in her veins. When it came down to it, Cas was exactly like his father. She knew this, yet still felt the briefest flicker of disappointment.

"We've been protecting the Ruined, but—" Iria said.

"Then why is Damian about to be executed?" Aren asked.

"We are helping hundreds of Ruined in Olso. The fact that only one has been captured is actually pretty impressive."

Em balled her fingers into fists, seriously considering punching Iria in the face.

"I'm very sorry that the one who was caught was your friend," Iria added, putting her hands up like she knew what Em was thinking. "But you need to pull yourself together. You look devastated. Mary would not be devastated about a Ruined being captured."

"He's not just our friend, he's the current leader of the Ruined," Aren said. "What are the Ruined going to do without him?"

"They're going to keep crossing into Olso, like they were ordered," Iria said. "Just because he isn't there doesn't mean everything will fall apart. They know what to do. Right now, it's more important for you both to stay calm and not give yourselves away."

Aren gave Em a pained expression, like it physically hurt him to agree with Iria. She was right, of course. Mary wouldn't care at all about a Ruined being captured. In fact, she'd probably go down there and kill him herself.

"The Ruined killed Mary's parents. She'd be at least a little upset to have one in the castle," Em said. "Maybe I can use that as an excuse to talk to Damian. Say I want to find out if he was the one who killed them?"

"Or I can try to get down there." Aren frowned in thought. "Maybe I can find a way to break him out."

"Maybe," Iria said. "I wouldn't do it at the expense of our plan, though."

It's unfortunate, but there are bigger things at stake here. The words Aren had said only a few minutes ago ran through her head, and she could tell he was thinking of them as well. It had been different when they didn't know who it was. When it wasn't their best friend.

"We'll think of something," she said firmly. "We're not going to let him die."

Cas was nowhere to be found that morning and through the afternoon. No one Em asked had seen him, and it appeared Galo was missing as well. They must have snuck out again.

She spent the afternoon circling the castle, hoping to run into Jovita or the king and queen, but they were behind closed doors all day. She wasn't sure she wanted to ask them for permission to see Damian anyway. She had a better chance with Cas.

The staff let her wait in his office after they found her pacing in front of his door for the fifth time. She settled into the chair in the far corner and stared up at the rows of books.

He finally walked through the door as the sun was setting in the window behind her. He was shoeless and carrying a book, a surprised expression crossing his face when he spotted her.

She jumped to her feet, glancing down at his knuckles. Of course they weren't bruised. Whatever they'd done to Damian, they'd had the guards do it for them.

She barely held back from curling her lip in disgust.

"I hope you don't that mind I waited for you," she said.

"Not at all. I was upstairs reading. I wanted some time to think." He dropped the book on the table, sliding his hands into his pockets.

"Oh. I looked everywhere for you."

"It's a hidden room upstairs. I'll show it to you sometime." He smiled. "Did you need something?"

"I heard about the Ruined you captured. You've seen him?"

He nodded slowly, an emotion she couldn't identify flickering across his face.

"What—what happened? Why is he here?"

"My father wants information."

She twisted her fingers together, her stomach churning. What kind of torture were they inflicting on Damian?

"Don't worry, you're safe," Cas said. "We've been draining him of his power."

"Are you going to see him?" she asked. Perhaps she could casually tag along.

"No, we have that dinner tonight."

"Dinner?"

"My father wanted to throw a celebration for the hunters before he sends them back." He gestured to his shoulder, where Em could barely make out a bandage beneath his white shirt. "Trying to appease them, so they won't attempt to kill me."

She'd completely forgotten about the stupid dinner. She let out a long sigh. "I guess I should go get dressed."

"I'll meet you outside your room in half an hour?" Cas's lips curved up. She quickly turned away, wondering if she'd be able to avoid looking at him for the rest of her time in the castle. It wasn't fair that such a terrible person had that smile.

"Half an hour," she said as she rushed out of the room.

Davina helped her into a red dress with a slit in one leg almost to her hip, then pulled a few strands of hair back in thin braids. The rest of her hair hung loose. The maid dusted powder on her cheeks and rubbed bright-red cream on her lips.

"There," she said, standing back to admire her work. "You look lovely. The queen will be very happy."

Em sighed. She *did* look lovely, but she was tempted to spread some dirt on her face just to spite the queen.

Cas appeared at her door right on time, his eyes sweeping over her as she stepped out of her rooms. His fingers brushed against her wrist, sending sparks up her arm, and she almost jerked it away.

"You look beautiful." He seemed like he might want to take her hand, so she quickly crossed her arms over her chest and started down the hallway.

They arrived at the ballroom, where the dinner was already in full swing. The hunters sat with the king, queen, and Jovita at the long table in front, and the dance floor was full of laughter and energy as people spun and swayed.

Em watched the hunters carefully as she walked with Cas to the table. She had rarely crossed paths with a hunter who didn't see the end of her sword, but a few had escaped her. She didn't recognize any of them, and it was unlikely they would have recognized her either. Not in this dress, with lipstick on and a prince on her arm.

Jovita introduced the four men as Em was seated with Cas on one side and a young hunter named Roland on the other. Roland had only two pins on his jacket, and luckily seemed more interested in draining his wineglass as fast as possible than talking to her.

She took a few sips of her own wine, letting the liquid warm her veins and ignite a fire in her stomach. Aren stood at the far corner of the room, dressed in his Lera guard uniform. His expression was blank, but she knew it was only because he was struggling to keep his emotions under control. He could snap the necks of most of the royal family just by looking at them, and she was tempted to tell him to go for it.

"Cheer up, Roland," one of the hunters—Willem, she thought—said, clapping the younger hunter on the back.

Roland tipped his wineglass back and wiped a hand across his mouth. "I'm cheerful on the inside."

Em swallowed down her disgust for all of them and plastered a smile on her face. "How are things out there? The king said the Ruined are trying to cross into Olso?" It was the last thing she wanted to talk about, but it would be helpful to hear the hunters' perspective. Find out how much trouble the Ruined were in.

"We keep spotting them near the border," Willem said. "Killed a couple before we heard from the king that he wanted one for questioning."

"Most are evading us," Roland muttered.

Willem gave him a sharp look. "We'll track them down eventually, Your Highness."

"Are you going back soon?" she asked, hoping the answer was yes.

"We're off first thing tomorrow," Willem said. He grabbed a chicken leg as a server put a plate in front of him. "Some of the guards are going to have to take over questioning that Ruined we captured."

"Better them than us," Roland muttered.

"You'll get used to it." Willem chuckled, and Em glanced down at his rows of pins. Eleven—no, twelve. "I gave the guards a few pointers. Told them to take his whole hand next time, instead of another finger. They start figuring out how many fingers they can get by with, and cutting off a few doesn't have much of an effect. But taking a whole hand"—he lifted his fist and lowered it quickly, miming chopping off a hand—"that takes them by surprise. Creates real panic so he'll start talking."

The room tilted, and she knew she was about to lose control.

No, not about to. It was gone.

"How lovely that you can talk so casually about torturing a fellow man," she snapped. "You must be so proud of the trail of bodies you've left behind you."

Out of the corner of her eye she saw Cas's head snap to her. Willem's smile faded, and Roland muttered something she couldn't understand, raising his glass in front of him.

She quickly stood, bile rising in her throat. She rushed away from the table so quickly she almost tripped over her dress. She had to hold the material away from her feet as she pushed open the ballroom doors.

"Mary!" Cas called from behind her. Footsteps pounded against the floor, and he was beside her, his fingers lightly wrapping around her arm. "Please wait."

Her eyes had filled with tears, but she stopped and turned to him anyway. His expression softened. "Are you all right? What did they say to you?"

She shook her head, blinking back tears as she pulled her arm away from him. His fingers left a trail of warmth down her skin, and the rage boiled over, screaming to be released.

"You talk about death here as if it's an achievement," she spat. "Like it's something to be *celebrated*."

"Sorry?" His eyebrows knitted together.

"Your father started all of this," she said, the words tumbling out of her mouth, almost against her will. "He marched into Ruina and murdered their queen and everyone else in sight. He solicited help from the king and queen of Vallos and then didn't send Lera soldiers to protect them from the inevitable retaliation from the Ruined. You act like things are so beautiful and peaceful and wonderful here with your cheese bread and fancy clothing and beaches, but it's all built on the backs of the people you murdered."

She took in a slow, shaky breath. She wanted to grab the words and shove them back in.

"Bit hypocritical, wouldn't you say?" he asked with a frown.

"Hypocritical how?"

"You killed the Ruined king in order to marry me. Doesn't that make you the same as him?"

She almost snapped that she hadn't killed anyone to marry him, though that was a lie. She'd killed Mary.

"That's different," she said, and he let out a disbelieving laugh. "It is! The Ruined were invading Vallos, and your father said they would only help if I helped them. I did what I had to do to survive."

"Maybe my father also did what he thought he had to do," Cas said, his voice rising. "Why is it different for you?"

"It just is!" she said, throwing her hands up in exasperation.

"Forgive me if I'm not convinced by that argument." He rolled his eyes.

"Are you really comparing your father murdering thousands of people to me—"

"Why is it that you get to set the rules for what is justified and what's—"

"I am not setting the rules!" she yelled. "I am saying that—"

"That what you did is acceptable," he interrupted. "But when it comes to my father, he's a murderer worthy of contempt."

"Fine!" She spread her arms wide. "I'm a monster. Is that what you want to hear? I've murdered people, and, if you want to know the truth, I'm not the least bit sorry. They had it coming."

Cas had his mouth open like he was going to yell again, but he closed it, hesitating for a moment. "I wasn't saying you're a monster," he said, his voice calmer.

She pushed her hands through her hair, a sick feeling clawing up her stomach. Maybe it was a lie to say she wasn't the least bit sorry. She thought about Mary sometimes. About that piece of hair dragging through the dirt as her dead body disappeared into the night. She wasn't sorry Mary was dead, but she wasn't totally comfortable that she'd been the one to kill her.

The door swung open and the king stepped through, turning a glare from Cas to Em. "What are you two yelling about out here? A staff member told me you were screaming."

"It's fine," Cas said quickly.

"I hope you're educating your new wife about how we treat guests in Lera." He jabbed a finger at her. "I expect you to at least be *nice*."

"Nice?" she scoffed. "You ordered me to kill someone in exchange for marrying your son, put me into a battle as soon as I arrived, and between murderous hunters and Olso warriors who *might* be plotting something, I've rarely felt safe since I set foot in this castle. *Nice* isn't high on my list of priorities."

The king turned so red he was almost purple, but he seemed incapable of getting words out. He sputtered, jabbed a finger at Cas for no apparent reason, and stomped back into the ballroom.

A sound like a laugh came from Cas. "I don't think I've ever seen my father rendered speechless before."

"I should yell at him more often, then," she muttered. "He could stand to be speechless occasionally."

Cas laughed, clearing his throat like he was trying to hide it. He painted a more serious expression on his face. "I'm sorry my father asked you to kill the Ruined king to marry me. I objected, if that makes any difference to you."

"It does. But I don't agree with what your father did in Ruina. You'll never convince me that he was right about that."

"I don't disagree," he said, startling her. He stared at the floor, rubbing at something with the tip of his shoe. "He got me out of bed last night, to see the Ruined when they brought him in. I'd never seen a Ruined before."

"And?" she prompted, expecting a fresh wave of anger. But the way his shoulders had curled in and his face had rearranged itself into a frown made her hesitate, made her want to hear what he had to say.

"And . . . it was impressive. And scary." He glanced at her. "When you killed a Ruined, would you provoke them to use their powers first? To weaken them? Is that how you killed the Ruined king? What was his power?"

"He ruined the soul. Could make you see visions and believe things that weren't true." She swallowed, the image of her dead father flashing across her vision. "And no, I didn't. I just snuck up on him. Attacked before he could react."

"Did you see his other daughter? Emelina? Is she still alive?"

"I didn't see Emelina." Her own name sounded strange, said out loud to Cas.

"My father wanted her dead too." Cas swallowed. "But she disappeared after her family was killed. And why would you care about a useless Ruined? If she doesn't have any powers, she's not dangerous." He seemed to be talking more to himself than Em.

"True," she said with a hint of bitterness.

"I've always thought it was kind of harsh, to call them 'useless.'"

"It's the most apt description," she said.

"They can resist a Ruined's power, if they want, right? That seems like something. I wouldn't mind having that ability."

"The Ruined don't attack each other," she said. "So that ability is just as they describe it—useless."

He looked at the ground again, his face drawn. It didn't seem like Cas was bothered by long silences, or even noticed they were happening. She waited a few moments, until he started talking again.

"He isn't much older than me," he said quietly. "I've been thinking about how I would feel if the tables were turned. If it were me, captured by the Ruined, waiting to die. I think I would be terrified. And really angry."

"Angry," she repeated.

"Because what did he do?" His voice was almost a whisper. "If I'm being totally honest, that's why I got mad at you when you said that about my father. I think you're right. We're executing all these people for a crime we think they *might* commit. We think they *might* be evil. They brought Damian in because he was trying to cross into Olso, which technically has nothing to do with us. What else has he done? Why does he deserve what they did to him last night?" He gestured at her. "If he was one of the Ruined who killed your parents, shouldn't you decide how he's punished?"

"Yes." Most of her anger had evaporated, leaving a heavy feeling in her chest and a sudden desire to wrap her arms around Cas. "And if it were up to me, I wouldn't do anything like your father."

He nodded, a sad expression on his face. It must have been painful, to realize your father was a monster.

She cleared her throat. "Are you going to tell your father any of what you said to me, or am I the only one brave enough to speak my mind to your father?"

He cocked his head to the side as he studied her. He took several quick steps forward, until he was right in front of her, and put both his hands on her cheeks. Her entire body collapsed in a heap when he touched her, and she couldn't stop herself from curling her fingers around one of his arms. His skin sparked and sizzled beneath her fingers. He was fire she could touch. She held on tighter.

"My father was wrong." His eyes burned into hers. "You should never be nice."

His gaze dropped to her mouth, and she thought for a moment that he might kiss her. But he noticed something behind them, and he stepped back as a staff member passed by.

She lightly brushed her fingers across her cheek, still searing from his touch. "I'll make sure to not be nice to you from now on."

His lips twitched up. "Good." He held out his hand and she slowly slipped her fingers through his. "Are you ready to go back in? We can go be not nice away from those hunters."

She barely moved her thumb against his hand, returning his smile. "Let's do it."

Em spent the evening avoiding the hunters, sticking to Cas's side as they moved around the room saying hello to governors, friends, and the king's advisers. Cas held her hand for most of the evening, ensuring that she forgot everyone's name as soon as they said it. She had only a vague recollection of the evening, except for how Cas's skin felt against hers. She remembered every detail of that.

"I need to go talk to Jovita," Cas said as the dinner began winding down. "She's been giving me that look for an hour."

Jovita was jerking her head with a frown, indicating that she wanted to talk to Cas.

"She probably wants to complain about me," Em said as Cas slipped his hand out of hers. "Tell you to get me in line."

"Would you let me get you in line?" Cas asked with a laugh.

"Oh, definitely not."

"That's what I thought." He grinned at her over his shoulder as he walked away, and she couldn't tear her eyes away from him until he was halfway across the room. A piece of his shirt had come untucked in back, and she wanted to grab it and pull him back to her.

She cleared her throat and pushed the thought away. She was being ridiculous. She had bigger things to worry about than Cas and his adorably rumpled clothes.

She glanced over at the hunters' table. Roland had left for the night, but Willem was still there, his cheeks red from the wine. His brow furrowed as he stared at something across the room.

He was staring at Aren.

An icy hand grabbed her heart. He was looking at Aren as if he recognized him.

Aren noticed his gaze but was obviously trying to pretend

he hadn't. He turned to the right, saying something to the guard next to him. He caught Em's eye for half a second, and she could read the fear in his expression. He recognized Willem too.

Aren stepped away from the line of guards, scratching the side of his face as he strolled out of the room. He was clearly trying to be casual, but Em recognized the stiff line of his shoulders.

Willem stood and followed him.

She instinctively reached for her sword but found nothing but her dress at her hip. She suddenly hated the stupid dress.

Cas was still talking to Jovita, and the king had moved across the room to flirt with a pretty woman. Em watched as the hunter pushed open the doors and disappeared through it.

She walked as fast as she dared, hitting the doors several seconds after Willem had slipped through. She pushed it open slowly, peeking out. Willem was rounding the corner to her right, headed for the back of the castle.

She took a step forward, her shoes clicking against the stone.

"Em—Mary." Aren's soft voice came from behind her, and she whirled around. He peeked out from behind a corner.

She rushed down the dark hallway to him. The sounds of the dinner drifted away. The curtains were drawn over the windows, and the lantern across from them wasn't lit. If she knew Aren, he'd extinguished it himself.

"You know that hunter?" she whispered.

"I ran into him a few months ago. I killed his two buddies. He got away."

"He's been drinking, and he didn't look like he was sure.

Maybe he'll give up when he can't find you."

"Or he'll tell someone his suspicions."

Footsteps pounded the floor, a dark shape suddenly appearing around the corner. The figure came toward Em and Aren until she could clearly see Willem's furious face.

"I know you." He reached for the dagger on his belt. "I *know*—"

Em grabbed his arms, twisting them behind his back before he could find his weapon. Aren grabbed the dagger and pressed it to Willem's throat.

"It needs to look like an accident," Em said quickly. "A murder will make the entire castle suspicious."

Willem sputtered as he fought against Aren's hold on his throat.

"Get out of here," Aren said, jerking his head at Em. "They can't find you with us."

Em opened her mouth to protest, even though she knew he was right.

"I have one more round before I can . . ." A laugh echoed through the hallway, and Aren and Em's heads snapped up to find the source of the male voice.

Willem opened his mouth, a squeak escaping. Em clapped her hand over it. Aren slammed his hands against Willem's chest, pushing him flat against the wall with the dagger jabbed into his throat. Willem kicked his leg, bucking his body wildly. Aren narrowed his eyes at the man's legs, using his Ruined magic to make them go limp.

RUINED

Willem tried to yell, the noise muffled by Em's hand. She pressed down harder.

"Em, get out of here," Aren breathed.

"Stop. I'll be there in a few minutes," the male voice said, closer this time.

Two guards appeared at the end of the hallway. Em stilled, not even daring to breathe. She recognized one of them.

Galo was the one who'd just spoken, and he smiled at the guard in front of him, oblivious to the three people only a few steps to his right.

The other guard grinned, leaning forward to plant a kiss on Galo's lips. He said something Em couldn't hear, then turned to walk away, throwing a smile at Galo over his shoulder.

Galo laughed, ducking his head as he slid his hands into his pockets. He began to turn to the right, in the direction of the dark hallway. Em sucked in a breath.

"Are we standing, or are we doing rounds?" a gruff voice called.

Galo's gaze snapped forward. "Sorry, Julio." He strode forward and out of sight.

Em's legs almost collapsed under her in relief.

"A round means he's doing a walk around the castle," Aren whispered. "He'll be back in a few minutes."

"Close his windpipe off," Em said, using her other hand to cover Willem's nose.

"You should get out—"

"If you lose hold of him after I leave, it will be even worse. Do it."

Aren fixed his gaze on Willem's throat. The hunter's legs started to move. Closing off a windpipe took intense focus, and Aren couldn't control the legs at the same time. Em shoved her body against Willem's in an attempt to keep him still.

"I was supposed to be done with this," Aren said through gritted teeth. "I was supposed to be done killing hunters before they killed me."

"I know," she said quietly. Willem's body went limp, his head slumping to the side.

"Damian was supposed to lead the Ruined into Olso, not rot in some Lera cell while I stand guard over the people torturing him." His voice was strangled, and getting too loud.

Em threw a glance over her shoulder, her heart beating in her throat. They were still alone, for now.

"I can't let go yet," Aren said more quietly. "He's not dead yet."

Em nodded and left her hands over Willem's mouth and nose for almost a full minute. When Aren finally took a step back, the hunter's eyes were open, staring blankly past them.

She braced her hands against Willem's shoulders, keeping him upright. "Help me get him over to that table. We'll bash his head on the corner. He reeks of alcohol. Won't be hard to believe he fell."

Aren grabbed the left side of his body, grunting beneath the weight.

"You all right?" she asked.

"Fine." But his legs shook, beads of sweat appearing on his

brow. Using his magic had weakened him.

"Do you still keep count? I used to count how many I killed," Aren said as they stopped next to the table.

"Nah. I stopped several months ago. Turn him a little." She grunted from the strain of Willem's weight.

"Right there?" Aren asked, pointing to the edge of the table.

"Yeah. The side closest to me. Really launch him into it, so it leaves a mark. Ready?"

They shoved Willem down, the right side of his skull cracking against the wood. Em winced at the noise, turning to see if anyone had heard. Nothing.

Willem toppled to the ground, blood seeping from his head and pooling on the stone floor.

"Well, it left a mark." Aren stared down at the hunter. He pointed at the pins on his chest. "I've killed fewer hunters than he has Ruined, though." He murmured the last line almost to himself.

"Put his dagger back on his belt," Em said quietly. Aren did as he was told, then stood motionless, staring at the dead hunter.

"I have to—" Em began.

"No, me first," Aren interrupted. "No one can see you in this area." He strode to the end of the hallway, the lantern lighting up his face. He jerked his head. "Clear."

She darted out of the hallway and started to rush past him, toward the sounds of laughter and clinking glasses. She turned back suddenly, grabbing Aren's arm and giving it a gentle squeeze. "Thank you, Aren. I know it isn't easy for you to be here, and it means so much to me that you chose to come."

He shrugged, rubbing a hand over the back of his neck. "Of course I came. I never considered the alternative."

He hadn't. The night she had proposed the idea, he had immediately volunteered to come with her, and then used a hot stone to burn off his one remaining Ruined mark. He hadn't even hesitated.

"Go," he said.

She wanted to stay with him, to sit next to him in front of a fire like they used to do after killing hunters. Aren always retreated into himself after he had to kill. But he never seemed to mind when she sat next to him quietly.

"Stay safe," she said, letting go of his arm. "Let me know if anyone is suspicious."

He waved her off without meeting her eye. She took one more glance at him over her shoulder, then pushed the door open and disappeared into the crowd of people.

FOURTEEN

CAS WATCHED AS the wagon rolled onto the south lawn. The guards and the king had been gone a long time with Damian. The sun had sunk low in the sky, casting a yellow-orange glow across the grass.

His father jumped off his horse and strode across the lawn to Cas. It had been a full day since Mary had told him off. The king scanned the area, and he seemed pleased to find that the prince was by himself.

"Did you get any information from Damian?" Cas asked.

The king shook his head. "No. I think it's highly unlikely this one will talk. He doesn't respond well to torture."

Was there anyone who responded *well* to torture? Cas opened his mouth to ask, but was distracted by the guards pulling a limp

Damian out of the wagon.

"He's not dead, is he?" he asked, glancing sharply at his father.

"Not yet."

Cas was determined to remain calm. His voice wasn't going to shake.

"I'm going down there to talk to Damian," he said.

"If you want," the king said with a shrug.

"I'd like to offer to let him live if he gives us information."

"You can offer it, but it would be a lie."

"Why? You've let Ruined live before. Olivia Flores is still alive."

"Olivia Flores is useful, and still young enough to be controlled."

Controlled didn't sound like what his father had said about Olivia's situation before. Mary was probably right about Olivia being a prisoner, not a guest.

"Where is Olivia?" he asked.

"Fort Victorra. Keep that to yourself. Not many people know where she is."

The fortress in the Southern Mountains was the emergency meeting place if the castle was ever taken, and had a good supply of cells in the dungeons. They were not nice cells, from what Cas remembered.

"Is she in one of the cells there?" he asked.

"Of course she is. She can't just roam around freely."

Cas blinked away the image of a young girl chained up in those depressing cells. He needed to focus on the problem in front of him.

Cas gestured to where Damian was being dragged down the stairs. "What are his crimes?"

The king frowned in confusion. "What do you mean?"

"Lera law dictates that all accused are informed of their crimes and allowed a trial before the judge of their province. What are his crimes?"

"He's a Ruined. That's his crime."

"Being a Ruined is a state of being, not a crime."

His father's eyebrows lowered, and he crossed his arms over his broad chest. "Excuse me?"

"He hasn't actually committed a crime. Who's to say that he ever would have used those powers against anyone if we'd left him alone? If we'd just left them all alone?"

"Yes, I'm sure all the people Wenda Flores tortured felt the same," his father said flippantly. "The people she captured to let the Ruined practice on? The people of Vallos she slaughtered when she attempted to invade?"

"Damian is not Wenda Flores. Wenda Flores was one person, and she's gone. We're punishing all the Ruined for the crimes of the few."

"The Ruined are not individuals. They act as a unit, always." He gestured to where Damian had disappeared into the ground. "This is the only one you've met. You don't understand."

"Just because I disagree with you doesn't mean I don't understand."

The king's jaw twitched. "What is this? Is this what Mary thinks?"

"This is what I think."

"What a coincidence that it comes out a few weeks after marrying that girl." He said *that girl* as if it were a dirty word.

"The girl you ordered me to marry," Cas reminded him.

The king grunted. "Nothing like her parents. Perhaps she forgot everything about them after they died, because those two detested the Ruined." He let out a heavy sigh. "I was wrong to make you marry her without getting to know her first. If I'd known . . ."

"What?" Anger flared in Cas's chest. "That she could think for herself? That she would challenge us, instead of going along with everything we said?"

The king frowned in thought, running a hand over his beard. "Maybe there's a way to get you out of it."

Cas reeled back, the words like a slap to the face. Unexpected panic crept in at the thought of losing Mary.

"You are not allowed to have an opinion on my marriage," Cas said, his voice like ice. "That contract is between me and Mary now. Do you understand me?"

His father looked so astonished that he didn't seem to have the words to reply to that.

"I'm going down to talk to Damian," Cas said. "Maybe he'll tell me if he's actually committed a crime. If he has, then we can talk about appropriate punishment. But if he hasn't, we're holding and torturing a man who has done nothing wrong. I don't know what's more horrifying—our actions, or the fact that you don't seem the least bit bothered by them."

He turned away from his father's startled face and descended the steps into the dungeon. He let out a slow breath, willing his heart to stop thumping a frantic rhythm in his chest. He was shaky but lighter, the weight of the words building inside him for so long finally gone.

"I—I can't do that again. I—I don't . . ." The male voice drifted up from below. Cas slowed his descent, listening.

"We'll rotate the guards out," Galo said. "No one will have to do this more than once." He paused. "Ric, don't you dare vomit down here."

Cas took the last step. Two guards stood at the far wall, and Cas knew immediately which one was Ric. He was young and pale, his hands shaking. The guard quickly put them behind his back when he saw Cas.

"There's no need for you two to be down here," Cas said. "Will you wait at the top?" The guards nodded and rushed past him.

Galo stood in front of Damian's cell, and Cas stopped next to him. Damian was crumpled on the floor, his face bloody and swollen. Fresh blood was smeared across his shirt.

"The hunters left, didn't they?" Cas asked quietly.

"Yes. This morning. Except for the one who cracked his head open."

"They never revived him?"

"No, he was dead when I got to him."

"So my father had the guards take the lead torturing Damian."

"Yes."

Cas pushed his fingers through his hair. "Torture isn't exactly in their job description."

"No, it's not. They asked for volunteers, but . . ."

"No one volunteered." Cas felt a swell of pride for the guards suddenly. "Good for them."

Damian's head jerked as one of his eyes opened. The other was swollen shut. He rolled onto his side, and it seemed to take him a moment for him to focus well enough to recognize Cas standing at his cell door.

He laughed, a sad, hollow sound that echoed through the dungeon. He rolled over onto his back, wincing as he put a hand to his stomach.

"I've died, haven't I?" he said, his voice laced with amusement. "Always figured there was punishment waiting for me after death. Your face is my punishment, isn't it?"

"You're not dead," Cas said.

"Too bad." Damian moved his jaw around, as if checking to see if it still worked.

"How old are you?" Cas asked.

Damian's forehead crinkled as he frowned. He took several beats to answer. "Seventeen. Or eighteen. I lost track."

"Do you have any family?"

"Yes. Though everyone related to me by blood has been murdered." He lowered his voice. "But yes, I have family."

"Is that why you were crossing into Olso? Are they there?"

He laughed, a genuine one that shook his chest. "No."

Cas paused, glancing over at Galo. The guard stood only

a few steps away, his brow furrowed as he watched them. He debated asking Galo to leave, but maybe Cas needed him to hear this conversation with Damian. He needed to know if Galo felt the same as Cas, or if his thinking was more in line with the king's.

"The hunters killed your family," Cas said. It wasn't a question.

Damian's jaw tensed. "*Your* hunters killed my family, yes."

"Our hunters killed your family," Cas repeated, because it was true. "What did you do before the Lera invasion?"

"What do you mean, what did I do?"

"You were about sixteen when we invaded, correct? Were you in school? Did Ruina have schools?"

"No. Parents educated their kids at home." He hesitated. "But I was educated at the castle with Em and Olivia."

"Em is Emelina?" Cas asked.

"Yes."

"You were friends with the Flores sisters? Or related to them?"

"Friends."

"Your parents must have known Wenda Flores, then."

"Everyone knew Wenda," Damian said, throwing an arm across his forehead. "It's not like here, where you isolate yourself from your people like you're scared of them."

"Did you have training?" Cas asked. "Battle training?"

Damian barely lifted his shoulders in a small shrug. He wasn't answering that question.

"Were you involved in the raid on the Vallos castle?" Cas

asked, thinking of Mary's troubled expression yesterday when she asked about Damian.

Again, Damian just shrugged.

"Were you raised to hate everyone who wasn't Ruined?"

Damian dropped his arm from his forehead, turning his head to look at Cas. "No."

Cas glanced at Galo. The guard had his arms crossed over his chest, a serious expression on his face. He barely nodded at Cas, as if telling him to go on.

"Did you ever kill anyone before Lera invaded?"

"Ruined don't kill each other. I didn't have much contact with anyone else." He snorted. "Can't say that you guys have made a very good impression."

"No, I guess not," Cas said quietly.

A crease appeared between Damian's eyebrows as he studied Cas. He opened his mouth like he was going to say something, then shut it, his frown deepening. Cas stepped back to join Galo against the wall. He ducked his head, his words only for the guard.

"Do you ever wonder," he said to the ground, "if maybe we're the dangerous ones, not the Ruined?"

Galo paused before answering. "All the time."

FIFTEEN

"PLAN NUMBER ONE." Em put one finger in the air as she paced across her bedroom. "We simply try to keep him alive until we're ready to launch the attack. Then the castle will be ours anyway, and Damian can go free."

Aren nodded, leaning against the wall and staring out the window. The sunlight streamed across his face and onto his blue guard shirt. "He'll have to endure torture for a while," he said softly.

"I know." Em swallowed. "Plan number two. You volunteer for a shift down there, kill the other guard, and you and Damian make a run for it."

"If he's in any shape to run. Not to mention that me freeing Damian and disappearing will cast suspicion on you."

She moaned, pushing her hands into her hair. "Forget plan number two. Or! Revise it. Make it look like Damian killed the other guard, used his Ruined magic to get out of the cell, and escaped by himself."

"He'd still have a tough time getting over the castle wall. And evading the guards once he's free."

"Do you have any better ideas?" she asked, exasperated.

"No. Is there a plan number three?"

"I find out where Olivia is as soon as possible, and all of us get out of here."

"That's the worst one yet. Destroying your cover before we're ready to launch the attack makes this all for nothing. They'll heighten their defenses."

"I never said they were good plans. And I don't hear you throwing out any ideas."

He turned so his back was to the wall, lifting his head to the ceiling. "Plan number four. Let Damian die."

Em grabbed one of the bedposts, squeezing it almost to the point of cracking.

"Don't look at me like that," Aren said. He blinked several times, but not before she saw the tears in his eyes. "It's taking all my willpower not to rush down there and kill everyone even in the general vicinity of his cell. But all of this is bigger than him. You know that."

She eased her fingers off the bedpost. "I know that."

"Plan number one. It's the only option. Get them to hold off as long as you can."

"Maybe he can give them a few pieces of information, pretend to be useful so they're less inclined to kill him," she said. "I want to talk to him. Can you volunteer for a shift in the dungeon?"

"Sure. They haven't assigned guards for the overnight shift yet."

"Is there more than one down there overnight?"

"Two. But I can use my Ruined magic to tie his stomach into knots. He'll be too sick to stay."

"Good. Tell me when we're ready."

Em walked across the south lawn that night, glancing over her shoulder for the fourth time. She hadn't told Cas she was going to visit Damian, and she didn't want him spotting her and tagging along. Cas and his parents would find out she'd visited him, but it was better to explain later rather than ask for permission now.

She descended the steps to the dungeon, lifting the hem of her light-purple dress. The world grew darker the farther down she went, the only light coming from the lanterns lining the walls every few steps. The walls were bare and gray, nothing like the bright colors of the castle. It was cool and quiet, and she was suddenly reminded of home. It looked more like Ruina in Lera's dungeon than anywhere else she'd seen.

She saw Aren first, leaning against the wall, keeping watch on the stairs. Another guard was a few paces from him, and he straightened when he spotted Em, surprise coloring his features.

She took the last step, pulling a breath into her chest and forcing every muscle in her body to relax. She screwed her face into a calm expression.

Damian was lying on the ground, his head turned to her. Dirt coated his arms and neck, his face was horribly swollen, and his hand had been bandaged. They'd taken care of his wound after cutting his finger off?

"May I help you with something, Your Highness?" Aren asked. But his attention was on the other guard. The man frowned and touched his stomach.

"I'd like to speak with the prisoner," she said. "Is it safe?"

"It's safe, Your Highness, but—" The guard made a retching sound, clapping his hand over his mouth.

"Go," Em said, moving away from the stairs. "Get some fresh air."

The guard nodded, sprinting past her and up the stairs. Damian's laughter echoed through the dungeon.

"Aren." Damian shook his head. "You did a little more than was necessary there."

"If I can't use my fist to punch him the stomach, I might as well use my magic." Aren moved to the stairs, leaning forward to keep watch.

Em rushed forward, wrapping her fingers around the bars of Damian's cell. He sat up slowly, wincing. He was more relaxed than she would have expected, blowing his dark hair out of his eyes and smiling his crooked smile.

"Nice dress."

"What happened?" she asked.

"Seriously. I haven't seen you in a dress in over a year. They suit you."

"Damian, stop. What happened?"

His smile faltered, and he scrubbed a hand down his face. "The hunters know we're crossing into Olso. They're all over the border. We were still managing to get through, but they picked off some of us. They captured me, and I got the special privilege of torture before my death."

"Think of information you can give them," Em said. "Something small. If we can keep you alive long enough, we'll be able to release you after the warriors take the castle."

He pushed off the ground, getting to his feet with a grunt. "I doubt I'll last that long."

"That's why you need to give them a few things. Even if they're lies, it will take time for them to confirm it. Play along."

"Play along." He laughed, wincing as he put a hand to his stomach. "Ow."

She swallowed, scanning his dirty clothes. "Are you all right?"

"Never better." He leaned his forehead against the bars. "Is Prince Casimir being kind to you?"

"Yes."

He raised his bandaged hand. "Cas comes in and pretends to be nice after his father tortures me. They must figure one strategy will work."

Em grasped her necklace, the words on the tip of her tongue. *He's not pretending.* Damian raised his eyebrows, questions all over his face.

"Cas doesn't have the stomach for torturing and killing the way his father does," Aren finally said, when Em didn't. "He'll grow into it."

Or not, since he'll be dead in a few weeks. Em couldn't say those words either. They sat in the pit of her stomach. Damian's baffled expression didn't do much to make her feel better.

"I'm glad he's being kind to you, at least," Damian said quietly, so only she could hear.

"Give the information to Cas, not his father," Em said. "Show that you respond better to reason than torture."

"They'll still kill me, Em. The king isn't going to keep a Ruined for more than a few days."

"I'm going to get you out of this," she said fiercely. "I won't let them execute you."

He shook his head, his expression turning serious. "You can't stop it without making them suspicious."

"The Ruined can't lose another leader. They're looking to you—"

"They're looking to you too, they just don't know it yet. When they realize what you did to save Olivia, they'll worship you as much as they do her." He lifted his head from the bars. "Have you found out where she is?"

"Not yet. But I've gained Cas's trust and—"

"I think you've gained more than his trust." Damian's lips

turned up. "But I'm not surprised, to be honest."

Her cheeks warmed, and she snuck a glance over her shoulder at Aren. He'd disappeared into the stairway, giving them some privacy.

"You're here to save thousands, not break me out of a Lera dungeon," Damian said.

She stared at her feet, nodding as she blinked away tears.

"If I can think of something to tell Cas, I will. An old location of a camp, maybe. But they're still going to kill me, Em." He wrapped his fingers around hers through the bars. "We knew we risked our lives with this plan. I honestly didn't expect to make it out of this war alive."

"*I* expected you to make it out alive." She took in a ragged breath. "I thought you'd be there when we went back to Ruina. I thought that you and I . . ." She thought she had more time to figure out what was between them. She *needed* more time. She needed her friend beside her.

"I appreciate that optimism." His fingers gripped hers tighter. He jerked his head. "Now go. I don't want that guard telling the king you were down here forever."

She wiped a tear off her cheek, forcing a smile before she headed to the stairs. Aren strode to the cell, leaning his head close to Damian's to speak to him.

She didn't care about the risks. Whatever it took, she would find a way to save him.

SIXTEEN

CAS RAISED HIS hand to knock on Mary's door, a flutter of nerves exploding in his stomach. He cracked a knuckle as he waited for her to answer.

No one answered the door, and he stepped back. A maid approached from the other end of the hallway with a handful of linens, and she paused when she spotted him.

"Have you seen Mary?" he asked.

"I believe she's in the sparring room, Your Highness."

He murmured a "thanks" and headed down the stairs to the back of the castle. Laughter spilled into the hallway.

He stopped at the open doorway of the sparring room and found Iria with a dull sword in her hand, Mary across from her.

Mary wore a determined expression as she took a step to

the side, her sword extended in front of her. The trainer, Rulo, watched them from the corner of the room.

Iria lunged first, and Mary lifted her sword to stop the attack. He leaned against the door frame, watching as they circled the room, the swords noisily crashing against each other. An Olso warrior wasn't an easy opponent, but Mary's skills with a sword were almost unmatched.

"I heard she went to visit Damian last night."

Cas jumped at the sound of the voice to find his mother leaning against the wall on the other side of the door. She was out of view from the two women inside, which wasn't a coincidence.

"Mary?" he asked.

"Yes. Did she ask you if she could do that?"

"I . . ." He watched as Mary ducked Iria's blade. "She doesn't really ask my permission to do things."

"She should."

He snorted. "Really. You ask Father for permission regularly?"

The queen's lips twitched. "I see your point." She peeked around the doorway. "She's very good. Odd for a girl from Vallos."

"Talent, I guess."

"That's not talent. That's hard work and training. The kind of training they don't usually have in Vallos."

"Why do you sound suspicious?"

"Not suspicious. Just impressed. Does she ever talk about her training?"

"No. But I've never asked."

"You know what I think is sad?" the queen said. She talked slowly, in that way she did when she was saying one thing but meant another. "She didn't bring any portraits of her family with her."

"I think they all burned in the fire when the Ruined attacked."

"I figured. I thought I might try to track one down, as a surprise. I've sent someone out to work on it." She smiled at him. "But don't tell her. I don't want to get her hopes up if I can't find one."

"That's nice of you."

"Don't sound so surprised, Cas." She squeezed his arm as she walked past. "She's about to beat that warrior. And I suspect King Lucio sent the best."

Cas turned to look. Mary leaned away from Iria's attack, knocking her arm away as she jabbed the dull tip into the warrior's chest.

"I win," Mary said breathlessly.

Cas returned his gaze to his mother to find nothing but empty hallway. He caught a glimpse of her skirts as they disappeared around the corner.

Iria laughed, drawing Cas's attention back to them. "I will get you next time."

"Or you could get me right now, if you'd like to go again." Mary spread her arms wide in invitation.

"I'd like to go," Cas said, stepping out of the doorway. The women turned, Mary's smile faltering as their eyes met.

"Your Highness, I didn't see you there," the trainer said,

straightening and adjusting his collar. "Would you like me to get your practice gear?"

"No, thank you," Cas said, stepping into the room. Mary's gaze followed him as he came closer.

"You know, I was told by castle staff that you don't allow people to watch you practice," Iria said, her hands on her hips, the sword dangling from two fingers. "They say it's so no one knows your secrets and tricks." She cocked an eyebrow. "I told them it was probably because you were terrible and didn't want anyone to know."

He laughed, holding his hand out for her sword. "Let's see then, shall we?" He looked at Mary as Iria dropped the dull blade into his hand. "If you'd like."

"If you promise not to let me win."

"Why would I let you win?"

A hint of a smile appeared on her face again, and he decided he would never let her win at anything, ever, if she was going to look at him like that.

"And let's not tell my father I let you stay while we did this," he said to Iria as he rolled his sleeves up.

"It's your father who doesn't want people to watch you?" Mary asked.

"He thinks a royal's skills in battle are better kept a secret."

"He may be right about that."

He walked across the floor to stand in front of her. "I never thought I'd hear you say my father was right about anything."

"Don't tell him I said so."

"Never."

She began to lift her sword, then stopped, cocking her head. "What battle is he preparing you for? You don't need a sword to battle the Ruined."

"He used one against Wenda Flores."

"I guess he did." She arched an eyebrow. "Had you ever met a Ruined before Damian was captured?"

"No." He glanced at Iria, uncomfortable having this conversation in front of a warrior. He held his sword out in front of him. "Are we sparring, or are we talking?"

Mary lifted her sword, narrowing her eyes.

Iria counted them down, and Mary made the first move. He easily blocked her.

She was deliberately being slow and careful at first, to assess how he handled himself. He could see it in the way she watched him. It was interesting, considering her temper seemed to get the best of her in other situations.

He lunged forward and she went back, the metal of their swords sounding off the walls as they met. He tried to back her into a corner, but she ducked suddenly, darting around to the other side of him.

Her eyes raged with something he didn't quite understand as their swords met again. It was more than anger, and he couldn't tell if it was directed at him. He hoped it wasn't, because if it had been a real sword in her hand, she might have killed him.

He moved forward, obviously quicker than she had been

expecting, because she stumbled and he lightly struck her on her left arm.

"One," Iria said.

She took a step back, her breathing heavy. They circled each other, and he waited for her to lunge first again. When she came at him he met her blow, moving forward and back as she attacked.

He'd only ever sparred with his trainers and Galo, and it was different with Mary. He was distracted by the way a piece of hair had escaped from its knot and hung down her cheek. The pink in her cheeks. The sound of her breath.

She spun when he almost touched the sword to her chest, and he lifted his eyebrows, impressed. She grinned.

He ducked as she lunged at him again, the blade barely missing his head. He darted around and grabbed her hand, spinning her into his chest. He held down her arm as he lifted his blade to her throat. She gasped, snapping her head to the right. He could feel her sucking air in and out of her lungs against him, and her arm was warm and soft beneath his fingers. Her dark eyes burned into his, lighting up like they were on fire. He found himself staring at her lips, wishing he knew what they felt like on his.

"Should we leave?"

Iria's voice snapped him out of his trance, and he quickly released Mary. Her gaze was downcast, and she was rubbing the spot where he'd touched her arm.

"Apologies, Your Highness," Iria said. Somehow she always managed to make "Your Highness" seem like an insult. "Clearly you have nothing to be embarrassed about. When it comes to sword fighting, that is."

He gave her an amused look. "Thank you, I think."

"I think I'd like to spar with you more often," Mary said. "You're better than Iria."

"I'm standing right here," Iria said.

"You know he's better than you," Mary said with a laugh. She focused on him again, a hint of a challenge in her expression. "I think he's used to being better than everyone."

"Galo often gives it a very good shot," he said, unable to keep a smile off his face. "Would you like to go again?"

"Absolutely."

SEVENTEEN

EM PULLED THE door shut behind her as she exited her rooms, the sound echoing down the hallway. Her dress caught under her heel, and she yanked it free with a little more force than was necessary.

Iria appeared around the corner, her gaze falling to the rip Em had just created at the hem of her dress. "What did that dress ever do to you?" she asked with a hint of amusement.

Em wasn't in the mood to be amused. It had been several days since her visit to Damian, and she hadn't even been able to talk to the king once. He just brushed her off every time she approached him.

"Most of the ships have already left Olso," Iria said under

her breath as they walked down the hallway. "The Ruined are on board."

Em's heart jumped into her throat. "How much longer do I have?" She hadn't found out where Olivia was yet. It was a delicate balance, finding a way to bring up Olivia without casting suspicion on herself.

"They're almost here. But you still have several days, at least. A week, maybe."

Even if she couldn't find a way to stealthily get the information, perhaps she could just torture it out of the king or queen during the attack. It would serve them right, after what they were doing to Damian.

They rounded the corner. Koldo and Benito stood outside the Ocean Room. Koldo was speaking animatedly, grinning at Benito as if the latter was supposed to be impressed by his story. Benito managed to lift one eyebrow.

Em stopped next to them, leaning over to peer through the open door. No one had arrived at the meeting yet.

Cas rounded the corner, and Em quickly ducked into the meeting room so he wouldn't see her near the warriors.

She took a seat and glanced over her shoulder as he walked into the room. His lips turned up when their eyes met.

He likes you, Iria had said to her a few days ago. *More than likes you. He looks at you as if he's falling in love with you.*

Em swallowed down a wave of guilt. Cas probably didn't love her. He liked her, maybe, but love? No. Surely not.

The guilt clawed through her chest and into her throat,

making it hard to breathe. She didn't know what was worse—
that he liked her, or that she was pretty sure she felt the same way.

The warriors entered the room, followed shortly after by
the queen and Jovita. The king came in a few minutes later and
grabbed the trade agreement from Iria without so much as a
"good morning."

"I'll discuss it with my advisers," he said after a moment.

"They're not coming this morning?" Iria asked.

"No." He didn't offer any further explanation. "You can go.
That's all for today."

The warriors couldn't hide their surprise, but they all stood
without comment. Iria glanced at Em as she left, a hint of worry
in her eyes.

The king stared straight at Em, and she pretended not to
notice. If they'd discovered something, they would have captured
her immediately, not let her wander into a meeting with the royal
family. Right?

"It's come to my attention that you visited the Ruined prisoner," the king said.

She tried to swallow without appearing nervous. "I did."

"Why?"

"I wanted to know if he was part of the attack that killed my
parents."

Jovita and the queen shared a look. The queen leaned forward, resting her arms on the table. "What did he say?"

"Nothing."

"That's mostly what we've gotten from him," the king said.

"Nothing. Time to give up, I think."

Em gripped the edge of her chair, her heart diving into her feet.

"But he told me the location of a Ruined camp a few days ago," Cas said before she could speak.

"And I've relayed that to my soldiers, but Ruined camps move all the time. He knew he wasn't giving us anything important." The king stood, grabbing the treaty agreement off the table. "I'm losing patience. I don't usually keep Ruined prisoners."

"No, you usually kill them right away."

Cas's words hung in the air like they'd been shouted instead of spoken calmly.

"Do you have something you'd like to say, Casimir?" The king straightened his shoulders, staring down his son.

Em gently pressed her hand to her waist, where she'd slipped a dagger inside her dress. The leather sheath was warm against her left side. She could get at the weapon in about three seconds, hurl it at the king's chest, take Cas's hand, and run as—

She shook the thought away, curling her fingers into a fist and trying to pretend she wasn't imagining Cas's hand in hers as they ran away from the castle.

"I think we should reevaluate our policy on the Ruined," Cas said. "I can no longer support murdering people who haven't committed a crime."

The king's beard trembled, like he was having a hard time keeping his temper in check. "Luckily, I don't need your support. And no one with any sense disagrees with Lera's Ruined policy."

"I do," Em said.

The king barely glanced at her, like she didn't count. He stomped away from the table. "I have more important things to do."

"Damian talks to me," Cas said, looking over his shoulder at his father. "At the very least you shouldn't execute him while he's still talking to me."

The king's face twisted, like he hated to admit Cas was right.

"And you keep another Ruined locked away," Em said quickly. "If you keep Olivia, why not Damian?"

"It's different," the queen said with a sniff.

"How so? Is she somewhere very well guarded?" She tried to keep the question light, but her chest tightened in anticipation.

"Not your concern." The king turned his attention to his niece. "Jovita, join me?"

Jovita's eyes lit up, and she scurried after the king.

"At least stop torturing Damian," Cas said as they headed for the door. "He's never talked during torture."

"Fine." The king threw the door open, and he and Jovita disappeared through it. The queen followed, sparing a deep frown for her son as she went. Em let out a sigh.

"That went about as well as expected," Cas said with a nervous laugh.

"That was brave," she said, meaning every word.

"Thanks."

She wanted to thank him for stopping Damian's torture, but she couldn't think of a way to do it without casting suspicion on herself. Plus, she couldn't let the opportunity to ask about Olivia pass her by.

"Is it a secret?" she asked carefully. "Olivia's location?"

"Somewhat. The family knows. Some of the advisers. My father is just being a jerk. She's at Fort Victorra in the Southern Mountains. Where we meet in case of an emergency?"

Her entire body went numb, but she managed to barely nod. *Olivia. Victorra. Southern Mountains.* A year of desperately wondering where her sister was, and Cas had laid it all out for her with one simple question. She wanted to throw her arms around his neck and hug him.

Guilt pushed out the happiness almost immediately. His expression was so open and honest that she wanted to scream the truth at him and ask for forgiveness. She wondered what would happen if she came clean and simply asked him to let Olivia go.

Actually, she could guess what would happen—the same scenario that had played out in front of her moments ago. Cas would be reasonable; his father would disagree and do whatever he wanted.

Or Cas would explode, grab a sword, and stick it through her heart. If Iria was right, and he really did like her, it would only make his anger worse. He might lose sight of all reason.

Truth wasn't an option. She had to stick with her plan, regardless of how he looked at her.

EIGHTEEN

EM WOKE TO the sound of her door creaking.

Her eyes flew open, and she rolled out of the sheets and onto the floor. She sprang to her feet, making a beeline for the dresser that held her knife.

"It's me," came Iria's soft voice.

Em squinted in the darkness to where Iria stood by the door.

"What are you doing? What time is it?" Fear slammed into her chest, and she clasped the handle of the dresser drawer, ready to grab the knife. "What's wrong?"

"They're executing Damian."

"Now?" She'd meant to yell it, but the word came out as a strangled whisper instead.

"The king just woke some of the guards. Aren is already out there."

She flew across the room, shoving her feet into her boots. She knocked against Iria's shoulder as she wrenched open the door.

"Don't!" Iria hissed from behind her. "If they see you . . ."

Em didn't catch the last of Iria's words as she ran out of her rooms and into the hallway. It was dark and quiet, the curtains still shut tight over the windows. Most of the lanterns lining the hallway were unlit.

She darted to the main staircase, but a tiny voice in the back of her head told her not to rush to the front entrance of the castle in full view of the guards. She spun around, sprinting down the hallway and taking the back staircase to the kitchen instead.

Iria's footsteps pounded behind her as she ran through the staff dining room and out the door. She was wearing only a white nightgown, and the morning air was cool against her bare arms and legs. The sky was deep blue with the smallest hint of orange beginning to appear on the horizon.

The gardens were empty, and Em looked over her shoulder at Iria. "South lawn?" She received no reply except Iria attempting to grab for her arm. She shook the warrior off and sprinted around the side of the castle, Iria's footsteps following her.

Aren came into view as soon as she rounded the corner. He was leaning against the wall, his hands braced on his knees, his lips moving in silent prayer. She'd walked in on Aren praying many times in her life, though never after the castle burned, with his parents in it.

She drew in a ragged breath and his head popped up, his eyes wide and wet. "You can't be here."

"Is he dead?" she whispered.

Aren put both hands behind his neck, ducking his face into his chest. "I don't know. I can't look."

She took a few steps forward. She didn't want to see, but her feet kept moving anyway. They were slow, heavy with the sinking feeling that there was nothing she could do for Damian now.

She curled her fingers around the corner of the castle, peeking onto the south lawn.

Damian was on his knees near the stairs down to the dungeon. His ankles were tied together, his wrists bound in front of him. A guard was behind him with a blade. The king and queen stood not far away, along with Jovita and a few more guards. Cas was not there.

It didn't seem as if the king and queen, who had their backs to her, had noticed her presence, but Damian stared right at her. He was filthy and bloody, one eye partially swollen shut.

She couldn't move. Tears welled in her eyes, but his were clear, his expression grim but steady. His lips twisted into the saddest smile she'd ever seen.

"Em, they might see you." Iria tugged on her arm. Em wriggled free. Iria grabbed her again. "If they see—"

"Let go of her." Aren's voice was a growl, and Iria's body shot backward, as if suddenly hurled across the lawn by an invisible force. Aren gasped as she hit the ground.

Aren raced across the grass to her crumpled body. "I'm sorry. I didn't mean—"

"I'm fine." Iria slapped his hand away.

Em turned back to the lawn. The king made a motion for the guards to proceed.

"Aren." Her voice came out as a strangled whisper. "I can't let him die."

He was behind her suddenly, his hand finding hers. "You will not die with him." His voice wobbled.

Damian was still looking in her direction, and she watched as he brought his bound hands up to his heart. He tapped his fist against his chest twice in the official Ruina salute to the queen.

The guard raised his sword.

Aren lowered his forehead onto her shoulder, whispering, "I can't look." She could barely hear him through the blood rushing in her ears.

"For the crime of murder and treason, the kingdom of Lera sentences you to death," Em heard the king say. "May the ancestors see something in you that we did not."

The king nodded at the guard holding the sword. He lifted it into the air, hesitating for a moment as he found his mark.

The blade crashed down.

NINETEEN

"HE WOULD BE *an excellent leader, Emelina.*"

Em looked up at her mother, then through the open window to where Damian stood outside. He ducked suddenly, barely missing the ball Olivia threw dangerously close to his head.

"Oops," Olivia said with a giggle. Her long, dark hair was pulled tight in a ponytail, and it swung back and forth as she bounced on her heels, extending her hand as she waited for the ball to return.

"I guess," Em said to her mother, turning her attention back to her book. "If Olivia likes him."

"I meant for you."

Em looked up, surprised. Wenda Flores stood with her back to the bookshelves, the red, green, and black spines extending far over her head, almost all the way to the ceiling.

She cocked one thin eyebrow at her daughter. "He likes you. I'm sure you've noticed."

"He's too powerful to marry someone useless," Em said with a hint of bitterness.

"Just because your Ruined power never manifested doesn't mean you won't pass it to your children. You're still a royal. You'll lead the Ruined, and he belongs in that position with you."

"Olivia will lead, not me."

"You will be your sister's most important adviser. You'll have almost as much influence over Ruina as she will."

Em shrugged, glancing out at Damian again. He caught her eye and smiled. He wasn't the worst choice. But she also didn't look at him the way her mother looked at her father. Like the world would go up in flames if something happened to him.

"Em!" Olivia ran to the window, bracing her hands on either side of it. Her eyes were wide with excitement. "They caught another spy from Lera. They're bringing him now!" She pointed past Damian, where a wagon and horses rolled toward the castle.

"That was fast," Wenda said, the skirts of her red dress swishing across the floor as she walked to the door. "Have you been practicing, Olivia?"

"Every day," Olivia said seriously.

"Good." Wenda smiled at Em. "Your sister is going to take that man's head clean off his body. Would you like to come watch?"

〜〜〜

The memory slammed into Em's brain just after waking. A sick feeling rolled through her stomach and she darted out of bed, gasping for air.

She'd forgotten that day. It had been shortly before Lera attacked, and the memory had faded in favor of the bigger, more horrifying events that followed.

Em had gone to watch. Olivia hadn't been able to do it (though she did break the skin around his neck), so a guard had eventually stepped in with a sword. Em had looked away when it happened.

But she hadn't wondered who he was. She couldn't even remember his face now. If he was young or thin or if he had a beard. She remembered blood dripping down his neck. She remembered the screaming.

It hadn't occurred to her at the time that he could have been someone's Damian. Someone's friend or husband or father.

She pushed her hands through her hair, tears welling in her eyes. Her room was too dark—the only light coming from the moon shining through the window—and the blackness brought images she didn't want to see. Damian on his knees. Her mother's smile.

She hastily pulled on a pair of pants and a loose white shirt. She walked through her rooms and into the hallway, avoiding a maid's curious glance as she passed. She wasn't sure what time it was, but the castle still murmured with noise.

Her feet took her to Cas's rooms. She considered going to

Aren, but something about that didn't feel right. Aren wouldn't understand this ache in her chest.

Cas answered the door only a few moments after she knocked. His shirt was rumpled and half-unbuttoned, though he didn't look like he'd been asleep. He tossed his book onto the couch as he opened the door wider.

"Come in. Are you feeling all right? I came by earlier, but your maid said you weren't feeling well."

"I'm fine," she said as she stepped inside the dark library. Light spilled out from his bedroom, and he led her in that direction.

"You heard they executed Damian this morning?" he asked as they walked through the door. Two candles near his bed were lit, casting a glow over his unmade bed.

"Yeah." She stopped in the middle of the room, crossing her arms over her chest.

"My father did it on purpose, to show he doesn't have to listen to us." Cas turned around to face her. "I wouldn't have handled this situation the same way, if it were up to me. If my father doesn't succeed in killing every Ruined in existence, you and I should find a way to make peace with them one day."

"Peace," she repeated, the word burning down her throat. She'd never considered peace, for even a moment.

"Does that sound stupid?" Cas seemed unsure suddenly.

She shook her head. "No, it's not stupid. Your father and Jovita treat you like your ideas are stupid because they don't like the way your questions make them feel. Remember that, all right?

You're not dumb, you're not naive, you're not any of the things they try to make you out to be."

A slow smile spread across his face. "Thank you, Mary."

She swallowed at the mention of the girl she'd killed, her gaze dropping to the floor.

Cas reached for her hand, his tone softening. "Are you all right?"

"Fine," she lied. "Just . . . lonely, I think." The admission was embarrassing as soon as it was out of her mouth, but Cas squeezed her hand tighter.

"I'm glad you came," he said quietly.

She rubbed her thumb across her necklace. The constant guilt in her chest had started to give way to a fiery ache. It was physically painful to imagine how much he would hate her after he knew the truth.

He closed the distance between them with one small step. He was too close, or not close enough, and she put a hand on his chest.

The room was so quiet she could hear him draw a breath, and she watched as the air filled his chest. His fingers brushed across her neck, and Em knew that if she looked up now, he would kiss her. She was going to let him. She was going to do more than *let him*, actually, she was going to drag him to her and feel every inch of his body next to hers.

His eyes met hers, his thumb gently nudging her chin up.

She burst into tears.

Surprise crossed Cas's face as he pulled her into his arms. She closed her fingers around his shirt. She felt like if she didn't hold on to him, he might start slipping away from her.

"Tell me what's wrong," he said quietly, his arms tightening around her waist.

"Damian's death made me think. . . ." She took in a shaky breath and let honest words spill out of her mouth. "I've seen so many people killed and never given it a second thought. I've killed. I planned to kill more."

She hadn't just planned to kill Cas. She'd imagined smiling as she sank a sword into his chest.

"I don't think this is who I want to be," she said, her voice shaking.

"You did what you had to do," Cas said.

"I did what I chose to do." Tears spilled over her cheeks, staining his shirt.

"Then choose better next time."

It was such a simple statement that she almost told him it was too late. But when she lifted her head and met his eyes, he stared at her with such sincerity that it was impossible to disagree.

"You're not who I thought you'd be, Cas."

"No?"

"You're so much better."

He smiled, his thumb rubbing a tear from her cheek. "Stay with me tonight?"

She nodded without hesitation. He took her hand and led her to the bed. She climbed onto the soft sheets. He slipped in beside her and pulled the blankets up, even though they were both still fully dressed. He scooped her back into his arms, his fingers tangling in her hair and his lips brushing across her forehead.

"Can I tell you a secret?" he asked, his breath tickling her forehead. She nodded. "I didn't want to get married. I was angry I didn't get to choose. But—promise you won't tell my parents I said this." His voice held a trace of humor. "I couldn't have chosen any better than you."

He brushed her hair behind her ear, and she reached up, lacing her fingers between his. She brought their hands in close to her chest, brushing a kiss across his knuckles.

"You're so much better than I expected too," he whispered, his lips grazing her ear as he spoke.

His legs intertwined with hers, and she knew that in the morning she would regret letting him hold her like this. She would think of how the contours of his body felt against hers, how she could feel him smile when he kissed her forehead. She would remember it tomorrow, and the next day, and the next day, and she could already feel the pain that would accompany it. The memory of how he felt when he cared about her was going to be the most painful thing after he began to hate her.

TWENTY

"I'M LEAVING TONIGHT."

Iria's head shot up at Em's words, her face crinkling in confusion. "What?"

Em turned to Aren, who was perched on the edge of a chair. They were in the library, at the far end of the room in case anyone got the urge to listen by the door. He was obviously surprised, but also maybe relieved.

"I have everything I need," she said. "It's time for me to go get Olivia."

"You do not have everything *we* need," Iria said. "We need for you to stay so you don't arouse suspicion."

Iria had a point about that. Surely there would be questions if she suddenly disappeared.

But she couldn't keep lying to Cas. She'd told him she would come to his room again tonight, and she wanted to do it so desperately, her chest ached.

But she couldn't look into his eyes and lie. Not even one more time.

"We were planning to attack within a week, probably less," Iria said. "You can wait a few more days."

"I need time to get to Olivia," Em said. "What if they move her after the attack?"

Iria pulled a piece of hair from her braid and twirled it around her finger. "Tell you what. We'll give you a two-day head start. I'll confirm when the attack is happening, and you can leave two days before that. At that point it will be too late for them to launch any kind of effective defense, even if your disappearance arouses suspicions. They'll still be trying to figure out where you went and why."

Em hesitated. That meant two to three more days in the castle.

Two to three more days with Cas.

What if she used those days to warn him? She couldn't just let him die when Olso attacked. Was it foolish to think she could attempt to make him understand?

"Fine," she said quietly.

"Good," Iria said. "I'll send word for some warriors to head down to the Vallos Mountains to help you."

"That's another thing," Em said, rubbing her finger across her necklace. "I'd like you to spare Cas in the attack."

Silence met her words, the only sound the clock ticking from the other side of the room. Aren's brow was so furrowed she thought it must have hurt to keep it that way.

"I'm sorry?" Iria finally said.

"Em . . ." Aren's voice trailed off, and he shook his head, as if trying to find the words. "Why?"

"Cas is not the same as his father. He shouldn't—"

"You have got to be joking," Aren said. "Em, please tell me you haven't fallen in love with him."

Iria snorted. "You're the only one who hadn't noticed, Aren."

"I'm not in love with him—"

"Of course you're not," Iria said.

"I *know* him," Em said. "He disagrees with all of his father's policies, and he'll change things. If you give him a—"

"I can't . . ." Aren laughed in a way that almost sounded deranged. "I don't . . ." He shook his hands in exasperation. "I don't even have any words."

Em pressed her lips together, fighting back the sudden urge to cry. Aren was staring at her as if she'd just disappointed him for the first time.

"Our orders are to kill the entire royal family," Iria said.

"Not Cas," Em said quietly. Aren sank deeper into his chair, moaning as he put his hands over his face.

"Yes, Cas," Iria said. "And the king, the queen, and Jovita. The entire royal line needs to be eliminated, which, I would like to remind you, was the plan all along."

"I know it was. But if you allow Cas to talk to your king—"

"I assure you that King Lucio has no interest in talking to Cas."

"At least give him the option of surrendering his kingdom willingly!"

"Do you really think he'd take that option?"

Em pressed a hand to her forehead. No. She couldn't see Cas bowing down to the Olso king and willingly surrendering the kingdom he loved. Even to save his life.

"Listen," Iria said, her tone softer. "I won't do it myself. If it were up to me, I wouldn't kill him. But it's not up to me. There will be a lot of warriors here—at your request, I might add—and they have orders."

"Fine."

"Fine? What does fine mean?"

She stood and walked to the door. "It means fine." She pulled the door open.

She absolutely had to warn Cas.

Cas rounded the corner, smiling at a staff member scurrying past. He'd felt light all day since waking with Mary by his side. He'd been thinking of nothing else but the expression on her face when she agreed to come back to his room tonight. And hopefully all the nights after that.

He turned into the open door of his mother's study to find both his parents waiting. His mother stood by her desk, tapping her fingers against it with such vigor she was in danger of denting it. His father was pacing the room.

A large portrait sat in the corner. It was of a man, woman, and young lady. Cas didn't recognize any of them.

"Shut the door," his mother said.

He pushed it shut, the sound echoing through the room. "Is everything all right?"

"The painting arrived." His mother's mouth was set in a hard line, and she had an expression on her face that he'd never seen before. If she'd had a sword, he might have taken a step back.

"The one of Mary and her parents?" He squinted at the painting. He'd never met the king and queen of Vallos, but he didn't think the dark-haired girl was Mary. Her skin was paler, her eyes lighter, and she had small, graceful features, like she might break if shoved too hard. The man and woman stood just behind her, a hand on each of her shoulders. The man had impressively bushy eyebrows, his light-brown hair pulled back at the nape of his neck. The woman was pale and thin like her daughter.

"I think you were lied to," he said. "But it was a nice thought."

His mother's chest started heaving, like she'd just been running. "They did not send the wrong painting. That is the king and queen of Vallos."

"Then who is that?" he asked, pointing to the girl in the painting.

"Oh, wake up, Casimir," his father snapped.

"That's Mary," his mother said, her voice shaking. She clenched her fingers into fists at her side. "The question is, who is the woman you married?"

The world tilted, and he grasped the edge of the chair as he lowered himself into it. That was preposterous. Who would take her place? Why? Where was the real Mary?

More importantly, who had slept in his bed last night?

"Why?" he managed to gasp out, because his mouth wouldn't form any other word.

His father started pacing at a speed that made Cas dizzy. "You need to stay calm."

"I'm calm." He was too dazed to be anything but.

"No, we have an idea of who she is, and we need you to remain calm when we tell you," his mother said.

"She was upset about that Ruined prisoner," his father said, pacing even faster. "It made no sense for her to be that upset about him dying."

"She thought the punishment was—"

"Quiet," his mother snapped.

"She handles a sword better than almost anyone." His father let out a hollow laugh. "And we all know Vallos soldiers aren't well trained. Even a royal isn't that good."

Cas looked blankly at his father. Whatever the king was getting at, Cas hadn't picked it up yet.

"And then she asked you where Olivia was. Didn't she?"

"Yes." Cas's stomach turned over. "She asked again the other day."

"What did you tell her?" A piece of hair had escaped from his mother's bun, like even her hair couldn't handle this situation.

"I—I told her the truth."

His parents gasped in unison.

The fog in Cas's brain suddenly cleared. "You think she's one of the Ruined."

His father ran a hand over his beard. "Not just any Ruined, because she doesn't have any marks. She's the right age, and the hair . . . the eyes . . ."

"What?" Cas was drowning suddenly, unable to breathe or think or move.

"I think that girl is Emelina Flores."

TWENTY-ONE

EM RAISED HER hand to knock on Cas's door. She could do this. Maybe. Probably.

She lowered her shaking fist, taking in a deep breath. She had to warn him, even if it meant angering the warriors. She wouldn't let him die.

"He's not there, Your Highness."

Em turned to see Davina standing a few paces away, a half-eaten breakfast tray in her hands.

"He went to see your painting," Davina said.

"My painting?"

"I—I thought you knew." The color drained from the maid's face. "It's a painting of you and your parents, after all. I just assumed . . ."

Em's throat tightened. A painting of Mary and her parents. They knew.

She scanned the area for weapons. Nothing.

"Please don't tell the queen I told you," Davina begged. "Maybe it was supposed to be a surprise, and if she knew I—"

"Your secret's safe with me." Em turned on her heel, resisting the urge to break into a run. She didn't want to alarm the maid.

She turned a corner and almost ran smack into Iria. Panic was etched across the warrior's face. "The queen has—"

"A painting of Mary, I know," Em interrupted.

"We're leaving. Now."

"I don't have a weapon or—"

"I have one." Iria pulled her sword from her belt. "Stay behind me."

Em looked at her in surprise. "You're coming with me?"

"Do you really think the king is going to believe we knew nothing about you? We arrived right after you." Iria leaned around the corner. She jerked her head, indicating it was clear to go.

"We need to get Aren," Em said.

"Koldo's getting him. We're meeting away from the castle." They reached the top of the stairs, and Iria glanced down at the staff moving around the castle. "I think running is best."

"It'll attract attention. Do you know if they've all seen the painting yet?"

"No way to know."

"WHAT?" Cas's scream echoed through the castle, hoarse

and furious. Em's chest tightened, her heart leaping into her throat. She couldn't think about him right now.

"Running is best," Em said, grabbing Iria's arm. "But not here. Back stairway."

They sprinted down the hallway and to the staircase, their shoes thumping against the steps as they ran. Em slowed until her feet were almost silent. Iria followed suit, whipping her head around as they reached the ground floor.

Em quietly darted around the corner and pushed open the door to the kitchen. It was empty, and she and Iria raced across the room. She dove outside, squinting as the late afternoon sunlight splashed across her face.

"Which way?" Iria asked. "The front gate is going to be tough."

"Impossible. There are too many guards." She pointed to the tree Cas used to sneak out. "There. If we can jump the wall, we'll only have to deal with one or two guards."

"Where is she?" The queen's screeching voice drifted out from a window. "Guards, go! Stop her!"

Iria took off and Em followed close behind, leaping over a bench as she raced for the back wall. The tree loomed in front of her, and she grabbed a branch and launched her body up the tree onto the top of the wall. They'd used a rope to climb down last time, and she swallowed as she judged the distance.

Iria hopped onto the wall beside her, and Em jumped before she could change her mind. She landed on her feet—hard—and she stumbled as pain sliced through her legs. She shook them out, relief coursing through her as she realized she hadn't broken anything.

A guard ran at them at top speed, and Iria crashed down next to her, sword already drawn. Em moved to help her, but a second body smacked into her, knocking them both to the ground.

Arms circled around her, the grip cutting at the air in her chest. She was on her stomach, her cheek digging into the ground.

"Who are you?" a man growled.

She twisted against him, kicking up dirt. One elbow thrust into the guard's face and she managed to wriggle free.

She scrambled to her feet. Galo stood in front of her, his eyes flashing with anger. He wore his exercise clothes, his hands free of weapons.

She raised her fist and launched it into his cheek as he came at her. He stumbled backward, blinking, and she took the free moment to check on Iria. She was still engaged in a heated battle with the other guard.

Galo moved in the corner of her eye, and she turned in time to get an elbow in her stomach as he swept her legs out from under her. She gasped as she hit the ground.

He reached for her and she quickly rolled out of reach. She jumped to her feet and threw two punches, one right after the other. He returned one that stung against her cheek, but he clearly wasn't used to fighting without a sword.

She raised her knee and shoved it into his stomach. Galo wheezed, hitting his knees.

A sword appeared next to Galo's neck. Em's head snapped up

to find Iria standing over him, a sword in each hand. The other guard was dead on the ground behind her.

Em shook her head, reaching for the sword aimed at Galo. Iria gave her a curious look, but handed the blade over.

A face appeared at the top of the wall, and Iria grabbed Em's arm, trying to tug her away.

It was Cas. He stepped onto the wall, and any hope of him understanding vanished when she saw his furious face.

I'm sorry. The words echoed in her head immediately.

"Let's go!" Iria yelled, pulling her harder. Em whirled around and took off, the sound of boots hitting the ground echoing behind her.

"Hey!" Cas's yell followed her, and she ignored it the first time. "Hey!"

She looked over her shoulder to see him standing next to Galo, who was still crumpled on the ground, his hand clutched against his stomach.

"At least tell me your name!" Cas spread his arms wide, his expression a crazy mix of anger and incredulity.

She turned, running backward as she called in a loud, clear voice, "Emelina Flores!"

TWENTY-TWO

EMELINA FLORES.

The name had nudged out all other thoughts and settled in his brain like an open wound.

Emelina Flores. He only heard it in her voice. Saw the way she lifted her chin when she said it, like she was proud of that name and the way she'd fooled him.

The rage burned through his insides so intensely that he could barely feel the sting of the medicine as the doctor treated a cut above his eyebrow.

"I told you to stay calm!" his mother yelled. "Not go chasing off after her!" She stood next to the painting of the real Mary, her face bright red with fury. His father was in a chair next to Cas, a blank expression on his face. He would grip the arms of the chair every minute or so, like his anger was about to burst out of him.

"She was escaping," he said through clenched teeth. She had gotten away. He could have chased her down, but he'd run after them without a sword, and Iria and Emelina each had one.

That was the excuse he told everyone, anyway. The truth was he'd been rooted to the ground as soon as she stared at him with those wide, sad eyes.

Why had she looked so sad?

The doctor finished treating his wound and quickly scurried out of the room, shutting the door behind him.

Cas leaned forward, resting his head in his hands. He was such an idiot for not grabbing his sword before chasing after her. Though he hadn't thought he'd need a sword today to chase down his wife as she attempted to escape.

He let out an almost hysterical laugh, and both his parents regarded him like he'd lost his mind. He had, maybe.

A knock sounded on the door, and one of the king's guards opened it. "The other two Olso warriors are gone, along with Aren."

His father waved the guard away, and the door banged shut as his mother gripped her hair.

"We know where they're going," the king said in an oddly calm voice.

"To Olivia?" Cas guessed.

"Yes. I'll send soldiers down that way. Add extra security to the building. We'll catch them before they get anywhere near her."

"Just kill Olivia," his mother spat. "Send word to have her executed immediately."

Something twisted inside Cas as he watched his mother's face contort with anger. "She hasn't done anything," he said.

"I think you lost all right to have an opinion about the Ruined when you told Emelina Flores where her sister was," the king said.

Cas jumped to his feet. "Who ordered me to marry her?" His yell echoed across the room, making his mother jump.

His father's mouth twitched, but he said nothing.

"Cas," his mother said, her voice gentle. She put a hand on his arm, but he shook her off.

"If there's anyone to blame in this situation, it's you," Cas yelled, his glare fixed on his father. "You ordered the murder of thousands of innocent people, and now you're surprised when one of them—"

"Innocent?" his father roared, practically leaping out of his chair. "The Ruined are not *innocent*!"

"What crime did Damian commit? What did the rest of them do?"

"She got into your head," his father said in digust. "You let Emelina feed you these ideas—"

"I'm not an idiot," Cas said sharply. "She didn't need to feed me any ideas."

"And so you blame me. It's my fault Emelina Flores pretended to be your wife."

Cas spread his arms wide. "I see no one else to blame. None

of this would have happened if you hadn't started a war with the Ruined. Now I'm *married* to one of them." His stomach clenched as he said the words, and he turned away, afraid his face would give away too many emotions.

"You're no longer married to her," his mother said, like that solved everything. "It's not binding."

He rolled his eyes as he faced them again. "Really? Because you say so?"

"Yes!" his father interjected. "She lied about her identity! We will have it declared illegal."

"Our souls are bound until death." He repeated the words the priest had said, just to make his father angry.

It worked. The king smashed his hand against the painting, sending it toppling to the ground. "Then I will kill her myself!"

Cas's first instinct was to yell *No!* He said nothing instead.

"Your father is right," the queen said, in a much calmer voice than her husband. "This marriage isn't legal. We'll take care of it."

Cas shrugged. Whether he was still married to Emelina mattered less than what he'd shared with her and how he felt about her and how much he currently wanted to tear her apart with his bare hands.

Why had she looked so sad?

"Perhaps we could arrange something else for you," his father said in a suddenly optimistic tone. "The governor of the southern province has a daughter. She was our second choice, after Mary."

"You must be joking," Cas deadpanned.

"She's lovely. Much prettier than Emelina."

"You. Must. Be. Joking," he repeated, slower. His parents were insane if they thought he was ever letting them choose his wife again.

"Not the time," the queen said, shaking her head at her husband. He raised his hands in surrender. She focused on Cas again. "Right now we need to assess the damage done. What does she know? What was she doing while she was here?"

"She was with Iria all the time," Cas said. "They'd become friends."

"Or they were already friends, before she got here," his mother said. "Given that the warriors have mysteriously disappeared with her, I think we can safely assume that they knew exactly who Mary really was."

Cas cracked all the knuckles on his left hand, one at a time. "We went down to the shore. She was interested in the towers and how we protected our borders."

"And you showed her all that?" his father exclaimed.

"It doesn't matter now," the queen said before Cas could reply. "We need to prepare for the possibility of an attack. Let's call in the hunters from Vallos and Ruina."

"It will take weeks to get them all back."

"We caught Emelina off guard," his mother said. "Hopefully we have some time. But we'll put the guards at the towers on high alert."

His father frowned at Cas. "I can't believe you just handed over that information to her."

"She was my wife! I trusted her!" The last words tasted bitter as he said them.

He'd thought she cared about him and was excited about the prospect of ruling the kingdom with him one day. He'd thought she was strong and brave and would be the best queen Lera had ever seen.

He'd thought she was falling in love with him.

Maybe she had fallen in love with him. Her tearstained face filled his vision. *I don't think this is who I want to be,* she'd said. His brain screamed that she was a liar who couldn't be trusted, but he couldn't help but think that last night had been real.

The thought flooded his body with a sudden burst of rage. If it had been real, why hadn't she told him the truth? He'd told her, *Choose better next time.* She could have chosen to tell him the truth. She could have trusted him to listen, to be willing to negotiate about Olivia. She'd chosen violence, and deception, just like her mother.

She'd chosen wrong.

TWENTY-THREE

EM AND IRIA spent an unfortunate amount of time hiding in a horse stall not far from the castle. By the time they were able to step out, they both smelled and were stiff from crouching.

The hem of her light-blue dress was covered in mud, and she wished she'd had time to change into pants before escaping. She had nowhere to put the sword she'd stolen, and now that the sun had set, there was a bit of a chill in the air.

"Give it to me," Iria said, holding out her hand. "I have a spot on the other side of my belt."

Em hesitated. She didn't want to be without a weapon while Iria had two. If she'd been smart, she would have put together a bag to easily grab on her way out of the castle. Now she was stuck out here with nowhere to put her weapon, no water, and no food.

"Would you prefer to carry it?" Iria asked, raising an eyebrow. "It will just attract attention."

Em handed the sword over, and Iria slipped it through the leather on the right side of her belt.

"We're supposed to meet Koldo, Benito, and Aren not far from here," Iria said, taking a glance around. The main road that led into the center of Royal City stretched out to the east.

Behind them, the wheels of a cart squeaked as a man pushed it toward the center of town. They were so close Em could hear the laughter coming from the cluster of buildings. A few more steps and maybe she'd be able to smell cheese bread.

The man glanced over his shoulder as he turned the cart around a corner.

"Let's get out of here," Em said.

"Follow me." Iria took off jogging, and Em hurried behind her. They ran across the road and through the tall grass until Em's legs and lungs burned. She'd lost some of her stamina while in the castle.

They headed away from the center of Lera. They were traveling west, to the jungle. Em had taken the main roads and skirted around the edge of the jungle on her journey to Royal City several weeks ago, but she'd already considered it as the best way to go south.

The heart of the jungle was still a half day's walk away, but Iria led them into the thick band of trees just outside Royal City. She slowed to a walk and Em coughed as she tried to catch her breath.

"You should have gone running with me in the mornings." Iria was annoyingly smug.

"I'll . . . be fine in a few days," Em said, taking in gulps of air. "I always adjust quickly."

Iria smirked. "I hope so. They've only just begun to send out guards after us." She took off at a quick walk, and Em struggled to keep pace behind her.

Two figures came into view, and Em frantically scanned the area around them.

"Where's Aren?" she asked, jogging past Iria.

Koldo's eyes were wide with regret. "I'm sorry. I got separated from Aren right after we left the castle. There were guards everywhere, and we were both just trying to get away."

Her heart squeezed painfully in her chest. "They didn't catch him, did they?"

"I don't think so. But I never got a chance to tell him where we were meeting."

She let out a relieved sigh. It was unlikely anyone would be able to catch Aren, especially now that he was free to use his powers. He would be better off than any of them.

"He'll head straight for Fort Victorra," she said. "We can meet him there."

"Are you sure you want to go?" Iria asked. "The king will assume you're headed that way, and he's going to send an army to hunt you down."

"What's my other option?"

"You can join Benito on our ships. Koldo and I will make

sure the warriors at the fortress rescue Olivia."

"No. I'm going."

"I figured," Iria said. "Koldo and I will be going with you. We've instructed a few warriors to meet us with supplies and horses in the jungle."

"Thank you." Em regarded the warriors suspiciously. Rescuing Olivia had never been part of their deal. She'd been under the impression that task would be completely up to her. "And after we rescue Olivia?" she asked.

"The king will want to meet you two, of course," Iria said. "You can accompany us back to Olso."

There it was. The warriors weren't helping her so much as keeping tabs on her and Olivia.

"Benito, you'll go inform our ships we're moving up the attack," Iria said.

"To when?" Em asked.

"Tomorrow night," Iria said. Benito nodded.

Em's stomach twisted, the fear for Cas immediate and stronger than she would have liked.

Iria gestured at Benito, who pulled the bag off his back and gave it to her. He tossed Em his coat.

Iria dug around inside the bag, producing a canteen. She held it out to Em. "That's yours. You're very welcome."

"Thank you," she said, and actually meant it. She'd be much better off with two warriors than she would be on her own.

And if Iria tried to force her to go to Olso after they rescued Olivia, she'd deal with that when the time came.

TWENTY-FOUR

CAS STRETCHED OUT on the couch in his library, folding his hands behind his neck. He'd had all his bedding thrown out and replaced with entirely new linens, but his bed still reminded him of her. Mary had left her presence in every corner of his life, but she'd left the biggest one in his bed, even after only one night.

Emelina, he corrected himself, trying to push the image of her out of his head. He'd promised himself he wouldn't think about her, but she wriggled into his brain at every possible moment. He could think of nothing else.

His parents had stopped all the summer activities, and the castle had been eerily quiet all day. The staff edged around him like they were afraid he was going to explode. He was used to making people uncomfortable, but this was something new and much worse. They *pitied* him.

He hated her. He hoped she'd tripped on one of her stupid dresses and broken something and was now hobbling around in terrible pain.

A wave of guilt followed the thought. He cursed himself for it.

I don't think this is who I want to be.

The words had been so sincere, and they were all he could think of. He'd spent most of the day trying to sort through what had been real. He'd known a little bit of the real Emelina, he was sure of it.

The night in her bedroom had been real. When she described her mother as powerful and angry, and her father as her quiet audience, that was the real Emelina. It fit with what Cas knew about Wenda Flores and her husband.

Everything she'd said about the Ruined had been real. She hadn't even tried to hide her sympathy for them.

But she'd said she was an only child. She said it was lonely, when in reality she had Olivia.

Or she did, before Cas's father took Olivia and locked her away.

He moaned as another wave of guilt washed over him. How had she managed to even look him in the eye? He'd known Olivia was locked up, and it had never even occurred to him to inquire about her before Emelina mentioned it. No wonder she'd seemed miserable on their wedding day.

But . . .

You're not dumb, you're not naive, you're not any of the things they try to make you out to be. She didn't have to say that to him. She didn't have to come to his room and sleep in his bed. He'd given her plenty of space, and she'd come to him repeatedly.

Was he an idiot to think she'd grown to care for him? Was it wishful thinking?

A knock sounded at the door, and Galo stuck his head in a moment later. "May I come in?"

Cas sat up and the guard eased onto the couch next to him.

"Are you drunk?" Galo asked.

"Do I look drunk?"

"No. But your mother said you probably were."

"My mother is the one who deals with her sadness by getting drunk."

Though it wasn't a bad idea. Maybe he'd do that later.

"I'm sorry," Galo said quietly.

"It's fine."

"No, it's not."

He'd said *It's fine* to his father this afternoon. His father had just patted Cas on the back and given him a look of approval.

"No, it's not," Cas repeated.

"I think she really did care about you," Galo said.

"Are you trying to make me feel better?"

"No! I think she did." He rubbed the blue bruise on his chin. Emelina had given it to him. "She didn't kill me. She took the sword from Iria and didn't let her do it."

"They needed to run," Cas said.

"There was plenty of time to kill me, to make sure I didn't run after them." One side of his mouth lifted. "And as much as I'd like to think it's because of my sparkling personality, I suspect she spared me because I'm your friend."

"They could have killed me too, I guess." Cas scrubbed a hand down his face. "I ran after them without a sword, like an idiot."

Though if Emelina wanted to kill him, she had plenty of other opportunities. She could have done it in his bed, as he slept.

That had to mean something, right?

Cas laughed out loud at the ridiculousness of it all. Was he really grateful that his wife hadn't killed him?

My wife didn't smother me with a pillow! Must be love!

He closed his eyes for a moment. "Are they sending you south? My father said he was ordering a few of my guards to join the search for her."

"No, I'm staying here. They've asked me to act as captain of your guard. Temporarily."

"They have?"

"Yes. If that's all right with you."

"Of course it is. You know you'll be captain of my guard one day, permanently."

A hint of a smile crossed Galo's face. "Thank you." He paused, his expression turning more serious. "May I make a request, as your temporary captain?"

"Sure."

"Don't run after Emelina again?"

"You ran after her as well."

"Cas," Galo said, with a hint of annoyance.

"You can make that request, but I won't promise you anything." He slowly got to his feet. The room felt too small suddenly,
like just talking about Emelina had filled all the space around
him. "I'm going to get some fresh air."

"You know that now isn't the time to leave the castle walls,
right?"

"Of course. I'll just be in the gardens."

Galo took the hint that Cas wanted to be left alone and didn't
follow the prince out of his rooms. The hallways and kitchen
were deserted, and he pushed open the back door to the gardens.

The cool night air blew across his face, and he took in a deep
breath as he walked across the grass. He sat down at the base of a
tree, stretching his legs out in front of him. Would people think
it was weird if he slept out here beneath the stars?

He leaned his head back against the tree, listening to the
hum of chirping crickets and the sound of the breeze tossing the
leaves around. He didn't care if people thought it was weird. At
least out here there was plenty of air. Even Emelina couldn't fill
up this space.

A *boom* woke Cas from his sleep. His eyes flew open.

A second *boom* sounded in the distance.

The yelling began so suddenly his body lurched, his feet slipping on the grass as he scrambled to his feet.

A bell started ringing.

Someone was sounding the alarm to warn of an attack.

Cas ran for the back door, throwing it open and racing through the kitchen and into the foyer.

"Cas? Cas!" Galo's voice echoed through the castle from upstairs as Cas ran through the foyer. The hallways were suddenly flooded with light as the staff rushed to ignite the lanterns.

"Here!" Cas called.

Galo's footsteps pounded above him, and he appeared at the top of the stairs, his face grim. He raced down.

"Olso is attacking on the shore. We have to get you out of here immediately."

Panic gripped Cas as the guards and household staff began running past him. They were unprepared for a fight. Emelina had been gone only two days, and they'd yet to call all the hunters back from Vallos and Ruina. Many of the guards were headed south, to search for her.

"We'll go out the passageways in back," Galo said, tugging on his arm.

Screams ripped through the air, and Cas twisted around to find his mother sprinting across the foyer with a guard close behind her. She wore a purple robe that had come mostly undone, her white nightgown peeking out as she ran.

"I won't go without Cas!" she yelled.

"I'm right here," Cas said, and she raced to him, her braid flying behind her.

"Into the passageways, now," Galo said, giving them a push.

His mother grabbed his hand, and Cas looked over his shoulder as she pulled him with her. "Where is Father?"

"His guards will take care of him," Galo said firmly.

The sound of glass breaking shattered the brief quiet, and Cas flinched, ducking his head as something hurtled through the front window.

Flames burst from the object, and the guards circled around it, stomping it out with their feet.

"Cas!" his mother yelled. He realized suddenly that her hand had slipped out of his, and he turned to find her being pushed and shoved toward the kitchen.

"Go!" he yelled. "I'm right behind you!"

Swords crashed together somewhere outside, and Cas let Galo shove him in the direction of the kitchen. He saw his mother's head disappear around the corner, and only a moment later, a swarm of people in white and red rushed through the doors.

Olso warriors.

Cas scrambled backward, turning and breaking into a run with Galo beside him. Another flaming ball rocketed through the window, and Cas hit the floor, covering his head with his hands. Galo knelt down next to him, using his body to shield Cas.

Cas felt the heat of the flames as the ball hit far too close to them. He ducked away, straightening to find Galo with his left arm on fire.

Galo ripped off his jacket and stomped out the flames.

Cas felt a hand on his arm, and he whirled around to find

his father next to him. He had to beat back the urge to throw his arms around his father's neck like he was five years old again.

His father handed Cas a sword. It was heavier than he was used to, the red band around the hilt identifying it as a warrior sword. His father's blade had blood smeared across it.

Cas took off behind the king, looking over his shoulder to find the Olso warriors spilling out of the kitchen. Screams echoed through the halls, and he could only pray that his mother had made it out and the warriors hadn't noticed the passageway.

Galo lifted his sword as two warriors rushed at him. "Go!" he yelled over his shoulder.

Cas ran behind his father, almost crashing into him when he came to an abrupt stop as they rounded a corner. Three warriors stood in front of them. Light flickered across their faces, and Cas started as he recognized one of them. Benito. The warrior's eyebrows were drawn together, his lip curling as he charged them.

"Here!" another warrior yelled down the hallway as he lunged at the king. "I've got the king and the prince!"

Cas lifted his sword, jumping back as Benito swung at him. The blade barely missed his neck, and he realized with a flash of horror that the warriors had been ordered to kill them. They wouldn't be captured or brought anywhere for negotiations.

Panic vibrated through his every limb, and when he swung his sword, a strangled grunt accompanied the effort. Benito's sword met his.

Out of the corner of his eye, Cas saw one of the warriors fall, and his father engaged the other. He sidestepped as Benito lunged at him. The warrior lost his balance, stumbling forward. Cas quickly turned, slamming his boot into the back of Benito's legs. The warrior hit the ground on his knees and scrambled against the stone. Cas drove his blade into Benito's chest.

The warrior made a horrible gurgling sound, the sword sliding out of his stomach as he toppled to the ground. Blood dripped off the metal and Cas tried to shake it off, his stomach rising into his throat. He only succeeded in splattering blood across the blue wall.

A hand grabbed his arm, and he jumped, almost hitting the king with his sword as he whirled around. The two other warriors were dead on the ground, and his father gave him a look of approval as he glanced at Benito.

Someone nearby started shouting, and his father tugged on his arm. Cas had to jump over a dead body as they ran down the hallway. His breath started to come out in panicked puffs, and he transferred his sword to his left hand, wiping his sweaty palm on his pants.

Flames licked up the walls at the far end of the hallway, and his father turned, pushing open the door to a sitting room.

"The window," he said, gesturing for Cas to go ahead of him.

Cas ran into the dark room and to the large window, unhooking the latch and pushing it open. A gust of smoky air blew across Cas's face.

"Where did they go?" a voice yelled.

He whirled around just in time to see a warrior running into the room, making a mad dash for the king. His father was ready, sword lifted. "Go!" he yelled.

Cas ignored him, lunging at the warrior instead. The knife in the man's left hand flashed across his vision, and he opened his mouth to yell a warning to his father.

The warrior drove the knife into his father's chest.

The king gasped, his sword clattering to the floor. The warrior gave the knife a shove. The king toppled over, hitting the floor with a thud.

Cas froze. Red spread across his father's shirt, but Cas was sure he wasn't going to die. He couldn't.

The warrior darted toward Cas, and his brain snapped to attention. He surged forward, surprising the warrior, and his blade immediately nicked the warrior's arm. The man sprang out of the way, and then lunged for Cas.

Cas blocked his attack, taking two quick steps back and darting around the warrior. He jabbed his blade straight into the man's side. The warrior gasped as Cas yanked it out of his flesh.

He sliced the blade across the warrior's neck.

Cas turned away as the man fell. The king was sprawled out on his back on the floor, his white shirt entirely red.

Cas dropped down on his knees, his body cold and shaking. Would he be able to pull his father through the window? Maybe Cas could put him on his back.

His father's eyes were drifting open and closed, his head lolling to one side. His lips parted, but only a weird squeaking noise came out. His chest stopped moving.

Cas's hands were on his father's chest, and they were red with his blood now, but he'd lost feeling in them. Cas's whole body seemed to have departed, actually.

He realized suddenly he was whispering his father's name over and over, but it didn't seem to be doing anything to wake him up.

He wasn't waking up.

His father was dead.

"Put the castle staff in the wagon!" The yell from behind him made Cas jump, and he quickly moved his hands off his father's chest as feeling returned to them.

"Find the prince!" the voice yelled. "Kill him on sight."

Cas stumbled as he got to his feet. The sounds of boots thumping and voices yelling echoed all through the castle. He was surrounded.

He wiped his bloody hands on his black pants and darted to the window, sparing a glance at the dead warrior on the ground. He had to resist the urge to drive his sword into the dead man's chest. The blood seeping from his neck and pooling on the floor didn't seem like enough punishment.

He peered around the windowsill. Smoke curled up into the night sky in the distance, near the center of town, and his heart jumped into his throat. Were they killing innocent people? Were they going to burn the whole city to the ground?

Was he the one who was going to have to decide how to retaliate, now that his father was dead?

He pushed the thought out of his mind. Now was not the time to panic about the fact that he'd just become the king. He wouldn't be ruling anything if they caught him.

He looked left, to the front of the castle, and saw two warriors standing at the corner, their backs to him. He squinted to the right, at the dark wall that led to the gardens. He couldn't see anyone in that direction, but there was a lot of noise very nearby. Light spilled out onto the grass, and he suspected there were quite a few warriors in the gardens.

He eased his foot out the window, his sword still gripped in one hand. He didn't turn back to his father. Somehow he knew that if he turned around now, that was the image that would stay burned into his brain forever.

His feet hit the ground with a soft thud, and he crouched down next to the wall, stilling for a moment as he made sure no one had caught his movement.

He had three choices: make a run for it, which was likely to draw attention; try to sneak out the front gate, which was near impossible; or try to make it to through the gardens to the tree in back and attempt to jump over the wall. The latter was probably his best choice. He suspected there were more warriors in that direction, but that might work in his favor. He'd be harder to spot in the chaos.

He stayed low to the ground as he ran next to the castle wall.

Kill him on sight. The words rolled through his brain again, and he looked down at his clothes. His shirt was gray, without any royal insignia on it. Many of the Olso warriors had never met him, but they must have seen drawings of him.

He leaned down, grabbing some dirt and rubbing it across

his cheeks. He ruffled his hair as well, pulling a few strands down into his eyes. It wasn't the best disguise, but perhaps they wouldn't recognize him right away.

He continued along the wall until he made it to the rear of the castle. He peered around the corner.

Horses led a wagon into the gardens. The wagon was a completely sealed wooden box on wheels, usually used to transport prisoners. The warriors must have stolen it.

Some of the castle staff were lined up to get in the wagon. Where were the warriors taking them?

He glanced out at the gardens. At least fifty Olso warriors milled around. Some ran back and forth, clearly in search of something.

"The king is dead!" someone yelled from the back door. "No sign of the prince."

A hand clapped over his mouth suddenly, and Cas's body jerked. He started to twist from the tight grip the man had on him.

"Your Highness," the voice whispered, "don't panic."

The hand disappeared from his mouth and Cas turned. A boy a few years younger than Cas stood in front of him. He had a scar across one eyebrow and looked vaguely familiar. He worked in the kitchen, maybe.

"I'm sorry I did that," the boy said, his eyes round with fear. "I didn't want you to make any noise and—"

Cas waved his hand for him to be quiet. "It's fine."

The boy started unbuttoning his blue shirt. "Take off your

shirt and give it to me, Your Highness. If we trade and you get caught, they'll think you're part of the staff. They're putting all the staff in that wagon."

"Oh." Cas blinked at him before reaching to unbutton his own shirt. "Thank you, that's very smart." His hands stilled as something occurred to him. "Will they think you're me, if you're wearing my shirt? Some of the warriors inside saw me."

The boy started to laugh, then quickly stifled the sound "No, Your Highness. I don't think there's any danger of them mistaking me for you."

The boy was tall and broad, his blond hair brushing his collar. He had a long nose and a pointed chin, and Cas realized he was right. The warriors must have had a vague idea of what Cas looked like, and this boy in no way resembled him.

He pulled the boy's shirt on. The sleeves were a little short and it was a bit tight, but it would do. "What's your name?" he asked.

"Felipe."

"Thank you, Felipe." A flash of red caught his eye. Behind the boy, an Olso warrior was coming around the corner of the castle, his head turned to call something over his shoulder.

Cas grabbed Felipe's arm and dashed to the left, his sights set on the bushes only a few paces in front of them. He dove behind one, crouching down next to Felipe. The Olso warrior was joined by three others, and Cas held his breath as their boots crunched against the grass.

He gripped his sword with two fingers and went down on his

hands and knees, crawling into the gardens. Felipe followed him. The row of bushes extended only a bit farther in front of him; then it was open space until he made it to the hedges. He would have a hard time making it through without someone seeing him.

"I'll create a distraction so it's easier for you," Felipe whispered behind him.

Cas wanted to argue, but the boy had a determined look on his face, like he'd already decided. He nodded.

Felipe shot to his feet and ran in the opposite direction.

"There!" a woman yelled. "There's someone behind that bush!"

Cas waited until Felipe was halfway to the front of the castle before he took off. The warriors were all occupied running after him, and if he could just make it a few more steps—

He was yanked back by his shirt suddenly, the collar straining against his neck so hard he choked. His feet came off the ground. A boot slammed into the back of his legs. His sword sprang out of his hand and bounced out of reach.

He hit the grass hard, gasping for air and taking in some dirt as well.

"Get up," a man's voice spat.

Cas slowly got to his knees, and then his feet. His heart thudded in his chest, and he was intensely aware of the sword the warrior had in his hand. It was half lifted in warning.

The man gave him another shove with his boot, almost knocking Cas to the ground again. "In the wagon with the rest."

Cas did as he was told, the warrior following close behind.

"Two more castle staff," the warrior said. Out of the corner of his eye, Cas saw Felipe being dragged across the grass by a warrior.

A female warrior stood at the back of the wagon, and she jerked her thumb for them to get in. "Any sign of the prince?" she asked the other warrior. Cas ducked his chin into his chest.

"No."

"Start spreading the word to the locals that there's a significant reward for finding him. Dead or alive," the female warrior said. "Preferably dead."

Cas dared a glance inside the wagon and saw about thirty members of the castle staff loaded inside. They were a mix of young and old, cooks and maids he'd seen only in passing. He even spotted two guards. A few eyes widened in recognition.

He took a step inside, swallowing as he realized any of them could give him up, if they wanted.

But everyone was silent as he stepped into the wagon. Felipe followed behind him. Cas felt gentle tugs on his left arm, and he turned to see the staff making a hole in back for him to sit. He slumped down, pulling his knees to his chest, and the staff immediately filled in the space around him, hiding him from view.

"Are you hurt?" an older woman he vaguely recognized whispered. Daniela. She'd worked in the castle gardens for as long as he could remember. She grabbed his bloody hands.

He shook his head. "No. It's—it's not mine." He tried wiping his hands on his pants again, but the blood had started to dry and it didn't budge. He noticed he was shaking, as were most of the people sitting around him. They were staring at him with tight, scared faces, and he quickly stuffed his hands beneath him.

"It will be all right," he said quietly. His voice shook, betraying the fact that he knew that was an outrageous lie. "They have taken the castle, but they have not taken Lera." That one wasn't so much a lie as a hopeful declaration, since he had no way of knowing. What if Olso was already in the Southern Mountains? What if they'd defeated all the troops headed there? His mother and Jovita would head straight for the mountains as soon as they escaped.

If they escaped.

TWENTY-FIVE

AT NIGHT, EM thought of Cas.

And also in the mornings, afternoons, and evenings. But especially at night.

Two days had passed since their escape. Em watched as the sun disappeared completely behind the trees and the world fell into darkness. They'd been walking since early that morning, and her feet ached as she slid down a tree trunk.

The jungle was noisy around her, even though everyone in their party was quiet and on constant alert. The jungle was an absolute gift—loud and crowded, with chirping bugs and squawking birds competing for space with vines, trees, and leaves as big as her face. The forests of Vallos and Ruina were different. Quiet, sparse, harder to hide in.

Iria passed her a small piece of dried meat, and she took it with a soft "Thank you."

She tore off a piece of meat with her teeth, looking down at the mess that used to be her dress. The blue fabric was now completely brown at the hem, and smudges of dirt dotted the skirt. There was even a smear of blood, from where she'd caught the sharp edge of a tree branch on her arm and wiped it on her skirt.

She'd fashioned a belt out of a vine and stuck her sword through it, and she found herself always watching the warriors' movements, waiting to see if they were still partners now that they were safely away from the Lera castle. Two warriors against one tired, useless Ruined. Not her best odds.

"Who's taking first watch?" Koldo asked, planting his hands on his hips as he surveyed the jungle.

"I will," Em said, even though she was exhausted. She didn't want to sleep. Every time she closed her eyes she saw Cas's face. When she drifted off for even a few minutes, the guilty ache in her chest would jerk her awake, and everything she'd done would come rushing back.

"You barely slept at all last night," Iria said.

Em shrugged, dropping her gaze to the ground.

"Koldo, you want to refill the canteens?" Iria asked.

"Sure," Koldo said, taking the hint and disappearing in the direction of a nearby stream.

Iria watched him go, the sound of his footsteps fading into the distance. "I know that you developed feelings for Cas and it's eating you up that he's going to die, but don't lose sight of why you did this," she said quietly. "Your people were headed for extinction, and you're the only one who stepped in to do something about it. You did what you had to do."

"I did what I chose to do."

"You chose right."

"Yes, you did," a voice said.

Iria scrambled to her feet, pulling out her sword. Aren stepped out from behind a tree, hands raised in surrender. Em jumped up and threw her arms around him.

Iria let out a relieved sigh. "I didn't hear you coming."

Em grasped both his arms. "Are you injured? Did the Lera soldiers hunt you down?"

He smirked. "They tried." He glanced around. "No horses? Are we traveling all the way to Vallos on foot?"

"Warriors will meet us with horses day after tomorrow," Iria said. "If all is going well, they should be launching their attack right about now." She looked up at the sky. "We've traveled too far to hear it, unfortunately."

Em's stomach dropped into her feet. Was Cas already dead? Would he be able to escape?

She rubbed her fingers across her forehead, the guilt burning so intensely in her chest it took her breath away. This had always been the plan. If the warriors didn't attack, then she'd have no hope of rescuing Olivia. They'd be completely outnumbered when they arrived at the Vallos Mountains. She'd known this was how her time at the castle would end.

Still, she felt like curling into a ball and screaming.

Aren nudged her arm. "Iria's right about sleeping, Em. I could use some sleep as well. I covered your tracks as best as I could as I followed you, but I'm sure we'll still encounter some Lera soldiers soon. We need to be prepared."

"I'll keep watch," Iria said.

Em's shoulders slumped in defeat as she let Aren tug her down to the ground. He put an arm around her, leaning back against the tree.

"Thanks for finding me," she said, resting her head on his shoulder.

"Thanks for not getting killed," he whispered, squeezing her arm. "That would have really put a damper on my day."

Her lips twitched up as she let her eyes drift closed.

TWENTY-SIX

CAS LURCHED FORWARD as the wagon stopped. A few of the people around him stirred, waking from sleep. Beside him, Daniela arched her back, wincing as she rubbed a wrinkled hand across her eyes. They'd been crammed in the closed wooden wagon all night, and it was incredible that some of them were able to sleep. He wasn't sure he'd ever sleep again.

It was dim inside the wagon, only wisps of sunlight leaking in through the cracks in the wood. It was almost unbearably hot inside, and Cas's clothes were stuck to his body.

The door at the back swung open, and Cas squinted in the bright sunshine.

"Men first," the warrior barked. He jerked his thumb, indicating they should get out.

For a brief moment Cas panicked, thinking the warriors were lining them up for execution.

"Over there in the bushes," someone said as the men started piling out. Cas sighed as he realized the warriors were just letting the prisoners relieve themselves.

He climbed out of the wagon, ducking his head into his chest. There were six warriors around the wagon, and Cas noticed that many of the saddles were Lera colors as they dismounted their horses. They must have taken them from the castle or the townspeople.

The warriors marched them in a straight line to the bushes, swords pointed at their backs. No one appeared to be thinking about running, as that seemed pointless. A few warriors had spread out in a circle, covering every corner.

"Quickly," a warrior barked as they approached a thick patch of bushes.

When they headed back, Cas snuck a glance around. They must have been traveling south, because the air was thicker near the jungle. Were they headed for the Southern Mountains?

Would Emelina be there?

Anger bubbled in his chest, so powerfully it almost knocked him over. She must have known the warriors planned to attack. She'd probably had a hand in planning it.

She'd known they were coming specifically to kill him and his family, and she'd let it happen. How strong could her feelings really be for him if she'd so easily sent him to his death? His father was gone because of her. Galo too, most likely.

His throat closed, and he forced the image of his dead father out of his brain.

The women streamed out of the wagon as the men approached, and Cas took a moment to appreciate the fresh air around him. How many days was he going to be in that wagon?

And worse, where was he going to be when they finally let them out?

The man in front of him stepped onto the wagon, and Cas put one foot up, tossing his hair out of his eyes.

"Wait," the warrior said.

Cas froze as a hand closed over his arm.

"Look at me."

Cas's heart stopped. The warrior gasped as their eyes met.

The warrior's hand found his sword. "You're—"

Felipe shot in front of Cas so quickly it was nothing but a blur. The boy kicked the warrior in the hand, sending the sword flying. The boy scrambled in the dirt to grab it, and Cas opened his mouth to scream for him to stop.

Felipe grabbed the sword and sank the blade into the warrior's chest.

Cas's eyes went wide as the warrior fell to the ground, his mouth forming silent words.

A female warrior lunged, easily blocking Felipe's attack. She sliced her blade across his neck.

Cas screamed. A sob caught in his throat as he fell to the ground. Felipe's blood pooled beneath his knees.

Someone grabbed him under the arms and he struggled

against them, kicking his legs and trying to get back to the boy.

"Get him in there or I'll slit his throat too!" the female warrior yelled.

Tears streamed down Cas's face as a staff member gently tugged him into the wagon. He wiped a hand across his face as he scooted on his knees to the corner of the wagon, but a fresh wave of tears came.

People moved in all around him. Daniela sat beside him again. She put a hand on his arm, and he had to fight back another wave of tears.

He took in a shaky breath, glancing at the people around him.

"Please don't anyone else do that," he whispered.

Daniela patted his arm. "I'm sorry, Your Highness, but I think we're all going to ignore that order."

His cheeks burned as he wiped tears from them. His people were probably looking to him for leadership and strength, and he was weeping like a child.

He cleared his throat, turning his gaze to his feet. They began moving again, and Cas spent most of the morning and afternoon struggling to hear the chatter outside. He needed a plan, and an idea of their location, but the warriors gave no indication as to where they were going. The only hint he got was that they were "sticking to the road and staying clear of the river," which he took to mean they were avoiding traveling through the heart of the jungle. It would have been very difficult with a wagon anyway.

He leaned his head back against the wood, noticing suddenly

that every head in the wagon was turned in his direction. He straightened, giving them a curious look.

Daniela pointed to something across from him, and Cas leaned over so he could see what she was trying to show him.

A young woman in the back left corner had her hand braced against the side of the wagon. She tilted her hand forward, an entire wooden panel coming with her. She'd managed to free a large piece of the wood and was only keeping it in place with her hand. It was big enough for someone to squeeze through.

"They have us surrounded," he said quietly.

"When we stop," the girl whispered, her dark, tangled hair falling in her face. "They're talking about stopping soon. Come to this side, and we'll make a distraction."

Cas hesitated. If he got caught, they'd kill him no matter who he was. But if he stayed, someone else would surely recognize him. If not on the road, then when they arrived.

The staff started making a path for him to crawl through.

"I shouldn't leave you," he said. "I don't know where they're taking you."

Daniela shook her head. "You can't stay. The king is dead. If they kill you too, what will happen to Lera? They will have won."

Cas swallowed. He knew she was right, though guilt still nagged at him.

"Only if it seems safe," he said, scooting forward. "If I get caught, they'll know you distracted them so I could escape." He wasn't letting anyone else die for him today.

"I think you might get a few splinters in odd places," the girl said as she squeezed next to him. She squinted at the small area he'd have to wedge himself through, then glanced over at him. She seemed to immediately remember to whom she was speaking, and her whole face flushed.

He laughed softly. She smiled through her embarrassment and ducked her head.

"What's your name?" he asked quietly.

"Violet," she said.

"Thank you, Violet."

They rolled to a stop a few minutes later, a blast of fresh air blowing through the wagon as a warrior opened the door.

Daniela lurched forward, falling on a few people in the process.

"Sir?" she croaked, reaching for the warrior at the door. "I'm going to vomit."

The warrior jumped back as she tumbled out of the wagon. Retching noises filled the air as she hit the ground. Another girl poured herself onto the ground and did the same.

Cas leaned forward, watching through a crack in the wood as two warriors dismounted their horses and walked to the back of the wagon to see what was going on. The left side of the wagon was totally clear, from what he could see.

"They need water," one of the warriors said. Cas glanced over to see a big clump of them standing at the door. The staff members in front of him were sitting as tall as possible, hiding him from view in the back corner.

He nodded at Violet, and she slowly moved her hand, letting

the wood fall away from the wagon. She gently lowered it to the floor of the wagon.

The narrow opening was only barely big enough. He eased his leg through first. Seemed preferable to getting his head stuck. He slipped the other foot through.

His feet found the ground, and he took a quick glance back to see the staff divided between watching him and keeping an eye on the warriors at the wagon door. The warriors' attention was still on the women, but they started to turn back to the wagon.

"Come on, come on out," one of the warriors said, waving his hand impatiently.

A man in front made a sound like a scream or a cry, causing every head to turn in his direction.

Last chance. Cas braced his hands against the wood, arching his back as he let his torso through. His feet slipped, the wood scraping against his stomach as he began to fall. Definitely a few splinters in weird places.

He hit the ground on his butt with a soft thud.

He was out.

"Come on, everyone out!" a warrior called impatiently.

Cas gingerly moved into a crouch, scooting behind the front wheel of the wagon. A warrior atop a horse was only a few paces in front of him, but he was facing forward, away from Cas.

"What's going on back there?" a voice yelled from ahead. The warrior near Cas started to turn.

Cas scrambled beneath the wagon, rolling onto his back

directly in the center, away from the wheels. He held his arms against his chest, willing himself not to breathe.

"They're getting sick from the heat," a warrior replied.

Boots hit the ground, spraying dirt across Cas's right arm. "Get them some water," a female voice said.

The boots disappeared, and Cas lifted his head to see them headed for the back of the wagon. His left looked clear, though it was hard to tell from underneath the wagon. He'd have to risk it, because he had to get out from under the carriage before they started moving again.

Cas eased himself to the left and slowly rolled over onto his stomach. He scooted forward, barely peeking his head out.

The horse at the front of the line was unmanned now.

He looked at the rear of the wagon. He could see the side of one warrior and the back of another. If they turned this way suddenly, he'd be done for. He ducked his head, peering out the other side of the wagon. A line of shoes walked away from him. The staff was all headed to the other side, so hopefully the warriors would stay there with them.

He moved his forearms against the ground, wiggling forward on his stomach until his body was halfway out from underneath the wagon. He didn't dare stand, as one of the warriors might catch the movement out of the corner of his eye.

"Men with me!" a warrior yelled.

Cas dared to go a little faster. He was completely out from under the wagon now, lying flat on his stomach in the middle of the road. The tall grass in front of him wouldn't be enough to hide him if anyone looked closely, but maybe if he stayed still. Very still.

A grunt made him peer over his shoulder, and he saw the two warriors closest to him now facing each other, talking.

He scooted into the grass until his feet were off the road, and then went a bit farther. He placed his palms flat in the dirt and rested his face on top of them. He was breathing heavily, but he tried to be perfectly still.

"Back inside!" a warrior finally yelled.

Horses' hooves thudded against the ground, and he knew the warriors had all gone back to their posts. All they had to do was glance over at the lump in the grass and he was dead.

Cas held his breath as the wagon creaked and the horses began to move.

"What is that?" a voice called.

Cas curled his toes in his boots, preparing to run. Maybe if he ran fast enough they wouldn't catch him. Maybe he could find a good enough hiding place.

"Is that my knife?" The voice was amused, and someone else laughed. "Get your own knife."

Cas said a silent thank-you as the sounds began to grow distant. He remained motionless for a long time, probably much longer than he needed to.

He finally lifted his head, slowly, and blinked against the sunlight. Everyone was gone. A warm breeze blew through the grass, making it tickle his face, and he almost felt like laughing for a moment. The urge left as soon as it came.

He got to his hands and knees, then to his feet. If the warriors were staying away from the river, then that was exactly where he needed to be. He could follow it almost all the way to Fort Victorra.

He pushed his hair out of his face and ran through the grass, headed for the cover of the trees.

TWENTY-SEVEN

EM WALKED BEHIND Koldo and Iria as they trekked through the jungle. It had been two days since Aren had found them, and she felt better with her friend next to her. He'd pointed out Koldo's slight limp and bloodied left leg yesterday and she'd been watching it ever since, getting a handle on how he moved in case she needed to defend herself.

They were all silent as the morning stretched into afternoon, and Em couldn't help but think of Damian. He was the talkative one, the one Aren and Em would have to shush and remind that they were trying to be quiet to avoid hunters. The weight of his absence mixed with her fear for Cas, and every step she took felt heavy.

"Should I carry you?" Aren asked, cocking an eyebrow when she fell behind again.

"Sorry." She took a couple of quick steps to catch up with him. "I miss Damian," she said, leaving out the second part of her sadness.

Aren kicked a pebble out of his way. "Me too."

"Sometimes I wonder what would have happened if we'd gone into hiding instead of doing all this," she said, letting herself picture it for a moment. "Like if we'd just found a place to be safe and took some people with us. If I'd married Damian and tried to forget everything that had happened."

Aren laughed, and she turned to him in surprise. He rolled his eyes at her.

"You never would have married Damian, Em."

"I . . . I don't know. Maybe it could have happened, if everything had calmed down."

Aren shook his head. "If you'd felt that way about him, it wouldn't have mattered how crazy our lives were. You managed to develop some pretty strong feelings for Cas despite terrible circumstances." He lifted an eyebrow, and she looked away. He had a point.

"He wasn't upset about it," Aren continued. "Disappointed, sure. But he wasn't waiting or hoping or anything."

She swallowed, crossing her arms over her chest.

"And you will never be the type to hide," Aren said. "Everyone else wanted to hide, and you insisted on fighting. I admire you for it."

"Don't admire me." She'd taken the king's tactics and made them her own. While trying to defeat him she had become him, and that seemed far worse than anything she'd ever imagined.

Aren bumped his shoulder against hers. "Too late."

Cas's stomach rumbled for food, and his mouth was so dry that he couldn't think of much else. The heat inland was almost unbearable, and he wondered why people would live in the jungle when they could enjoy an ocean breeze near the shore.

He was entirely alone, and had been for a full day, but the sounds of the jungle seemed far too loud. He'd never realized how accustomed he was to the sounds of the castle—the hum of the staff moving about, the quiet voices that echoed through the halls, the way the wind would gently rattle his window. Even in the wagon he'd been more comfortable, surrounded by the voices he'd known all his life.

But out here, without another soul anywhere near, the sounds were deafening. The crickets were singing a constant, manic rhythm, and a frog would croak every now and then, as if trying to accompany them. The noise only increased his panic about being completely alone.

He wiped the back of his arm across his forehead and batted a giant green leaf away from his face. He had to be close to the river by now. He couldn't hear it yet, but he'd headed west after leaving the wagon. Unless he'd drifted off course, he'd be there at any moment.

He trudged forward. His feet had begun to ache, but it was

nothing compared to the thirst, and he forced his legs to move faster, until he finally heard the sounds of the water lapping against the shore.

The homes appeared as soon as he was able to see the river, and he stopped, startled that anyone lived out here. He'd known a large number of the Lera people lived in the jungle, but he'd never actually seen them.

The homes directly on the river were built on rafts, floating right on the shore. The homes a bit farther up the shore were built high off the ground, pieces of wood taller than him elevating the homes so they were safe from floods. The roofs were made of woven palms, and some of the homes didn't have walls. They wouldn't have needed them, since it was never cold this far inland and they probably welcomed the frequent rain.

He looked from the rushing water to the homes, reluctant to leave the safety of the trees. A woman emerged from one of the raft homes, wearing clothes that must have been brought in from a Lera city. Her skirt was knee-length and bright red, and she wore a white sleeveless shirt. The clothes were old and worn, and she must have had them for a long time.

Another woman followed her, outfitted in a skirt made of dried grass and only a scrap of fabric to cover her chest. They both headed away from Cas.

A whispered voice sounded from behind him. Cas's body went cold. He slowly looked over his shoulder.

A spear was pointed right between his eyes.

He turned, raising his hands in surrender. Two men stood in

front of him. One was about Cas's age, the other much older. The young man had a sword dangling from his hand, letting the older man handle the spear that was pointed at Cas.

"I was just going to the river," Cas said. "For water."

The young man stepped closer to him, moving toward Cas so quietly that it became very obvious how these two had managed to sneak up on him so easily. He wore pants that ended above his knees, and a stained gray shirt. The older man wore the same kind of pants but no shirt at all.

The old man jabbed him in the chest with the spear and Cas gasped, stumbling backward. He'd poked Cas just hard enough to break the skin, and a dot of red started to appear over the castle insignia.

"You're from the castle," the man said accusingly. Cas flashed back to the warriors saying they were going to let the locals know there was a price on the prince's head.

"I—I stole it." His lie came out hesitantly. "The person wearing it was dead, so I took it. The Olso warriors attacked the castle."

"Did the warriors kill the people in the castle?" The older man was so hopeful suddenly that Cas had to beat down a swell of rage. The image of his father's white shirt turning red flashed through his memory.

"Some of them," he said quietly.

"Good." The man nodded, as if this satisfied him.

"You can have some water," the young man said, sheathing his sword. "Then you'll leave."

Cas tried to appear grateful. The old man ran ahead, skipping over rocks until he reached the shore. The other man walked behind Cas, a little too close for comfort.

The old man walked to a large bucket and grabbed a cup hanging from the side. He scooped it inside, then held it out to Cas. "It's clean."

Cas took a quick, covert sniff of the water before tipping it to his mouth. It was clean, though it had an earthy taste, with a hint of fish. He gulped it down anyway, wiping a hand across his mouth when he was done. The man scooped out another cup for him, looking at Cas like he was an idiot as he drained that one as well.

"You should have stayed in the city," the man said.

"Olso has taken over the city." Cas handed him the cup. "They could come here. You should be careful."

The man laughed. "Olso warriors have no problem with us."

Cas just shrugged. "Thank you for the water."

The man pointed in the direction Cas had come from. "Royal City is back that way."

Cas didn't tell him he wasn't going to Royal City. Let them think he was.

"The others aren't coming this way, are they?" the young man asked.

"What others?" Cas asked.

He pointed into the jungle, but Cas saw nothing. "I've seen others. Everyone is going south."

Perhaps he'd seen the Lera troops headed to the Southern Mountains. Cas felt a burst of hope. If he was able to find them, he'd be safe again. He'd have a horse and a sword and an army to take back the castle.

"I'm sure they won't bother you," he said, even though he had no idea. He thanked the men again, turning to walk away. A child stood directly in front of him, and he stopped short, giving her a weak smile. She stuck her thumbs in her ears, shot her tongue out, and made a face at him. She shrieked with delight as she ran away, like she'd waited most of her life to do that.

Cas cast a glance over his shoulder as he started walking again. The men followed him with their eyes, their mouths set in hard lines. He picked up his pace, telling himself it was because he hoped to find the Lera soldiers, not because he was afraid of two strange men.

He began to search for signs of horses or anything that indicated someone had come this way. He spotted a footprint here and there, though that could have been from the people he'd just met. But the footprints seemed to be headed south, so he followed them.

A rustling sound behind him almost made him turn, but he caught himself just in time. He took a careful step forward, trying not to let his shoulders tense. If someone was watching him, he didn't want them to know he was aware of their presence.

He pushed a branch out of his face, using the opportunity to peek over his shoulder.

Something slammed into him. He hit the ground.

The young man grabbed the back of his shirt and yanked Cas to his feet.

The old man stood in front of him, spear aimed directly at Cas's neck. He drew the spear back, preparing to plunge it straight into Cas's flesh.

Cas grabbed onto the arm holding him, using the anchor to lift his legs off the ground. Cas launched his feet into the man's chest. The man stumbled backward, tripping over a vine and hitting the ground.

The arm around him loosened as he returned his feet to the ground. Cas lifted his elbow and slammed it into the young man's side. He grunted, and Cas spun out of his grasp.

The old man lunged at him with the spear, and Cas dove out of the way. The man swung the spear wildly, and Cas quickly ducked. He popped right back up, grabbing hold of the wooden handle of the spear as it came at his head again. He yanked it out of the man's hands.

He took a step back, away from the man's flailing hands. He used both hands to sink the sharp tip of the spear into the man's neck.

The old man made a strange gasping sound as he fell, the blood draining down his bare chest.

The young man had disappeared, and Cas whirled around, frantically scanning the area. The man was standing on a fallen tree right behind Cas, sword poised. He jumped before Cas could react.

Cas darted out of the way, but not before the blade sliced across his bad shoulder. He stumbled as he felt blood start to trickle down his arm.

The young man grabbed him by the hair, and Cas tried to pull away, yelling as the pain shot through his scalp. He dropped to his knees. The young man stepped in front of him. Cas felt the metal of a blade against his skin, and he squeezed his eyes shut.

TWENTY-EIGHT

TWO WARRIORS AND four horses waited near the river-bank. Iria and Koldo greeted the two men, but Em hung back with Aren, surveying their weapons and supplies. The two new warriors were fresh and clean next to the four travelers—their red-and-white coats were crisp and their faces weren't drawn and exhausted. They both had swords, and probably a knife or two hidden somewhere.

"This must be the famous Emelina Flores," a warrior with a mustache said, striding over to her. "I'm Miguel."

"Em." She jerked her head to her friend. "Aren."

"Nice to meet you both." He gestured at his warrior buddy. "This is Francisco. I'm glad we found you. We were starting to think you weren't coming."

"We've had to travel on foot," Iria said.

"Did you come from the castle?" Em asked hurriedly. "What happened?"

Matching grins spread across Miguel's and Francisco's faces. "The castle is ours. The king is dead."

Relief and dread smacked against her all at once.

"The rest of the royal family has gone missing," Miguel continued, and she almost collapsed from relief. "We assume they're headed for Fort Victorra, so we'll take care of that when we arrive. We've informed some of the locals out here that there is a sizable reward for killing any member of the royal family."

Iria's eyes flicked briefly to Em before she smiled at the warriors. "Wonderful. Should we keep going then? Aren and Em, you'll need to share a horse."

The sounds of a man grunting echoed through the trees. Em whirled around, searching for the source of the noise.

She could hear rustling and heavy breathing, followed by a yell. A fight, maybe. Everyone remained still. She wrapped her fingers around her sword.

A flash of blue streaked across her vision and disappeared from view. She stepped to the side, craning her neck to see around the trees.

Her heart stopped.

It was Cas, on his knees with a blade to his throat. A man with a sword set his mouth in a determined line, preparing to slice Cas's neck.

She was moving before she realized she was going to him,

ignoring the shouts from behind her.

Cas was out of sight suddenly, and for a terrible moment she thought the man had succeeded in killing him. But he rolled away from the blade and jumped up, moving faster than she'd ever seen. And she'd thought he was giving it his all when they sparred.

She leaped over a vine, her fingers sweaty around the hilt of her sword. Cas slammed his body against the man, knocking them both to the ground.

Cas scrambled to his feet. He had the sword. She skidded to a stop a few paces from him just in time to see him plunge the sword into the man's chest.

He whirled around, bloody sword still poised in front of him. Their eyes met.

He was dirty and his pants were smeared with something dark—probably blood. He wore a blue staff shirt that was only half buttoned and covered in grime. Deep, dark circles marred the flesh under his eyes. He'd aged three years instead of three days.

His face twisted, and she caught a full glimpse of just how much he hated her. He hated her with everything he had, hated her with more intensity than he'd ever felt about anything.

He lunged at her, and she barely raised her sword in time to block his attack. The sound of their blades crashing together echoed through the forest, and her heart began to beat so fast she felt sick.

"Cas—" She gulped back the words as he dove at her again.

He nicked her neck with the blade and she scurried back, away from him.

He followed, shoving his sword dangerously close to her chest. She blocked it and lifted her sword against the next attack.

He slammed his foot into her knee. Her legs buckled and she hit the ground, keeping a tight grip on her sword. She started to scramble to her feet.

Cas had his blade aimed at her neck.

She sucked in a breath. He was gasping for air, his expression twisted and furious. He wasn't just angry; he was going to kill her.

She considered saying she was sorry, but she wasn't sure she wanted those to be the last words she ever said.

The blade in front of her face shook a tiny bit, and she looked from it to Cas. He pressed his lips together, the saddest defeated expression crossing his face.

He started to lower the blade.

Every part of her body crumpled in relief. She opened her mouth, desperately trying to think of what to say that wouldn't make him change his mind and kill her immediately.

"I—"

Her words ended in a gasp as an arrow whizzed past her face. Cas stumbled backward as it sank into his flesh.

TWENTY-NINE

CAS FELL TO the ground, the arrow sticking out of his left shoulder. Em frantically scrambled across the dirt to him.

"You missed," Iria said from behind her.

"Tell her to move out of the way, and I'll make sure the next one's in his heart," Miguel said.

Em yanked the arrow out before Cas could protest. He pressed his lips together to muffle his scream. He looked like he wished he'd killed her.

"Move, Emelina," Miguel said.

Her eyes met Cas's. His father deserved to die. Lera deserved to be burned to the ground. But Cas didn't deserve any of this.

"No," she said, her voice sounding stronger than she felt. Boots stopped next to her, and Aren frowned down at her.

"If you're going to kill him yourself, do you mind being quick about it?" Miguel asked. "I know your mother was fond of extended torture, but we don't really have time—"

"No one is killing him," she said. Some of Cas's anger melted into confusion.

"Em . . ." Iria's voice trailed off, and she glanced at Miguel.

"We have to," Miguel said. "King Lucio ordered the royal family killed."

"I do not take orders from King Lucio, and I say that he lives." Em looked at Aren. "Will you help me move him to the river? That arrow was probably filthy. We should boil some water and clean the wound."

"We should *what*?" Miguel let out a disbelieving laugh.

"No one needs to help me," Cas spat, sitting up with his hand braced against his bloody shoulder. "I can walk."

"Oh good," Miguel said. "He can walk. Let's catch him some fish and make him a lovely meal while we're at it, why don't we?"

Cas eyed his sword, just beyond his reach, and Aren quickly scooped it off the ground. He knelt down next to Em, lowering his voice so Cas wouldn't overhear. "He tried to kill you, Em."

"He wasn't going to do it. He was lowering his sword."

"It looked like he was going to kill you from where I stood."

She glanced over her shoulder to see the four warriors in a huddle, talking among themselves. Miguel kept throwing his arms around in annoyance.

"Come on," Em said, jumping to her feet and extending her

hand to Cas. He glared at it. "You have to get that wound clean."

He struggled to stand on his own, almost falling over in the process. He blinked, obviously light-headed from the loss of blood. "Why? Just kill me and get it over with." He let out a strangled laugh.

"No one is killing you." She gestured for him to walk in front of her, because she didn't trust that he wouldn't take off running. He didn't stand a chance out in the jungle with that wound and no sword.

He walked past her and toward the river, casting a quick glance at the warriors. They all followed him with their eyes, and Em kept careful watch on Miguel's bow and arrow. There were four warriors, and only she and Aren. Em didn't think she could count Cas on their team, even if he weren't injured. She had Aren, at least. He made their odds much better.

"Tell them you want to offer him as a trade," Aren whispered to Em.

She looked at him quickly. "What?"

"Tell them you want him alive so you can trade him for Olivia. Fort Victorra will be well protected by Lera soldiers by the time we get there—tell them you have doubts that the warriors will be able take the area. He's your backup plan."

"That's a good idea. They may actually go for that."

"I think you should kill him, for the record," he said. "But if you really can't, I trust your decision."

"Thank you," she said as they approached the river. Cas stood near the water, a muscle in his jaw twitching. He looked at them suspiciously, obviously wondering what they were whispering about.

"How do you expect to boil water out here?" he asked.

Aren snorted. "How sad. Prince Casimir doesn't even know how to build a fire. Life's a bit tough without Mommy and Daddy's maids, isn't it?"

Cas flushed, his eyes sparking with fury, and Em cleared her throat.

"Aren, would you mind gathering some branches and kindling?" she asked. She pointed at Cas. "You. Sit down."

He stood there for several seconds, like he wasn't sure he wanted to obey her. But then he slumped to the ground, blowing a piece of hair out of his face. The warriors hadn't moved; their heads were still bent together as they talked. She knelt down in front of Cas, careful to keep the warriors in her sight.

"What. Are. You. Doing?" He spit out every word, like it pained him to talk to her. "Why are you helping me?"

"It looks like you need it." She knew what he meant, but she didn't think she had the words to explain why she was helping him. *Because I have feelings for you* was too pathetic now, given the utter fury on his face. "Where are your guards?" she asked. "Why are you alone?"

"I imagine most of my guards are dead, thanks to you."

"And almost everyone I ever cared about is dead, thanks to you," Aren said as he dropped an armload of branches off.

"Aren," she said softly, in a warning tone. He stomped away. She passed Cas her canteen. "You should have some water."

He snatched it from her and took a few gulps.

Miguel turned away from the group of warriors, planting his hands on his hips. "Why are you giving him water? What do you expect to do with him?"

"He's coming with us," Em said. "As our prisoner. When we get to the Southern Mountains, I want to trade him for Olivia."

Cas laughed, a hollow, almost manic sound. "Your prisoner. Wonderful. It's so lovely to meet the real you, Emelina. You're just how my father described."

Em struggled to keep a neutral expression as she ignored him.

"Trade him and Lera will have their king back," Miguel said.

"No, they'll have a new king. A powerless one, since Olso will have full control of the country by then, I assume?"

Miguel just frowned.

"I'm not letting you kill my biggest bargaining chip. I made it clear when we entered into this agreement that my most important goal was to get Olivia. Once I have her, you can resume hunting down the royal family, if that's how you want to spend your time." *After Cas has had time to get far away from you,* she added silently.

"And if he tries to kill you again?" Miguel asked.

"Then I guess I'll be dead."

Miguel took the bow and an arrow off his back. He pointed the arrow straight at Em. "Enough of this. Koldo, Iria, grab her before that other one comes back. Move her out of the way."

Koldo strode toward her and Em scrambled to her feet, reaching for her sword.

Iria jumped forward, grabbing Koldo by his jacket. "Wait, wait, wait." She moved between Em and Miguel, extending her arms in either direction. "Let's just calm down."

Koldo stopped in his tracks, looking worriedly from Miguel to Iria. Miguel didn't lower his arrow.

"She is not our prisoner," Iria said. "We have control of the Lera capital because of her. All of this is because of her."

"No kidding," Cas muttered.

Iria ignored him. "If she wants to take Casimir as her prisoner, that's her choice. She's earned at least that."

"I don't take orders from Ruined," Miguel said through clenched teeth.

"And they don't take orders from you," Iria said.

"I certainly don't." Aren emerged from the forest, dropping another armful of branches off for the fire. Miguel spun to face him, arrow still ready to launch.

Miguel's legs flew out from under him suddenly, the arrow soaring to the sky as his butt hit the ground. Aren strode forward, kicking the bow out of Miguel's grasp. He grabbed the warrior's collar, leaning down to bring Miguel's face in line with his own.

"Point that thing at me again and I'll crack every one of your ribs in half and pull them out through your belly button."

Miguel swallowed. Aren shoved him away and straightened. He grabbed the bow and held it out to Iria, some of the anger draining from his face when he looked at her.

"Maybe you should hold on to that."

She took it with a nod. Aren spun on his heel, walking past

Miguel and grabbing the sticks to start arranging them for the fire.

"Thanks," Em said quietly to Iria.

One side of Iria's mouth turned up. "Sure." She glanced back at Cas. "It's your choice. But if he kills you, I'll never hear the end of it from those guys."

"I'll try to avoid it."

"Good." She took a step away, turning to face Em with a smile. "I'd be a little sad if you died."

"Only a little, huh?"

Iria held up her thumb and pointer finger, leaving a small amount of space between them. "A tiny bit."

Em laughed, turning back to Cas. The sound died in her throat as soon as she looked at his angry face. "Thank you for not killing me earlier." She kept her voice low, only for him. "And please understand that if I die, no one else here will hesitate to kill you. I'm on your side."

His lip curled, and he leaned closer to her. "You have never been on my side. You're a liar, and a murderer. Maybe my father was right to exterminate every last one of you."

She stood, clasping her hands behind her back to hide the fact that she was shaking. "He was right to kill my mother and slaughter almost everyone living in the castle? Even the staff? Children?" She cocked her head. "At least he'd be proud to see you've turned out the same."

Em marched away from Cas, blinking away tears.

THIRTY

CAS TRUDGED BEHIND the horses, his hands bound together in front of him. His shoulder ached and burned, but he kept his expression neutral and walked in silence.

Emelina was next to him. Aren and the three male warriors were on the horses, and Iria walked beside them. She kept glancing back at him and Emelina.

He stole a quick look at Emelina. She wore the same dress she'd had on last time he saw her, but now it was smeared with dirt and grime and ripped in places. Her dark hair was pulled back, her expression grim. She'd cleaned his wound and spread some berol root on it without a word, and she'd barely acknowledged his presence since they'd started walking.

Guilt tore through his chest, and he hated her even more for making him feel it. The words had tumbled out of his mouth without him pausing to think about them—*maybe my father was right to exterminate every last one of you*—and Cas couldn't stop replaying them in his head.

He hadn't meant it. He knew, with absolute certainty, that his father had been wrong to kill the Ruined without cause. He'd killed them out of fear, and he'd died because of it. Even if Cas hated Emelina with every fiber of his being, he didn't blame the entire Ruined species for her actions.

"What happened to the real Mary, Emelina?" he asked, breaking the silence.

"I killed her. When she was on her way to Lera."

"You just killed her. Without provocation."

"She killed my father and left his head on a stick for me to find. I wouldn't say I wasn't provoked."

Cas swallowed, determined not to feel sorry for her. But he also didn't feel particularly sorry he never had the chance to meet the real Mary.

"And it's Em," she said, quieter. "Most people call me Em."

A flash of memory—*I was educated at the castle with Em and Olivia*—and Cas drew in a breath. "You knew Damian."

"Yes. He was a friend."

"And I let you argue to set him free. I'm such an idiot."

"You're not an idiot. You were kind to him. You don't know what that meant to me."

He didn't know how to respond to that. He could have told her that he would do it again, because Ruined didn't deserve to die simply for being magical, but he wasn't in the mood to be nice to her. He kept his mouth shut.

"Do you have to walk so close to him?" Iria called over her shoulder. "It makes me nervous."

"He's not going to hurt me, Iria," Em called, and Cas felt a surge of anger that she didn't seem to think he was actually a threat to her.

Maybe because he'd squandered the opportunity to kill her. He could still see her face as he pointed his sword at her head. His blade had been locked in place, the terror at actually having to go through with murdering her making his stomach rise up into his throat. Even now, as he stared at the scratch on her neck where he'd nicked her, he felt a little sick.

He should have been able to kill her. He should have enjoyed it. She hadn't just betrayed him, she'd made him care about her so thoroughly that he couldn't even hate her properly. And now he was a hostage, injured and still at her mercy.

"I do want to apologize, Cas, for—" Em began.

"Don't apologize to me," he spat. "You're not sorry. You manipulate people. You say and do what you think they want and then turn around and use it against them. Your apology means nothing to me."

"Well, I'm apologizing anyway!" she yelled, making everyone turn around and stare at them.

He rolled his eyes. "I'm sorry if I doubt the sincerity of an apology *screamed* at me."

"I tried being nice. That just seemed to make you more angry."

"When were you being nice? Was it somewhere between you taking me hostage and yelling at me?"

"I saved your life."

He snorted. "Your bar for *nice* is awfully low."

"I don't—"

"Would you two be quiet?" Iria interrupted. "The entire jungle can hear you."

Em shut her mouth, casting an angry look in Cas's direction.

"I don't accept the apology," he whispered.

She took in a breath, like she was preparing to really let him have it. Then her body deflated, the last wisps of anger leaving her face as she shrugged.

"I understand. But I am sorry, Cas."

He didn't want her to understand. He didn't want her to act all quiet and contrite. He wanted to see her being haughty and unashamed. He wanted her to laugh in his face and tell him he was stupid. He wanted to scream at her, to shake her and tell her he would never forgive her. But the traces of her last words—*I am sorry, Cas*—lingered in the air, and he couldn't bring himself to say anything at all.

"Should we tie up his legs?"

Em looked over at the sound of Iria's voice and shook her head. "No, I think he's fine."

Cas glared at Iria. They'd stopped not long after the sun set, and he'd collapsed against a tree without a word. Em suspected he was far too tired to run.

Em sat down on the ground near him, watching as Miguel leaned over and muttered something to Francisco. It was dark, but the moonlight cast a glow over their faces, and they both seemed to be very pointedly avoiding her.

Koldo stopped in front of her, offering some dried meat. She took two pieces and passed one to Cas.

"Thanks, Koldo," she said, smiling at him.

He mumbled, "You're welcome," without meeting her eyes, pink spots appearing on his cheeks.

She tore off a hunk of meat with her teeth and watched as Koldo handed a piece to Iria. None of the men had talked to Iria much since she'd defended Em, but Koldo looked visibly uncomfortable just being near her. Iria stretched her legs out in front of her, apparently oblivious.

"I'm going to see if I can find some bananas," Aren said.

"No," Em said quickly, hopping to her feet. "I'll do it. Will you stay here and watch him?" She gestured at Cas.

Aren's head tilted, like he knew something was wrong. She touched his arm as she passed him.

"They're planning something," she murmured. "I'll stay close by. Let them think I've left you and Cas alone."

He barely nodded, and she let her hand drop from his arm as she walked away. She walked into the thick trees, making noisy footsteps as she jogged into the darkness. Then she stopped, silently doubling back.

She ducked under a vine, crouching behind a bush. Francisco, Koldo, and Iria were exactly where she'd left them. Miguel was gone.

She slowly removed her sword from her belt, casting a quick glance around her.

A cricket jumped across the ground in front of her, and she watched as it disappeared into the darkness. Rustling noises and chirps echoed from the jungle, making it difficult to hear if someone was nearby.

She waited several minutes, barely breathing. Finally, Miguel emerged from the trees behind Aren, making a slow and silent approach. A piece of cloth dangled from his hands. Probably for Aren's eyes. If they blindfolded him, he wouldn't be able to use his Ruined magic, and she and Cas were screwed.

Francisco had moved in front of Iria, standing over her and blocking her view of Aren. Em watched as Miguel took another step toward Aren.

"Aren, behind you!" she yelled.

Aren sprang to his feet and whirled around. Miguel's arm swung straight up, the blindfold fluttering to the ground. The arm twisted backward with a horrible crunch.

Miguel's scream echoed through the trees as Em darted out of the bushes. Cas scrambled to his feet, stumbling as his bound wrists threw him off balance. Francisco rushed at him, sword drawn. Cas barely jumped out of the way in time.

Francisco lifted his sword again, and Em ducked beneath it, planting herself between him and Cas. The warrior's blade crashed against hers, and she quickly blocked his next attack.

Miguel's screams made Francisco glance away for half a second, and Em lunged. She drove her sword into his side, aiming to wound, not kill. If she was ever going to make peace with the warriors, it was best not to leave them dead.

She grabbed Cas by the ropes around his wrists and sliced her blade through them.

"Aren! Sword!" she yelled, holding her hand out.

He turned away from Miguel, tossing her Cas's stolen sword. She caught it and thrust it into Cas's hand.

"The horses," she said, jerking her head in their direction.

Cas's eyes widened at something behind her. He slammed his hands down on her shoulders so hard she crumpled to the ground. He leaned back as Koldo's blade sailed over Em's head.

Em kicked Koldo's knee, and the warrior went down with a yelp. "Go!" she yelled at Cas.

He ran past Iria. She stood a few paces away, her mouth in an O as she surveyed the scene.

Koldo scrambled across the dirt, his hand reaching for Em's ankle. His wrist cracked suddenly, the back of his hand hitting the top of his wrist. He howled, cradling the arm against his stomach. Aren was slumped against a tree, his chest heaving up and down.

She took off after Cas. A body slammed into hers and she hit the dirt, hard. Two hands pinned her to the ground.

"Punch me," Iria said in her ear. "Make it look good."

Iria loosened her grip and Em wriggled free, springing to her feet. She whirled around and swung her fist, connecting with Iria's jaw. The warrior hit the ground with a grunt.

Em winced and gave Iria an apologetic look before turning back to Cas. He'd just freed the second horse. Koldo sprinted toward them, and she took off running, grabbing the reins of the horse. Cas moved toward the third horse, but she shook her head.

"Leave it!" she yelled.

He jumped on the horse. Em mounted the other horse, aiming her boot straight for Koldo's face as he tried to pull her off. He stumbled backward, landing on his butt as she rode past.

Aren still stood by the tree, and he reached his hand out as Em's horse galloped his way. She grabbed his arm and pulled him up. His body was limp from the exhaustion of using his magic, and he slumped against her back as soon as he was on the horse. She kicked at the side of the horse and they took off at a gallop, leaving the warriors in the dust.

THIRTY-ONE

CAS COULD HAVE easily left Em and Aren behind as they rode away from the warriors, and he considered it as he stared into the black jungle. Em's horse carried two people, and was far slower than his as a result.

Em slid off her horse, leaving Aren hunched over on the saddle by himself. He looked like he might be asleep. She walked to Cas, holding out her canteen. He took a small sip and handed it back.

He didn't have a canteen, or any idea where he was going in the dark. Once the sun rose he could figure out which way was south, but he'd lost track of their position after being captured. He had a sword now, at least, but what chance did he really have by himself? If he'd come across Iria and the other warriors alone, he'd be dead.

He squinted at Em as she put the cap back on the canteen. Was this all part of the plan? Was she pretending to save him in order to use him further? Did she really want to take him prisoner and trade him for Olivia?

The dark jungle suddenly seemed like a better idea than staying with her. He must be at least halfway to the Southern Mountains. He could make the rest of the trip by himself.

"I won't blame you if you take off." She turned around and walked back to her horse. "We should be to Gallego City by morning. If you want to ride with us until then, I promise you'll be safe."

Gallego City meant Lera soldiers. It meant finding out if his mother and Jovita were alive, and having a guard to protect him. He hadn't even realized they were close to Gallego.

"I'll ride with you," he said, and almost added the words "thank you," but they died in his throat.

Em nodded, and it was the last time she looked at him that night. They rode in silence, her and Aren in front, and he found himself drowning in the frenzied sounds of the jungle, wishing one of them would speak. Now that he was temporarily out of danger the weight of the last few days felt like it might crush him. The images from his final moments in the castle played over and over in his head, until his chest was so tight he thought he might never take an easy breath again.

When the sun finally started to rise, he almost cried with happiness. His body was stiff and sore from a night on the back of a horse, but he sat up straighter, taking in the bright-green leaves around him, the colorful bird perched on a tree not far away.

Aren had apparently regained his strength, because he slid off the horse and walked alongside Em. She glanced over her shoulder at Cas.

"We're close," she said.

He craned his neck. "How can you tell?" he asked, his curiosity overruling his desire not to appear stupid.

"The area is well traveled."

He glanced around, baffled. It was exactly the same jungle he'd been in the past three days. "What makes you think that?"

"Footprints, broken branches, crushed leaves, trash. When you're being hunted every day of your life, you learn how to look for signs of other people."

He stared right back at her, refusing to show an ounce of sympathy. Because of her, he was the one being hunted now. She didn't deserve any sympathy.

She turned back around, and Cas ignored Aren's withering stare. After seeing what he could do last night, Cas thought it best to leave Aren alone.

They rode for several more minutes, until Em stopped and slid off her horse. Cas did the same, shaking out his aching legs as soon as his feet hit the ground.

"There's a chance the warriors have taken the city," she said. "It's best to go by foot, to make sure. We won't want to be spotted."

"We?" Aren exclaimed. "No. He can go by himself."

"I'd like to know if the city is still under Lera control," she replied. "Will you stay here with the horses?"

Aren looked from Cas to Em and back again. He pointed a finger at Cas's face. "If you hurt her, I will break every bone in your body."

Cas's fingers itched for his sword, even though he knew it would be useless against a Ruined as powerful as Aren. He crossed his arms over his chest instead. "She'll be fine," he said through gritted teeth.

"Come on," she said, jerking her head for Cas to follow her.

They walked until the signs of people became so obvious even Cas could spot them. The trees were thinner, a distinct dirt path free of leaves and debris winding out of the jungle. He'd only been to the city named after his ancestors once, a few years ago, and he was embarrassed to admit that he didn't even remember what route he and his parents had taken to get there. They had gone by carriage instead of taking a boat down the shore, but he hadn't paid attention to the path the guards carved out for them.

Em's hand hovered over her sword, though she didn't seem aware she was doing it. It stayed there as they walked, poised to pull the blade out at a moment's notice. He tried doing the same, but found that his mind wandered and he'd push a hand through his hair or cross his arms over his chest. If anyone snuck up on them, Em would have her sword immediately and he'd be stuck fumbling around for his.

She moved smoothly through the jungle, even in her dress. Her boots barely made a sound against the ground, and he noticed her stepping around twigs and leaves he wouldn't have thought twice about stepping on. He followed her example, putting his boots in her smaller footprints.

"Was this all for Olivia?" he asked suddenly. The words shot out of his mouth as if they refused to be contained a moment longer.

"Yes," she said, without turning around. "And a little bit of vengeance, if I'm being honest."

"What if you had died in the castle?" he asked. "What if you hadn't escaped in time? You must have known that was a possibility."

Her eyebrows knitted together as she glanced back at him. "It was more than a possibility. That's why Aren was there. The hope was that one of us would make it out. Given how strong his Ruined magic is, my money was on him." She shrugged. "And if that failed, at the very least I had the warriors and a promise from the Olso king that he would do his best to stop Lera from executing all the Ruined."

The word *executing* vibrated through his body, pricking emotions he didn't want to feel. If his father were here, he would say that Em's actions only proved his point—the Ruined deserved to die. They were too dangerous to live.

And Cas would have told him that Em was only one person, like her mother was only one person. He hadn't met Olivia, but perhaps the whole family was a black mark on the Ruined.

Or maybe we did this to them. He beat down the words as soon as they bubbled up, but the sick feeling they brought remained. What kind of life must Em have lived, to be perfectly willing to walk into that kind of danger? To marry him, knowing full well that it might lead directly to her death?

He wondered suddenly what Em had been like before— when she still had her parents and sister and before she knew how to walk without making a sound. Had she been angry and bitter about her lack of Ruined power? Or had she thrown herself into other things, like learning to wield a sword? Her skill with a blade certainly hadn't developed over the past year. She'd spent a lifetime honing that skill.

He shifted his gaze to her to find her glancing back at him again. Something about her face was different since he'd found out who she was. It wasn't just that he knew who she was; it was as if something had shifted inside her. He hadn't realized she'd been tense around him, but he recognized the absence of it now.

He quickly looked away. He wished he could shut off his brain and stop wondering about her. It must have been easier to be his father, to be certain in his hate for the Ruined, to be unable to see shades of gray.

She stopped, putting a hand out behind her to indicate he should stop as well. Her fingers curled around the hilt of her sword, but she didn't pull it out, and he followed her lead.

Two figures passed through the trees. Cas and Em both hit the ground at the same time, crouching in the dirt. The men's voices were low, muffled, but their white-and-red jackets were clearly visible from this distance. Warriors.

A small open-air wagon passed by with two Lera soldiers bound together in back. He swallowed, wondering how many of the soldiers had been captured on their way to the Southern Mountains. Would his mother and Jovita even be able to make it? What would they find when they arrived?

He stood as the warriors headed in the direction of the city. He took a few steps forward until he could see a small cluster of wooden buildings. Warriors swarmed all over the area. They'd taken the city.

"I'm sorry," Em said softly.

His anger at her flared up without warning, and he barely held back from screaming *Whose fault is that?* at her. But the last thing he needed was to attract the attention of those warriors, or any others in the area. His jaw tightened, and she lowered her eyes, like she could tell what he was thinking.

They turned away and headed back into the cover of jungle. His shoulders slumped as he walked, and Em kept glancing at him like she wanted to say something. Apparently there was nothing to say, because she was quiet on the walk back.

Aren's voice rang out suddenly, loud and clear. "I told you, she's not here."

Em came to a halt.

"Keep him quiet," another voice hissed, barely audible.

Cas crept forward with Em until they could see the source of the voice. Iria, Koldo, and Miguel stood a few paces away, Miguel with his arm in a makeshift sling and a sour expression on his face. There were three others, and Francisco was on the ground with a gruesomely twisted neck. The other three were in a circle around Aren, who had his hands bound and a strip of white cloth tied around his head as a blindfold.

"She took off. We had to split up," Aren said, much louder than necessary. He was trying to warn Em.

Cas glanced over to find a pained expression on her face as she watched. She reached for her sword and began pulling it out, like she was going to attack.

He grabbed her hand, stopping her. She swallowed, throwing another desperate glance at Aren.

"Spread out," Miguel said. "She can't have gone far, if he's here." He jabbed a finger at Iria. "Not you."

She crossed her arms over her chest, taking a step closer to Aren. "I'd prefer to stay with him anyway."

"Koldo, watch her," Miguel spat. "Otherwise the Ruined might be gone when we get back."

Em wrapped her fingers around Cas's, tugging him gently. Regret was etched across her features as she glanced back at Aren. She was going to leave him.

They stepped away from the warriors carefully, quietly, then broke into a run. Cas jumped over vines and weaved around holes in the dirt as he followed Em. His legs were longer than hers, and he could have gone faster. He could have sped around her and taken off in his own direction and left her behind. He didn't. He stayed behind her, for no other reason than it seemed exactly the right thing to do.

When they slowed to a stop they were both breathing heavily, and Cas put his hands on his hips as he surveyed the area. A rustling sound came from somewhere to his left, and he spun around, searching for the source. Nothing.

Em darted behind a tree, pressing her back to it, and Cas did the same across from her. He carefully withdrew his sword. Footsteps echoed through the jungle.

The footsteps slowed, then stopped.

A bead of sweat trickled down Cas's forehead, but he didn't dare move to wipe it away. He was still breathing heavily, and he worked to become silent.

The footsteps drew closer, until the tip of a white jacket appeared in Cas's peripheral vision. Miguel.

He turned. His eyes met Cas's.

Cas spun away from the warrior, before he even attempted to attack. Miguel dove for him. Cas flicked his sword up, shoving it straight into the warrior's stomach. Miguel opened his mouth to yell, his sword spinning in his wrist haphazardly.

Em's sword sliced across the warrior's neck. His head toppled to the ground.

The body slumped into the dirt, and Cas noticed that Em had to look away, her face crinkling in disgust.

"Take his sword," she said. "It's better than the one you have."

Cas dropped the rusty sword and grabbed the warrior's.

"Let's go." She broke into a run.

When they came to a stop again, Cas pointed in the direction of the river. "A boat would be easier."

She took a sip of her water and handed it to him, wiping a hand across her mouth. "Of course it would. But we don't have one."

"A lot of the people who live around here have rowboats," he said. "I remember it from my last visit to Gallego City. We could snatch one."

"Sure, we could try."

"I want to be clear about something," he said slowly. "We were sending Lera soldiers to hunt you down and bring you to Lera for execution."

"I figured."

"You should be brought to justice for what you did."

"And your father should be brought to justice for what he did." She held his gaze.

"That doesn't excuse what you did."

"I'm not saying that it does. I'm merely pointing out the facts."

A hundred different emotions surged through Cas's chest at once—anger, guilt, sadness, helplessness—and he tried to find one to cling to. Anger was easiest. Anger could cover up all the other emotions, swallow them whole, and leave him with nothing but a burning fire in his stomach.

But a king had to be calm. Rational. He needed to act the way a king would.

"We're going to the same place," he said, trying to keep his voice steady. "It would be easiest for us to stick together. But as soon as we get there, I will have no problem ordering the Lera guard to arrest you."

"So I should abandon you as soon as we get close, is what you're saying."

"I'm saying I'm not your friend. But I need your help, and

you need mine, and I can put my anger aside for a few days if you can."

She pressed her lips together, sadness stamped across her features so suddenly that Cas wanted to take his last words and stuff them back in his mouth. "Agreed." She cleared her throat. "But can I explain something?"

He sort of shrugged, unwilling to give her permission but too curious to stop her.

"None of this was ever about you," she said quietly. "I'm sorry I used you. You—"

"You had to marry me, but it wasn't about me?" he interrupted.

"You know what I mean. I'm sorry I had to hurt you to—"

"You didn't hurt me," he snapped. "You hurt my kingdom."

She rubbed a finger across her necklace, her eyes on the ground.

He wanted to ask her why she hadn't warned him about the attack. He wanted to ask if he was a complete idiot to think she'd developed feelings for him, despite everything. He wanted to know how she could leave him to die if she actually cared for him.

He couldn't find the words to ask. Maybe he didn't want to know the answer.

"I was trying to leave as soon as possible," she said, her voice wavering the smallest bit. "I would have been gone in a matter of days if it weren't for that painting."

He shot her a furious look. "Is it supposed to make me feel better that you were miserable and trying to escape?"

"That's not what I meant."

"I know what you meant."

"No, you don't!" Her voice rose. "I thought you'd be the same as your father. I didn't expect you to be . . . to be . . ."

She twisted her hands together, her brow furrowing. His breath hitched in his chest. Every part of him was waiting, hoping, praying she was about to say she'd fallen in love with him. To confess that her feelings had been real and she wasn't just pretending in order to get information out of him.

He almost laughed out loud at his pathetic state. Was he really hoping that a girl who had conspired to ruin his kingdom was actually in love with him?

"Well?" he asked, as the silence continued. "You didn't expect me to be what? Gullible? Stupid?"

"Kind!" she practically yelled. "Reasonable! Thoughtful!" She hurled the words at him like they were insults, and he wasn't sure how to react.

She whirled around and resumed walking without waiting for a response. He hesitated for a moment, letting the words sink in.

Kind, reasonable, thoughtful. It wasn't *love* or an admission of wild, passionate feelings, but he realized he liked her three words more. *Love* would have been easy, another easy lie in a long line of lies. *Love* would be easy to dismiss.

But *kind, reasonable, thoughtful* couldn't be brushed off. They wriggled in and made themselves at home and breathed air in between the ache in his chest.

THIRTY-TWO

CAS HAD SAID nothing to Em since she'd stupidly told him he was kind. And *reasonable*. Did anyone like being called *reasonable*? She wouldn't blame him if he hated her even more now.

She'd noticed he'd learned to step carefully and cover their tracks without her having to explain. He might have been ignoring her, but he was clearly taking mental notes about everything she was doing.

They were still fairly close to Gallego City, and small wooden homes dotted the river. It didn't seem like the warriors had expanded past the city, but they walked carefully, both her and Cas's hands constantly poised over their swords.

"There." Cas pointed to a nearby home, with a dock

stretching out into the river. A small rowboat was tied to a post on the dock.

She looked out at the sun, which had almost fully disappeared. She'd been skeptical about the boat when he mentioned it, because they'd be easily spotted on the river in daylight. But the warriors would be less likely to spot them at night. And they wouldn't have to worry about leaving a trail.

Cas walked to the river and she followed, casting a glance over her shoulder as they reached the dock.

He crouched down next to the metal loop that the boat was tied to and tugged at it. "Get in," he said to her as he worked on the rope.

She carefully stepped into the boat, keeping her hand on the dock as the boat tilted beneath her. "Is now the wrong time to mention that I've never rowed a boat?"

Cas smiled, cocking one eyebrow. "Seriously?"

His smile knocked her even further off balance, and she had to take a moment to steady her feet on the boat. "There aren't a lot of rivers in Ruina. And we traveled by foot in Vallos because the hunters always congregated at the rivers."

"See those hooks right there?" he asked, pointing. She nodded. "Put the oars through those."

She grabbed the oars and sat down.

"And you're definitely facing the wrong way." One side of his mouth turned up as she felt her cheeks flush. She wasn't sure if she was blushing because of his adorable amused expression, or because she was embarrassed to not know what she was doing.

"Hey!" The scream made both of them whirl around, and Em saw a guy standing in the doorway of his house. He took off toward them.

Em spun around and stuck the oars through the loops, keeping a tight grip on them. Cas yanked the rope free and tossed it away.

The man tore across the grass, his face furious.

"Move," Cas said to her as he hopped into the boat. She did as instructed, handing him the oars. He leaned back, moving the oars over the water, and they pulled away from the dock.

The man pounded onto the dock and seemed to seriously consider jumping in. But Cas rowed quickly, smoothly, and had put a good distance between them and the dock within seconds.

"I'm sorry!" Cas yelled at him, and Em pressed her lips together to keep from laughing. He caught her expression and laughed. "What? I am."

"First time you've ever stolen something?" she asked.

He cocked his head. "Yes. Unless you count all the fig tarts I've stolen from the kitchen."

"Those fig tarts technically belong to you, so no, I don't count them."

He began to smile wider, but the grin abruptly disappeared. The familiar lump settled back into her throat. One minute of the old Cas was even more painful now that she knew that he would never smile at her like he used to.

"What was the first thing you stole?" he asked.

His smile was gone, but he hadn't said the words like he was picking a fight. He squinted at the water, leaning backward and forward as he moved the oars.

"Food," she said, after considering for a moment. "A few weeks after my father died. Me and Damian and Aren had gone on the run to Vallos, and none of us were experienced hunters. I was starving and this woman had dried beans sticking out of her bag. I swiped them and we ate for several days."

"Did you feel guilty?"

"Not at the time, no. I didn't really feel anything except rage then. Thinking back now, I wonder if she'd intended to eat that for several days as well."

He nodded, still staring at the water. She didn't know what that nod meant, and he didn't offer a response, so she kept her mouth shut.

"And you really don't have any Ruined power?" he asked.

She shook her head. "No."

"Did your mother intend for you to inherit the throne?" he asked.

"No, Olivia was next in line. I was supposed to be her closest adviser." She ran her fingertips over the water. "I was fine with it."

"Really." He lifted his eyebrows.

"Yes. She's even more powerful than our mother was. Our people shouldn't have denied me the throne after Olivia was taken, but I never disputed that she should have been the one to rule if she'd been there."

"Ruined power is the only thing that matters when inheriting the throne?" he asked skeptically.

She shrugged. "It's no more arbitrary than the firstborn inheriting."

"I guess." He looked at her for the first time since they'd started the conversation. "Was your mother disappointed?"

Em shook her head. "No. She thought I had other powers. Nonmagical ones, I mean."

"Like what?"

"She said my strengths were being rational and calm. The ability to make people fear me. She said I inherited that from her. She had big plans for me, apparently. Leading armies and working as an extraction specialist."

"An extraction specialist," Cas repeated.

"Extracting information from people," she said. Her guts twisted, and she had to look away from him. Would her mother have given her a choice? Or would that have been her job, whether she liked it or not?

"My father always said that *extraction* was Wenda's specialty," Cas said, his tone betraying a hint of bitterness.

Em stared at the water, wishing he hadn't asked about her mother.

"He said her torture methods were unlike anything he'd ever seen. It was one of the reasons he had to invade."

"And was that also why he took Olivia?" she snapped.

"Maybe he feared that her daughters were going to turn out exactly like her, considering she was already preparing one of them for a career in torture." His voice rose, the oars moving faster.

"I can think of worse things than turning out like my mother!" As soon as the yell left her mouth she regretted it, but the anger swirled inside of her too violently to back down.

"I can't think of *anything* worse, actually," he spat. "She tortured people for fun—"

"Your father just tortured one of my best friends!" she interrupted.

"And your mother would have tortured every person in Lera if given the chance!"

"Well, she wasn't given the chance, was she?" Em shouted.

"And maybe that's not such a bad thing," Cas said tightly.

"Lovely. Please go on about how you think it's so great that my mother is dead."

"Really. You're telling me that you aren't celebrating that my father is dead."

She pressed her lips together. He had her there. Lera—and the rest of the kingdoms—were much better off without him.

And maybe she could understand why Cas felt that way about her mother.

"Perhaps we should just both agree that both our parents were horrible people," Cas said drily.

She let out a startled laugh. Cas cocked one eyebrow at that reaction, and she felt a fresh wave of almost hysterical laughter bubbling to the surface. She leaned over her knees, her giggles echoing across the river, and she clapped a hand over her mouth to stifle them.

She caught a glimpse of Cas's stony face, and she knew the

laughter was going to dissolve into tears. The ache of keeping them in pushed at her throat, and her attempts to force the tears away were entirely unsuccessful. They spilled down her cheeks. She pressed her forehead to the tops of her knees.

"Are you *crying*?" Cas asked, like it was the first time he'd ever seen anyone do it.

She didn't want to admit it out loud, so she remained silent and tried not to let her shoulders shake.

"You've lied to me, attempted to destroy my kingdom, basically killed my father, and now you're *crying*?"

She sniffled. The boat tilted slightly, and she peeked up to see him scanning the area, holding the oars out of the water.

"I . . . I can't even go anywhere," he said. "I'm stuck on this boat with you, watching you cry."

She wrapped her arms around her legs as she tried to get ahold of herself.

"It's been a bad few days," she mumbled.

He was quiet for several seconds. When he finally spoke, his voice was softer, calm. "It really has."

Em woke to Cas yelling her name.

She jerked awake, her brain cloudy and her body stiff. She'd fallen into a deep sleep, and it took several seconds to pull herself out of it.

When the fog cleared, she realized the boat was going very, very fast.

And the noise . . . what was that?

She whipped her head around, squinting in the dim, early morning sun. A waterfall. It was still too dark to see it, but from the speed they were going, they must be rapidly approaching it.

Cas grabbed her hand, the boat lurching dangerously to the right. "Get out of the boat!" he yelled. "We're going over—"

His sentence ended in a gasp as the boat tilted down.

She lost Cas's hand as the water swallowed them both.

THIRTY-THREE

CAS GASPED AS he surfaced from the water. His entire body stung from the impact, but he hadn't hit anything solid.

He couldn't say the same for the boat, however. Pieces of wood bobbed on the dark river.

Em was nowhere to be seen.

"Em?" He splashed in a circle, desperately squinting in the darkness. "Em!"

He didn't see her. His chest started to tighten, panic creeping in. What if he lost her like this? What if, after everything, he lost her going over a stupid waterfall?

"*Cas!*" Her yell came from behind him, and he whipped around and swam toward it as fast as he could.

He heard her breathing before he saw her. Em's head barely

bobbed above the surface, and she sucked in air before disappearing under. She resurfaced a second later.

He reached for her, his fingers finding her under the water. He tried to tug her up, but her body resisted.

"It's . . . stuck," she gasped, her arms flailing. "My foot is stuck."

"Which foot?"

"The left one." Her face disappeared underneath the water for a moment, and she spit out water when she surfaced.

He took in a deep breath and dove down. It was too dark to see anything, so he had to feel his way down her leg. At her foot he felt something slimy and stringy wrapped around it. He tugged at it, but it didn't budge.

His lungs burned and he kicked to the surface, sucking in a deep breath. "I've almost got it," he said. "Try to stay still."

She nodded and he dove back under, grabbing her leg. He yanked on the vine as hard as he could. It finally released Em's leg.

He swam back up, his hands finding her waist. She was shaking, and she immediately clung to him, wrapping her arms around his neck.

He circled one arm around her waist, using the other to keep them afloat. "It's all right," he said softly.

"Thank you," she said, lowering her face into his shoulder.

"You're welcome."

For a moment the only noise was the water rushing and Em breathing against him, and he realized that he wasn't supposed to be saving her. If he'd been thinking clearly, he might have remembered that he hated her. He should have been ordering her execution, not saving her life.

His last thought hit him like a blow to the head, and his stomach lurched. Was he really going to order her execution? Stand by and watch a soldier chop off her head, the way his father had with Damian?

No. The answer came immediately. He cleared his throat and tried to think more sensibly. If she were standing in front of him, being judged by Lera law, of course she would have to be executed. There was no other option.

Still, he couldn't imagine giving that order.

He held her tighter. He would save her again, and again, no matter how angry he was with her.

"Can you swim?" he asked quietly.

She nodded, and his fingers brushed against her arm beneath the water as she untangled herself from him. She swam slowly, and Cas stayed next to her until they reached the riverbank. He grabbed onto his sword as he left the water, relieved it hadn't been lost.

Her dress clung to every curve of her body as she walked out of the water, and he tried to avert his eyes, but he found it hard to focus on anything but her. She turned and met his gaze. Something in his expression must have given him away, because a blush crept up her cheeks.

She wouldn't look at him like that if she didn't have feelings for him. He was almost sure of it, but the tiny sliver of doubt made him want to scream.

"I think I need a moment to rest." She clumsily plopped to the ground.

His anger disappeared almost as soon as it had come, leaving nothing but an ache in his chest. He wanted to scoop her into his arms and tell her everything would be fine.

"I'm going to see if there's some fruit nearby," he said, spinning on his heel so he wouldn't have to look at her anymore. Was he really that pathetic? Was he really still harboring feelings for her, after all she'd done?

Yes. He definitely was.

Cas returned from the jungle with a few round yellow fruits. His cheeks and the bridge of his nose were a bit pink from the sun, and it made him even cuter, if that was possible. And he'd taken his shirt off and slung it over his shoulder. Em found herself staring at one particular drop of water making a journey from the base of his throat down the center of his chest. She watched as it rolled down, sliding across his skin and disappearing into the ridges of his abdominals. She had never wanted to be a drop of water so badly.

He cut open the fruit with his sword and handed it to her. They scooped out the sweet fruit with their fingers and ate it in silence.

He caught her staring and she quickly looked away. He wasn't acting like he hated her anymore, and it was almost worse. It was easier not to stare at him, not to dream about his arms around her, when he was glaring at her like she was his worst enemy.

"Are you ready to get going?" she asked, getting to her feet. Her dress was still wet, but it kept her cool in the warm jungle, and she didn't think she'd mind as the sun continued to rise. Cas put his shirt back on, though it had turned see-through when it got wet and didn't hide much.

They trudged into the trees. Her body was heavy with hunger and exhaustion, and her pace was much slower than it had been the day before. Cas didn't seem eager to go faster. He stayed right next to her, his gaze on the ground.

The sun rose higher in the sky, and she caught him watching her often. She recognized that he was working his way through something, trying to find the words, and she waited patiently.

Finally, he opened his mouth and asked a quiet question: "Why did you look so terrified on our wedding day?"

She couldn't keep the surprise out of her voice. "What?"

"On our wedding day. You were terrified. I'd thought it was because Mary didn't know me, because she was nervous about marrying a stranger. But you'd planned everything. Why were you nervous?"

She grasped her necklace tightly. "I was still marrying a stranger, even if I had orchestrated it all. I didn't know how to act or what to say. I was terrified about that night, because I've never . . ."

"Oh."

"Thank you for that, by the way. It was very nice of you not to assume I'd be ready to sleep with you right away."

"You were a stranger as well, and I didn't particularly look forward to my first time happening because my parents declared it."

A smile tugged on her lips. "Good point."

"Did you ever consider telling me who you really were?" he asked. "We talked about the Ruined often. You knew I had different opinions than my father. Did you ever consider what I would have done if you'd told me?"

"Every day," she said quietly, immediately. "Especially after you tried to save Damian. I wondered what your reaction would be."

"But you didn't."

"No." She paused. "What would you have done?"

He pulled on his fingers, cracking the knuckles. "I don't know. Maybe I would have been able to listen to you." He shook his head. "Maybe not. I got really angry when my mother showed me that painting. But it could have been different, coming from you."

"I'm sorry, Cas." Her voice was strained, and he couldn't help but believe that she said the words with sincerity. "I'll be sorry for the rest of my life about what I did to you."

"And when I . . ." He trailed off before finishing the question.

"And when you what?"

He cleared his throat. "Nothing."

"You can ask me anything, Cas. I'll answer you honestly."

He let out a hollow laugh, kicking a rock. "Honestly, huh?"

She swallowed as she watched the rock dart across the dirt.

She deserved that, but she still wanted to yell at him that she had been honest about plenty of things.

He stuffed his hands in his pockets, his eyebrows knitted together. He grabbed her arm, bringing them both to a stop.

"Did you care about me at all? Because you acted like you cared about me, and then you just left me there to die." His voice shook. "You didn't even try to warn me."

She opened her mouth, but only a strange sound came out. He was right, of course.

"Or am I an idiot to think you actually had feelings for me?" Cas asked before she could get a word out.

"You're—"

"Were you just pretending to like me, because that's—"

"Of course I wasn't pretending!" The words exploded out of her before she could stop them. Heat spread across her cheeks.

Cas's mouth had been open, ready with a reply, and he snapped it shut.

She cleared her throat. She'd already embarrassed herself horribly, might as well finish it off. "I fully intended to ignore you, but it turns out you're very hard to ignore. I never pretended to feel anything for you, Cas. All of that was real, and definitely never part of the plan. And I should have . . ." A lump formed in her throat, and she swallowed, her voice shaking. "I should have warned you about the attack. I should have trusted you. I'm sorry."

He stood motionless, staring at her. She was either relieved to get that off her chest, or hoping that the ground would break open and swallow her whole. The latter option was burning particularly bright at the moment.

Then his arm was reaching for her. He grabbed her around the waist, roughly tugging her to him. Her chest bumped his and his eyes burned with fire as he lowered his mouth to hers. She wrapped her fingers around his shirt, rising up on her toes.

He kissed her like she was in danger of slipping out of his arms. His lips were hot and insistent against hers, his hands pressing into her back and crushing her against him. She wound her fingers into his hair, and every piece of her melted into him with no hope of return. Even after he pulled away she would leave pieces of herself all over him, and none of those pieces were ever coming back.

She slid her hand down to his waist, tugging his shirt up and running her fingers over his warm skin. He sucked in a breath, his chest shifting against hers. She ran her thumb up his spine, hoping for that response a hundred more times. She wanted to feel his body reacting to her touch every day for the rest of her life.

She lost herself in the kiss for so long she felt a bit dizzy when he finally pulled away.

"I don't know if I should have done—" Cas began.

She didn't want to hear the end of that sentence. She cut him off with another kiss, putting both her hands on his cheeks. Her fingers grazed over the stubble on his jaw and trailed down his neck and to his chest. She wanted to memorize how he felt against her.

He wrapped his arms around her so tightly her feet almost left the ground. His lips left hers, but he didn't pull away. Their foreheads touched as he spoke softly. "Promise me this wasn't part of the plan."

"I promise," she whispered. "I tried so hard not to fall for you and failed miserably."

One side of his mouth turned up, and he brushed her hair away from her face as he leaned down to kiss her again. He was slow this time, letting his lips linger and his breath tickle across her mouth. She let herself collapse into him, let herself forget where she was and what she had to do.

When they finally broke apart, his hair was messy from her fingers, his mouth red. She imagined she looked about the same.

"I should be most angry about you conspiring with Olso to start a war," he said breathlessly. "Or about the fact that my father died because of events you put in motion. But I was most angry that you pretended to have feelings for me." He shook his head, a short laugh escaping his mouth. "How stupid is that?"

She smiled, biting her bottom lip to try to keep her grin from spreading too far across her face. "You underestimate yourself if you think any woman would have to pretend to have feelings for you."

He grinned, his cheeks turning pink. The expression fell off his face almost as soon as it came, and she knew what he was thinking. It didn't matter how they felt about each other. There was no world where the king of Lera could be with a Flores, even if she hadn't destroyed his kingdom.

"I was scared to tell you the truth," she said. "I know it's no excuse, but a tiny part of me was afraid you would immediately send someone to move or kill Olivia if I told you about the attack. I asked for them to spare you. But you saw the warriors. They're not exactly taking orders from me."

He nodded slowly. "You can have your sister when we get to the Southern Mountains. I'll release her. Then I want you to run away as fast as you can."

Gratitude swelled inside of her, and she had to swallow down tears. "Thank you, Cas."

"You'll probably need to stay hidden when we arrive. If my mother or Jovita sees you, I don't think I can provide them with a reason why you shouldn't stand trial." He winced, like he was suddenly in pain. "I can't order your execution. I don't even think that's what you deserve, and I would never recover from that."

"Thank you," she whispered again.

"Assuming the Olso warriors don't kill me, I'll convince my advisers that it's best to focus on them, and not you. I think we'll have our hands full for quite a while." His expression turned serious. "If you promise not to attack Lera again."

"If you promise not to execute the Ruined simply for their magic."

"Agreed."

"Agreed." She began to smile at him, but the relief of their arrangement was quickly overshadowed by the fact that this meant they would likely never see each other again. He wore a matching expression, and she reached out, finding his hand.

When the jungle fell into darkness that night Em's eyelids felt heavy and her feet and legs ached. She suggested they rest for the night and Cas agreed. He pulled her close to him as soon as they sat down in the dirt against a large tree trunk. Her body began sending off sparks immediately, the exhaustion she'd felt a few seconds again vanishing.

"Don't let them take away your rightful position as queen," Cas said quietly, resting his chin on top of her head.

"What?" She put one hand on his chest.

"You should be queen of your people, whether you have Ruined magic or not. Maybe especially because you don't. Your mother's biggest failing was her overreliance on magic. You proved that you don't need any to defeat your enemies. They should be celebrating you, not telling you you're useless."

"Quite a compliment, coming from one of my 'enemies.'"

"You can tell them I said that. Or maybe don't, if you think it will actually hurt the cause." She smiled, and he put one hand on her neck and ducked his head down to kiss her. Her body responded immediately, and she was suddenly shifting, sliding onto his lap with one knee on either side of him.

His fingers burned fire across her neck. His lips joined them and she had to grab his shoulder with one hand to keep herself steady. But it was a hopeless act, because she was anything but steady.

He whispered her name, "Em," as his mouth found hers again and she felt a rush of relief that they'd never really kissed before. It would have torn her apart to hear Mary's name when he was kissing her, to wonder if he would still want to kiss her if he knew who she really was.

She ran her fingers through his hair and was rewarded with a moan of approval. Cas sat up straighter, one hand on her waist to keep her in his lap. She thought he couldn't get any closer, but he drew her against him until she could feel his heart beating next to hers. If he'd asked her in that moment to run away with him, to take his hand and hide from everyone, she almost certainly would have said yes.

A light touch on her knee made her grasp his hair tighter. He pushed her dress up her thigh, his fingers trailing sparks over her skin. That spark was going to catch and she was going to be consumed by flames at any moment. She was sure of it. But there was nothing that would stop her kissing him.

His hand disappeared from her thigh and was on her back, finding the buttons of her dress. There were far fewer than the last time he'd unbuttoned her. He quickly had three undone and her dress slipped down her arms.

His hands pressed into the bare skin of her back, his fingers curling like he was about to completely lose control. She was right there with him.

Cas's hands stilled suddenly, and she heard the noise half a second later. Horses.

She pulled away from him and his hands disappeared from her back. Her body still buzzed from his touch, and it took a moment for her eyes to focus.

A group of warriors surrounded a wagon in the distance. They weren't scouting the area, but it looked like they were keeping whatever was in the wagon heavily guarded.

"It's a wagon," she said quietly. "Is that the one you were in?"

He shifted beneath her, and she slid off him so he could see. He squinted in the dark, then leaned back against the tree. "That's the one."

She lifted her shoulders, straightening her dress, and Cas motioned for her to turn around, a smile on his face. He buttoned her back up, planting a soft kiss on her shoulder when he was done.

"Could have been bad, if they were closer," she said, a hint of amusement in her voice. She turned around, settling next to him. "We never would have heard them coming." Five or six armed warriors against her and Cas? They would have been dead for sure.

"I could think of worse ways to go." He glanced back at the road. "I wish I could help them."

"There are too many of them. Maybe if we still had Aren, but without him . . ."

"I know," Cas said softly. "I just feel helpless. I'm supposedly the king now, and I've never felt less in control."

She laced her hand through his, lifting it to her lips. "You'll be in control again. If there's anything I can do to help with that, you know I'm more than willing."

He released her hand, pulling her closer to him and planting a kiss on top of her head. "I know, Em."

THIRTY-FOUR

THREE STEPS SEPARATED Cas and Em. If three steps were too many, what was he supposed to do when there were thousands?

He closed the distance and brushed his hand against hers. She smiled at him as she stepped over a patch of leaves, letting her fingers curl around his for a moment.

They'd spent most of the day walking to the Southern Mountains, and Cas felt his heart sink further with every step. Once they arrived he would know for sure what had happened to his mother and Jovita, and probably Galo as well. And he would lose Em.

His brain kept trying to come up with a scenario where she could stay with him, where he could convince his mother and advisers and everyone in the kingdom that Em wasn't their enemy.

I know she deceived us all and is partially responsible for Olso's attack on the castle, but I promise she's not as bad as you think, Mother! He could already see her face. She would probably slap him.

He wouldn't blame her. He knew he'd lost his mind, that his feelings for Em had clouded every shred of good sense he had.

But then . . . she also made excellent points. The decisions his father and his advisers had made were not perfect. They were horrifying, in some cases. His father had always seemed convinced that his actions were for the best of Lera, and Cas wished he'd prodded him further. He wished he'd had more honest conversations with his father, like he'd had with Em yesterday.

He glanced at her again. His body was always trying to lean into her, to be closer, to touch her.

"I think it's best you don't tell them we traveled together," Em said.

"You're right," he said softly. "I'll tell them I made the journey by myself."

"They'll all be very impressed. Maybe they'll start saying you're very handsome *and* tough."

"I can only hope."

Her smile faded and she dropped her gaze, her walk slowing. "I'll miss you, Cas."

Two steps this time; he jumped across them and pulled her against him. She always sucked in a tiny breath when he put his arms around her, and it made it impossible not to kiss her. He ducked his head and pressed his lips against hers. He let his hands slide down her back, taking in the shape of her and convincing himself for a moment that he'd never have to let her go.

He wished he'd kissed her before, when they were sleeping in his bed. He would have spent all night kissing her, tracing his fingers over her shoulders, memorizing the shape of her mouth. He'd thought he had all the time in the world then, and now he looked back with exasperation at all the moments with her that he'd squandered.

"I'll miss you too," he said when they broke apart. "More than you know."

She shook her head, brushing her lips against his again. "I know."

When she looked at him like she was now, it was impossible to think that her feelings were fake, or part of the plan. She looked at him like she never wanted him to let her go, but also like she was about to cry. Like she was desperately, irreversibly sad. He recognized it as guilt, and the worst part of him was glad she felt it. He hadn't completely forgiven her, and she hadn't asked him to. She must have known that was an impossible request. He wanted to forgive her, and his father—and himself, while he was at it—but the heavy weight of disappointment was stubbornly sticking to his chest. Clawing it out all at once didn't seem to be option. Letting it slowly drip away until the hurt became bearable seemed like the more likely scenario. Every time she looked at him, he felt a little piece fall away.

He reluctantly let her go. Selfishly he wanted to ask her to stall, to spend one more night with him under the stars. But neither of them could afford to delay, so he bit back the words.

They walked in silence, occasionally intertwining their hands and holding on to each other.

Voices drifted over the trees, and they both immediately stopped and went perfectly still. Cas couldn't quite make out what they were saying, as they were speaking softly, but they weren't far away.

Em crept forward and he followed, letting his hand linger on her back.

A blur of gray and blue flashed through the trees. Cas's heart leaped and then immediately sank.

Lera soldiers.

"You should go," Em said quietly.

He swallowed the lump in his throat. She laced her fingers through his.

"You'll be the best king Lera ever had," she said, blinking back tears.

He tugged on her hand until her body was against his, her face in his neck. "I don't know about that."

"I do."

He hugged her as tightly as he could and kissed her forehead. "When I find your sister, I will make sure she's set free. Keep watch on the lodge, when you get there. I'll send her out the front and straight into the trees. You can meet her there."

"Thank you." She gave him a shaky smile as he pulled away.

He pressed his lips to hers, for only a few moments, because he was afraid if he held on for any longer he would grab her hand and run away.

He glanced over his shoulder at her once, but that was all he could manage. He didn't know if she stayed and watched him go, or if she left after that first look.

He ducked under a vine, and the voices abruptly stopped as his footsteps echoed through the jungle. A man with his blue-and-gray coat tied around his waist suddenly appeared from behind a tree, a sword in one hand and a dagger in the other.

Galo. Cas had to blink back tears at the sight of the friend he'd feared the worst for.

The guard's eyes widened with shock. "Cas?" he said very quietly, still aware of their surroundings.

The other guards immediately jumped out from their hiding spots, their faces etched with disbelief.

Cas held up his hands since one of the guards still had his bow and arrow aimed at him. He quickly lowered them, a sheepish expression on his face.

"What are you—how did you—" Galo rushed forward. He appeared to be going in for a hug, then seemed to think better of it. "Are you all right, Your Majesty?"

Cas stepped forward and embraced Galo. "I thought you were dead."

Galo looked like he might cry when Cas released him. "We feared the same, Your Majesty."

"Please stop calling me that."

"Sorry." Galo surveyed him. "Are you injured?"

"My shoulder was reinjured, but I'm fine. Did my mother make it out?"

Galo gestured behind him. Cas followed his gaze to see two guards on horses, their hats pulled low over their foreheads.

One of them looked up, and Cas's heart leaped into his throat. His mother.

She slid off her horse and ran for him, almost knocking him over as she threw her arms around him.

"I knew you weren't dead," she said, her voice thick with tears. "I told them you would have found a way to escape." She released him, holding on to his arms as she inspected his clothes. "Why are you wearing a staff shirt?"

"Some of the staff helped me escape."

Jovita was on the other horse, and she jumped down and briefly hugged Cas. "I'm glad you're all right," she said.

"Sure you are," Cas said with a laugh. She smiled tightly, not quite meeting his eyes. Perhaps his cousin hadn't been entirely sad about his disappearance, and her sudden direct path to the throne.

"Come on," the queen said. "We should keep moving. Tell us your story on the way."

"Is Fort Victorra still under our control?" Cas asked.

"Yes," his mother said. "We sent one guard to ride ahead and check, and he said it's still secure and they're preparing for an attack. We've sent soldiers to protect the Vallos border as well. We want to keep the warriors in the north for now."

"And Olivia?" he asked.

"We'll dispose of her when we arrive," the queen said. "I

didn't send word for them to kill her. I figured there were more important things to take care of."

He flinched at the casual way his mother talked about killing Em's sister. They definitely needed to get to the Southern Mountains, to safety, and to prepare for an attack. His mother and Jovita were right about that.

"Have you seen the warriors come through with a wagon?" he asked. "I saw them last night."

"One of our scouts saw a wagon," Galo said. "They're ahead of us."

"They have a lot of the staff in that wagon, and a few guards," Cas said. "I was in there with them for a while. Last night there were only five guarding the wagon."

"Six, last we heard," Galo corrected.

Cas surveyed the group, counting. Eight guards, that he could see, plus his mother and Jovita. "Is this all of you?"

"No, there are four scouting the nearby areas," Galo replied. "Two ahead and two behind."

"That's plenty. Do you think we can catch up to the wagon?"

"No," Jovita said sharply. "We don't have time."

"We're headed that way anyway," Cas said. "And given how we were treated in the wagon, I can't imagine the warriors have anything good planned for them." He turned to Galo. "How far ahead and behind are the scouts?"

"Not far. One of the two comes back often with reports."

"Good. Next time they come back, we'll have them stay with us. At least four guards will go with my mother and Jovita, and they can continue on to the mountains. The rest are with me, and we'll be taking that wagon."

"No, you will not," the queen said. "There is no one of use in that wagon, and we are not risking our lives to save them. Everyone back on your horses. Joseph, Cas will ride yours."

The guards looked from the queen to Cas, clearly unsure what to do. His mother put a hand on his arm.

"Cas, your safety is more—"

"It wasn't a suggestion," he said, his voice rising. She blinked, dropping her hand from his arm. "There are thirty people in that wagon, and they all helped me escape. Thirty people we will take with us to the Southern Mountains, to help defend our hold on Vallos."

Jovita put her hands on her hips. She gave Cas a look like he was an absolute idiot.

"Pick four guards to accompany you," he continued.

Joseph immediately stepped forward, and the queen motioned to a few others.

"Leave Olivia alone for now," he said, trying to keep his voice casual. "The last thing we need is her causing any trouble. Focus on securing the building. We'll deal with her later."

The guards all nodded, but his mother studied him, a hint of suspicion in her eyes.

He quickly turned away. "Let's go."

It took less than an hour to catch up to the wagon, and a guard who went ahead informed Cas that the warriors were resting, letting their prisoners out for a bathroom break.

Only two of the Lera guards had bows and arrows, and all eight stood in a circle around him. There were five men and three women, and he didn't know any of them particularly well, except Galo. But they all listened intently as he outlined his plan, nodding as he gave orders.

"I'm going to make it my mission to open that wagon," he said, his voice low as they weren't that far from the warriors. "Either the men or the women will still be inside, because they only let one group out at a time usually. No one in that wagon has a weapon, but we could use the extra bodies."

"Are you sure you won't wait here?" Galo asked, and Cas immediately shook his head. "Or just let us go ahead and you can come in after we've killed a few of them."

"No. I'm good with a sword; you need my help."

"I'm sticking close to you, then," Galo said. "If you die, we have to take orders from Jovita."

This produced a few chuckles from the tense guards, and Cas smiled. "Fair point." He looked at each of them. "Thank you for this. I know our main priority is to get to the mountains and defend the rest of Lera and Vallos, but I can't just let the warriors take the castle staff. Especially not after they helped me escape."

A young man with dark curls—one of the guards with a bow and arrow—took a glance around the circle. "I think I speak for all of us when I say that we're honored to be with the one who wanted to save the staff, not leave them to die."

The guards nodded in agreement, and Cas looked at them

gratefully. "Thank you." He pointed north. "Let's go. Get in position."

The guards scattered, and Galo grabbed the curly-haired one by the wrist and planted a quick kiss on his lips.

"Don't die." He released the guard, who shot Galo a quick smile before he took off.

Cas watched him go, then turned to Galo. "How long has that been going on?"

"A few months." Galo started walking, drawing his sword. Cas did the same.

"Months! You didn't say."

"I don't think now is the time to talk about my love life, Cas," Galo said, amused.

"Fine. But you're telling me later."

Cas stopped behind a tree. He could see the wagon in the clearing ahead. The women were in the wagon, the men in a line outside, getting ready to be loaded back in. The warriors were in the same positions they'd been in when they'd had him—two in front, one on either side of the wagon, and two in back. The two in back were off their horses, supervising the prisoners.

Cas glanced to his right. He couldn't see the guard, but he was probably almost in position, getting ready to shoot off an arrow.

"How is—what's his name?" Cas glanced at Galo.

"Mateo."

"How is Mateo with that bow?"

"Excellent."

An arrow whizzed through the air. It landed squarely in the back of a warrior at the side of the wagon. Her body convulsed once before she toppled off her horse.

A second arrow flew through the air, but the other warriors were already off their horses, swords drawn.

"In the wagon!" one of the warriors yelled to the prisoners. The men froze, ignoring the order.

Cas broke into a sprint, Galo at his side. Two more arrows flew through the air. A warrior screamed as one lodged in his arm. A few of the male staff members jumped on top of him.

A warrior immediately planted himself in front of the door to the wagon, and Cas swung his sword as he approached. The warrior blocked the attack, his feet kicking up dust as their swords met.

Galo crept around behind the warrior, grabbing him by the throat. The warrior's eyes widened, his sword jerking sideways. Cas lunged, sinking his sword into the man's chest Galo dropped him, his body making a thud as it hit the ground.

Cas jumped forward, releasing the latch on the wagon and swinging open the door. Gasps echoed through the group as they recognized him.

He gestured for them to get out, quickly whirling around to survey the damage. He spotted one Lera guard dead on the ground, but the staff had swarmed the warrior.

Two warriors were fending off an attack from four guards, and clearly losing. A guard sliced his blade into the chest of one of the warriors as Cas watched.

RUINED

In a matter of minutes, five of the six warriors were dead, and Mateo was engaged in a heated battle with the last one. The guard was clearly not as good with a sword as he was with a bow and arrow.

Cas ran for them, slamming his body against the warrior's. They both tumbled to the dirt, the warrior keeping a grip on his sword as he went down. Cas barely ducked his head as the man swung at his neck.

The warrior scrambled to get up, but a few of the women from the wagon had him pinned.

Cas quickly rolled away from the warrior, and Mateo put both hands on his sword, driving it into the warrior's chest. He smiled at Cas as he withdrew the blade.

"Thank you, Your Majesty."

Cas nodded as he got to his feet. The clearing was almost silent, the warriors' dead bodies littering the ground. Only the one guard had died, but Cas found himself unable to look in that direction. The death felt heavy in his chest.

He looked back at the wagon to see Daniela, the older woman he'd met earlier in the wagon, climbing out. She teetered to him and threw her arms around his neck.

He gave her a gentle squeeze before releasing her. He regarded the dirty, exhausted faces around him. "Is everyone all right?"

Heads nodded in unison.

"Did they feed you?"

"A little dried meat yesterday," one man said.

"It's not far to Fort Victorra," he said. "Feel free to get back in the wagon if you're too weak to walk." He gestured for a couple of guards to take over the wagon.

"Thank you," Daniela said, her eyes shining with tears. Several more thank-yous rumbled through the crowd, and he gave a tired smile before turning away. Galo stood behind him, watching the staff.

"I think you've just created thirty people who would do anything you say," the guard said.

Cas walked to his horse. "It looks like a few died since the last time I saw them."

"That's not your fault."

Cas shrugged as he mounted his horse. The guard climbed atop his as well, and the rest of the guards spread out in front and behind him as they started down the trail.

"I'm sorry about your father," Galo said after a long silence.

"A warrior came through the window and stabbed him before I could react," Cas said. "I couldn't save him."

"No one expected you to," Galo said. "You shouldn't have had to face a warrior alone anyway. I failed you."

"No, you didn't," Cas said, frowning at him. "If I remember correctly, you stayed behind to fight off a rather large number of warriors. I'm surprised you made it out alive."

"I am too."

"It's a good thing. I don't know who else I would have named captain of my guard."

Galo looked at Cas in surprise. "I'm too young to be captain of the king's guard."

"Well, I'm too young to be king, but here we are."

"Here we are," Galo repeated quietly. He gave Cas a sad smile. "All right. Thank you." He paused, glancing at Cas for several moments. "We haven't found a trace of Emelina Flores."

"Ah."

"You hadn't asked."

"I guess I figured you would say if you had."

Galo gave him a thoroughly suspicious look but didn't push further. Cas would confide in him eventually, but not when the other guards were so close.

Cas glanced at his friend, realizing for the first time that Galo was the only person he trusted enough to tell the truth about Emelina. His mother and Jovita would have a nervous breakdown. None of his father's advisers had ever taken him seriously enough to build any kind of relationship.

"I'm glad you're not dead, Galo," he said softly. He wanted to say more, to tell Galo everything and ask for advice, and he could see Galo reading that emotion on his face. Cas turned away, kicking his horse until it began galloping. "Let's go."

THIRTY-FIVE

LERA SOLDIERS SWARMED the fortress. Jovita had described Fort Victorra to Em as "simple," and she wasn't wrong. While the Royal City castle was all windows and lavish decorations, the fort was nothing but a square pile of bricks.

Two towers flanked the main building, with openings at the very top, presumably for the soldiers to keep watch. A brick wall ran around the entirety of the building, though it wasn't so high that it couldn't be climbed if necessary. But it would be hard to climb it without drawing attention from the guards.

Em crouched on a hill not far away, where she could see the soldiers milling around behind the wall. A huge number had made it to the Southern Mountains without being captured by Olso guards.

Em pressed her hands into the grass, craning her neck to peer at the winding road leading to the fort. The queen and Jovita had arrived several minutes ago, but there was no sign of Cas yet. Hopefully he wasn't far behind.

A flash of movement caught her eye in the woods beyond the fort. A few red jackets came into view. Warriors.

She jumped to her feet, keeping her body low to the ground as she jogged down the hill. She needed to find Aren before Olivia was released. She wanted to hightail it out of Lera as soon as she had Olivia, and she wasn't leaving without Aren.

She broke into a run as she entered the cover of trees. The woods were too quiet. No animals scurrying around, no insects chirping. A lot of people had been through the area recently.

A powerful gust of wind blew across her face, too strong to be natural. She whirled around, searching for the Ruined. Dirt sprayed across her face, and she blinked, her eyes watering.

A body smashed into hers, and Em grunted as she hit the ground. She threw her elbow back, connecting with soft flesh, and managed to wriggle away as the woman cried out in pain.

She scrambled across the dirt, her sword half drawn before she caught a glimpse of her attacker's face. She froze.

"Mariana?"

The Ruined girl blinked, giving Em a baffled look. "Emelina?"

Footsteps pounded the dirt, and Em whipped her head around to see two Ruined men running toward them.

"It's fine, it's just Emelina." Mariana jumped to her feet,

dusting the dirt off her pants. "What are you doing here? We thought you were dead."

"Nice to see you too." Em pushed off the ground, adjusting the sword on her belt. "What are *you* doing here? Did you come in on the warrior ships?"

Mariana nodded. "The warriors wanted us to help take Fort Victorra."

Em looked at the empty space around them. "Where are they?"

"They're getting into position for the attack. We were doing the same." Mariana cocked her head, her thin dark braids falling over her shoulder. "Why are you here? I was sure you died months ago."

Em ignored the question, glancing at the two men. The man with gray streaks in his hair was Weldon, and must have been the one to spray dirt in her face. The younger man, Nic, was also able to control the elements, but the power was so weak he was practically useless.

"What are you wearing?" Nic asked, grimacing as he surveyed her tattered blue dress.

"I'm on my way to get Aren," she said. "You three come with me. I may need the backup."

"Aren's alive?" Mariana instantly perked up.

Weldon lowered his bushy eyebrows. "We thought you finally got him killed."

"The warriors have him."

"Maybe you should wait here," Mariana said, like she was

talking to a child. It was a tone any useless Ruined knew well. "We can handle it."

Em rolled her eyes and turned away from them, breaking into a run.

"Seriously, what is she wearing?" Nic asked from behind her.

"Come on!" she yelled over her shoulder. Footsteps followed her a moment later, and she led them through the trees to the south side of the fort. She slowed as she approached the area where she'd seen the warriors. She didn't make an effort to be quiet. She was negotiating with the warriors, not attacking.

Iria's face appeared from behind a tree, and she glanced over her shoulder. "Emelina's here." An angry murmur followed her words, and Iria frowned.

Em slowly stepped forward. Iria stepped aside, revealing Koldo and a female warrior standing over Aren. He was seated on the ground, still blindfolded but apparently unharmed.

"I just want Aren," she said, raising her hands.

The female warrior shook her head. "He's too dangerous. He killed a warrior earlier, and we're not taking a chance that he'll kill more. We're keeping him until we can transport him to the Olso king for evaluation."

"Petra, we don't need—" Iria began.

"Move, or I will make you move," Mariana interrupted, stepping up beside Em. She narrowed her eyes at Koldo and the warrior screamed, batting at invisible images with his bandaged wrist. He whirled around, slamming straight into a tree.

He moaned as he hit the ground. "I hate you people."

Petra reached for her sword, making a beeline for Mariana. Em jumped between them, putting her hand over Mariana's face before she could use her powers.

"Get off," Mariana said, jerking her head away.

"Everyone just calm down." Em turned to Petra. "Put the sword away."

"Make me."

"I'd be happy to." Mariana lunged and Em shoved her.

"We're on the same side!" Em yelled. "Will everyone just shut up for a minute? Nic, take off Aren's blindfold."

"If you take off his blindfold, he'll kill us all," Koldo said, shakily getting to his feet.

"Probably not," Aren said. "I'd say there's only like a sixty percent chance I kill you all."

"Aren," Em said in a warning tone.

He let out an exaggerated sigh. "Fine. Fifty percent."

Iria stepped aside, giving Nic access to Aren. He tugged off Aren's blindfold and untied the rope binding his hands. Aren hopped to his feet.

"Are the warriors in position to attack?" Em asked Iria.

"Yes. There are a few Ruined scattered through the woods as well. They're part of the second wave." She pointed at Mariana. "Weren't you given an assignment?"

"Yeah, but then I ran into Em wandering aimlessly around the woods."

"I wasn't aimless, I was looking for—" Em cut herself off, taking a deep breath and turning back to Iria. "I need for you to wait. Cas promised to release Olivia."

Mariana gave her a baffled look.

"Olivia is in there," Em said before Mariana began asking questions. "She's still alive, and she should be walking out that door any minute."

"Wait." Mariana put her hands out in front of her, like *stop*. "Cas, as in Prince Casimir?"

"King Casimir, now," Aren said.

"He told you he would release Olivia." Mariana's face twisted into utter disbelief. "Why would he do that?"

"It's a long story. But—"

"It's a long story you need to hear," Aren interrupted. "Em married Cas. She's the reason we were able to launch a successful attack against the Lera castle. She's why we're all here."

Silence fell over the group, and the three Ruineds looked at Em in confusion.

"Married?" Weldon repeated.

Mariana made a disgusted face. "Ew."

"Can you hold off on the attack?" Em asked Iria.

"No. It happens after sundown. Everything is already in motion."

Em looked at the sky. About another hour until sundown. Hopefully that was enough time.

"Fine. Aren, come with me. We're going to keep watch on the fort and see when she comes out. Mariana, Weldon, Nic, get in your positions." She pointed at the warriors. "You three. No more taking Ruined as prisoners. We're on the same team here."

Koldo and Petra frowned at the Ruined warily, but Iria agreed.

"Got it?" Em asked Mariana.

Mariana blinked, throwing a baffled look at Weldon and Nic. "When did you start giving orders?"

"When I executed this entire plan while you were all hiding and running away."

Mariana turned to Aren. "She really did all this?" He nodded. Mariana still didn't look convinced.

"Get in position or get out of the way," Em said.

Mariana hesitated for a beat, then gestured to Nic and Weldon. "Let's get in position."

THIRTY-SIX

CAS FOLLOWED GALO through a tall metal gate, a chilly wind causing goose bumps to rise on his arms. Fort Victorra cast a shadow over the lawn, and Cas raised his head to look at it. He hadn't been to the fortress in years. It already felt oppressive, and he wasn't even inside yet.

Lera soldiers and guards swarmed all over the lawn, and every head turned to watch him. A chill raced down his spine. They all took orders from *him*. They were all expecting *him* to have the answers.

He forced a smile as a familiar guard's face lit up at the sight of him. Galo pulled open the thick wooden doors, stepping back to let Cas go first.

The guard to his right straightened as Cas stepped into the building. There were no windows, so it was dark and cool. The entryway was small and cramped. Cas went through a second door and found himself in a large, mostly empty room. Lanterns hung from the walls, casting a soft glow onto the stone floors. The stairway to his left led up to most of the rooms, if he remembered correctly, and also allowed access to the two towers. Several guards stood nearby, one positioned at each wall.

"Where are my mother and Jovita?" he asked.

"Upstairs in the east tower," a guard said.

"And the prisoners? Is anyone besides Olivia down there?"

"No, Your Majesty. Just Olivia Flores."

Cas leaned closer to Galo, lowering his voice. "Will you go down there and relieve any guards? Tell them they're needed out front. I'll meet you there in a minute."

Galo gave Cas a questioning look, but he nodded and headed out of the room. Cas walked to the stairs, jogging up them and into the east tower. His mother and Jovita stood by the window in the small room. They both turned when he walked in.

"Tell me what's going on." He moved to the window, nudging Jovita aside. The sun was setting, and a soldier was lighting the torches around the building. It was quiet, the air thick with fear and tension.

"We've spotted some movement in the woods," his mother said. "We think they'll be attacking tonight. They were probably waiting for us to get here."

"We're their target," he said.

"It might have been safer for you to stay hidden in the jungle," Jovita added.

"Safer, maybe, but not a very brave choice considering we're at war." He cracked a knuckle as he said the word *war*.

"Why do you have a warrior's sword?" Jovita asked, eyeing the blade at his waist.

"I took it from one after I killed him."

"Did you come all this way by yourself?" Suspicion crept into her voice.

"Does everyone have orders?" he asked, ignoring the question. He gestured at the soldiers outside. "Do they . . . know what to do?" He knew nothing about leading an army into battle, and the question sounded stupid as it left his mouth.

"Colonel Dimas is the highest-ranking officer here," the queen said. "I'd hoped General Amaro would make it in time, but she hasn't arrived." She paused. "Or she's dead."

"There are already plans in place to defend Fort Victorra in case of an attack," Jovita said. "You should know that, Cas."

He vaguely remembered those plans, and he rubbed his fingers against his head. "Forgive me if I can't remember everything clearly right now, Jovita. I didn't have guards to escort me through the jungle. I've barely slept since we were attacked."

"Your Majesty?"

Cas turned to the source of the voice to find a short guard standing in the doorway. He looked at Cas nervously.

"I'm sorry to interrupt, Your Majesty, but I'm not sure who I'm supposed to be reporting to right now."

"It's fine," Cas said.

"We were just told to leave the dungeons—me and the other guards—and I just wanted you to know that we don't usually leave Olivia with less than three guards and—"

"Is she dangerous?" Cas interrupted.

"Well, no, not anymore, but—"

"Then we need you fighting."

The guard nodded and scurried away, mumbling an apology as he went.

The queen and Jovita regarded him with matching suspicion. He tried to keep a neutral expression on his face.

His mother touched his arm. "Cas, let's get you something to eat and hide you in one of the rooms. Jovita and I can handle any problems that arise."

Cas's gaze flickered to Jovita, an uneasy feeling unfolding in his chest. "I'm not hiding away while our soldiers fight." He turned to his cousin. "Jovita, go get Colonel Dimas and tell him to meet me downstairs. I want a briefing on the plan."

"Your mother and I already talked to him," Jovita said.

"Good. Now go and tell him the king wants to speak with him in a few minutes."

Jovita's jaw twitched, but she walked past him and ran down the stairs. He headed after her, his mother following him.

"Part of being a good king is making sure you stay alive to actually rule," she said, her shoes pounding the floor as she ran after him. "Charging into battle to save a few staff members in a wagon and—"

"We saved them and I'm still here, Mother."

"It's not smart." She grabbed his shirt, pulling him to a stop. "Why did you take the guards off Olivia?"

"We need everyone fighting." He tried to keep his face blank, but his mother frowned suspiciously.

Cas turned away, jogging down the stairs. His mother stayed put, and he could feel her eyes burning into his back. He stepped off the stairs and out of her line of sight. He was going to have to sneak Olivia out, and he wasn't looking forward to the fallout once his mother realized what he'd done.

Colonel Dimas walked through the front door and nodded at Cas. "Your Majesty. I'm glad you made it here safely." He led Cas outside and took him around the entire building, giving Cas a brief rundown of their defense strategy as they walked. Many of the guards and soldiers were obviously weary, their uniforms wrinkled and dirty from travel. But they stood tall in straight lines, ready for battle. Cas looked down at his grungy blue staff shirt.

"Can I get a guard uniform?" he asked the colonel as they returned to the front lawn. "It'll be easier to fight if I blend in."

"Will you be joining us, Your Majesty?"

"Yes."

"I'll have someone find one."

Cas thanked him and turned on his heel, shaking his head when a guard made a move to follow him. "I'll be back in a minute."

He walked through the front doors and across the large room.

There were two arches on the back wall leading to the rear rooms, and he glanced over his shoulder before ducking through the left one. The guards watched him, but none made a move to follow.

He headed across the parlor, sidestepping the table and cluster of chairs in the center of the room. If he remembered correctly, the doorway at the back left corner of the room led to the dungeons.

He pulled open the door and quickly descended the stairs. A heavy wooden door was at the bottom, and he pushed it open to reveal a long hallway with cells on either side. Galo stood in front of one of the last cells, and he looked up at the sound of the door opening.

"This is Olivia?" Galo asked, pointing to the cell in front of him. His face was pulled tight with worry, and Cas quickly walked toward him. All the cells he passed were empty. Oddly, it smelled strongly of flowers or perfume the farther he went into the cells.

"Is she all right?" Cas asked.

The last cell was the only one occupied. It held a teeange girl. She was chained to the bed, facing the wall instead of out at the bars. A blindfold covered her eyes. She wore loose pants and a white shirt, both smudged with dirt and grime. Her dark hair was wild. She had more Ruined marks than Damian. The pale lines covered her arms and crept up her neck into her hair.

"I think that's her," Cas said quietly.

"Have they had her chained to that bed the whole time?"

Cas ran a hand down his face with a long sigh. "I don't know."

What had he expected? That she had several rooms and a nice bed? That she was allowed to bathe regularly and given enough to eat? Neither had happened, given the state of her.

He held his hand out. "Do you have the keys?"

Galo handed them over. "They're labeled. It's the green one."

He held the green key up to the lock. "Olivia—"

The dungeon door banged open and he jumped away from the cell. His mother and Jovita strode down the hallway, followed by four guards.

The queen extended her hand as she stopped in front of Cas. "Keys, Casimir."

He took a step back, his shoulder brushing against Galo's. He cleared his throat, trying to sound authoritative. "Could you all please give me a moment?"

"You can't release her." The queen shook her head. "I know that's why you're down here. I know Emelina put ideas in your head about the Ruined, but you can't just let Olivia go. You don't know what she's capable—"

"She's chained to the bed!" He pointed at her, anger rising in his chest. "She's not capable of anything!"

"It's a failed experiment, Cas," Jovita said. "We'll admit that. We learned a few things, and we thought Olivia's healing powers could be useful, but she couldn't be conditioned to—"

He pointed at the guards. "Get them out of here."

None of the guards moved. His mother looked at him apologetically. "I'm sorry," she said quietly.

The guards sprang forward. Hands closed tightly around

Cas's wrists. He tried to jerk away, but they held firm. One of them pried the keys out of Cas's hand.

"I'm sorry, Your Highness," one of them murmured.

Galo's fingers curled around his sword.

"You're too emotional," the queen said.

Cas fought down a swell of rage. "You—"

"Lera isn't about the opinions of just one person," the queen interrupted. "Even if that person might be the next king."

Might be the next king. *Might?* He swiveled his head to Jovita. She didn't meet his gaze.

"We're engaged in war," his mother said. "Now isn't the time to drastically change policies. If you were thinking clearly, you would see that. You've barely slept in days—we can all tell—and I can certainly understand you still being traumatized by the death of your father."

His mother gestured at a cell. "Only for a few hours, until we fend off an attack from the warriors. You'll be safe down here." She grabbed her necklace, pulling it over her head and then throwing it over his head. The metal was still warm from her skin as it slipped beneath his shirt. "It has the Weakling flower in it. It protects you from Ruined magic."

He looked down at it in surprise, turning a questioning gaze to her.

"It's one of the reasons we had Olivia. We needed to know their weaknesses, in case of a situation like this. You should have it, if you're going to be down here with her." She pointed to Galo, who still had his hand on his sword. "Put him in there with Cas."

Cas twisted against the hands holding him. He couldn't get free. "You need all the guards fighting!" His mother just shook her head in reply. He shot her a furious look as a guard took Galo's sword.

The guards gave Cas a gentle push to the cell. He stubbornly refused to budge, so they had to drag him through the open metal door. The two men released him and stepped out of the cell, then pushed Galo inside. The guards banged the door shut behind them and twisted the key.

Cas crossed his arms over his chest, noticing that his mother was avoiding his gaze. He stared at each of the guards in turn, making a mental note of their faces. He didn't want to forget the faces of traitors.

"Let's go," the queen said. "One of you stay at the post outside the door. No one in or out."

"I'll stay," a guard offered. The queen nodded, gesturing at Jovita to follow her. They disappeared through the door, the guard who'd elected to stay shutting it behind him as he followed.

Cas looked from Galo to Olivia, in the cell across from them. Was Em going to think he'd betrayed her? Would she attack with the rest of the warriors now? Dread curled at the bottom of his stomach.

He let out a long sigh, pushing a hand through his hair. He turned to Galo. "I need to tell you what happened in the jungle."

THIRTY-SEVEN

EM LAY FLAT on her stomach at the top of a hill, Aren stretched out beside her. She'd been watching the front of the fort for an hour, and there had been no sign of Cas or Olivia. The Lera soldiers had disappeared inside the fortress, and the front lawn was deserted.

"Em."

She glanced over her shoulder to see Iria crouched behind her. "Everyone is almost in position. Are you and Aren helping?"

Em searched the front lawn again, like Olivia was suddenly going to appear if she wished for it hard enough. Why hadn't Cas released her? Had she been moved? Was she dead?

Had he changed his mind?

She looked at Aren.

"I'm going to help," he said quietly. He got to his feet. Em sighed, slowly standing and following him and Iria down the hill.

"We're doing two waves," Iria said as they walked. "We've got a Ruined in position to take down a section of the front wall, and then the warriors are going in. The Ruined will attack shortly after. We've got them scattered in safe positions. Once they've exhausted their magic, we'll move back in."

"I want to try and get into the building and grab Olivia," Em said.

"Your best bet is to wait until after we've taken it," Iria said.

"What if you don't succeed?"

"We will." They'd reached the bottom of the hill, and she pointed into the thick of the trees. "Aren, there are a couple of Ruined that way. If you go meet up with them, they'll get you in position."

Aren shook his head. "I'm staying with Em. We're going for Olivia. I'll take down as many Lera soldiers as I can, though."

"Fine." Iria took off, her footsteps quiet in the grass as she disappeared into the trees.

"Do you want to go in the front with everyone else?" Aren asked Em.

She shook her head. "All the attention will be there. Let's be sneakier." She headed into the trees, gesturing for him to follow her. Mariana stood with two warriors, and her eyes brightened when she saw Em and Aren coming.

"Did he release Olivia?"

"No," Em said. "We're going in after her. Is there anyone set up at the back of the building who could blow a hole in it?"

"Sure, we have Weldon back there, and he can do it," Mariana said.

Em turned to Aren. "Can you hang back with Weldon and take out any Lera soldiers in the immediate area? I'll go in by myself."

"I should go in with you," Aren said.

"No, you'll be more useful if you can get the soldiers off me so I can get in. And I know how much energy that will take. You should be in a safe place."

He paused, then nodded. "All right."

"You need to hurry," Mariana said. "We're attacking any minute. You'll hear the wall come down soon."

Em and Aren took off, whispers of "Good luck" following them. The sun had completely set, and it was dark and silent as they ran. Her feet ached and her stomach had given up on the hope of food and just twisted sadly, but she ignored the pain.

They found Weldon in a tree not far from the back of the fortress. His legs dangled on either side of a branch, and he listened carefully as Aren explained the plan.

"We need you to blow a hole in the wall first," Aren said. He pointed. "Then take out that spot right there at the back of the building. And if you could make it big, we'd appreciate it. Take some people out with it."

Weldon grinned. "Absolutely."

A low whistle echoed through the quiet night, and Weldon

twisted his face into a more serious expression. "The front wall's about to come down. Go!"

Em drew her sword and ran. The area at the back of the fortress was nothing but grass, and anyone in the tower could have seen her coming.

A loud *boom* sounded from the front of the fortress. The ground beneath her shook, and she fell to her knees, watching as the stones of the rear wall of the fortress rumbled. A large section exploded, sending pieces of stone and wood shooting out in every direction. She ducked her head, covering it with her hands.

She jumped to her feet, squinting in the dust and darkness. Weldon had blown a huge hole in the wall and the building, and two men lay crumpled in the rubble. Another was stumbling around, blood pouring from his scalp.

There were more guards inside. She could see at least four running toward the wreckage, and she headed right for them. Aren could take out at least three; that left one for her and her sword.

She hopped over the stones, pointing her sword to her left. Aren took care of the guard rushing toward her immediately. His body made a crunching sound as it slammed into the ceiling and then to the ground.

The guard right in front of her also flew out of reach, and she raised her sword to the one rushing at her. She kept one eye on the scene around her, frantically searching for Cas. Where was he?

She ran her blade into the guard's chest when he lost his

balance, and quickly darted away from him. Footsteps pounded the floor somewhere nearby, and she ran in the opposite direction. She didn't want Aren to use his magic anymore. He needed to conserve his energy.

She slipped around the corner. Where would they keep Olivia? Locked in a cell, for sure. All the cells in Lera had been underground, so it was best to assume it was the same here.

She found a kitchen and a small dining room first, but no doors leading downstairs. She waited for the sounds of footsteps to fade, then darted across the destroyed room to the other side of the fortress.

She opened a door to find a small parlor. There was a door at the back of the room, and she ran to it and threw it open.

Stairs leading to the basement stretched out in front of her. A guard stood at the bottom, protecting a closed door, and his head popped up. He drew his sword.

She flew down the steps and the guard charged at her with a yell. She blocked his sword, raising her boot and slamming it into his chest. He fell backward, crashing into the door.

She seized the handle, pushing it open. The guard fell backward and scrambled to find his footing. She drove her sword into his chest.

"Em."

She pulled her blade out of the guard, looking up at the sound of the familiar voice. A hallway of cells stretched out in front of her, and she stepped forward, toward the sound of the voice. Cas stood in a cell, his fingers wrapped around the bars. Galo was behind him, an utterly baffled expression on his face.

"What are you doing in . . ." Her voice trailed off as she noticed the dark-haired girl in the cell across from them. Olivia.

"I'm sorry," Cas said. "I tried to free her, and my mother and Jovita stuck me in here."

She rushed forward, gripping the bars of her sister's cell. "Olivia? Are you all right?"

Her sister's head popped up, and she turned her blindfolded eyes toward Em. She was too thin, her hair a crazy mess. Olivia was nearly sixteen, but she was so tiny it was almost as if she'd aged backward since Em had last seen her. Her Ruined marks had almost doubled, covering more skin than Em had ever seen. She had even more than their mother.

"Where are the keys?" She whirled around and Cas pointed at the guard. She ran over and snatched them off his belt.

"The green one," Galo said. Then softer, to Cas, "Is she going to let us out too?"

"Of course I am," Em said, running back to Olivia's cell. She stuck the key in the lock and the door swung open. She darted inside and yanked the blindfold off her sister's face.

Olivia blinked several times, her gaze resting on Em. Her lips twitched, the chains around her wrists rustling as she reached for Em, but she didn't say a word. She just stared.

"Which one unlocks these?" she asked, reaching for the chains. The iron cuffs were locked at the wrist, and the long chain attached to them went all the way to the wall.

"I don't know," Galo replied. "Maybe one of the smaller keys?"

She sorted through the keys, trying two small ones before one clicked in the lock. She tore the cuffs off, taking Olivia's hands and pulling her to her feet.

"Can you walk?" she asked. She put her hands on her sister's cheeks. "Say something. You're scaring me."

Olivia scrunched up her face, glancing over her shoulder at Cas and Galo's cell. She turned back to Em, lowering her voice to a whisper.

"Did you really marry him?"

Em laughed, but the sound died as screams sounded from upstairs. Footsteps pounded the floor above them. Olivia lifted her chin, her head cocking in interest at the noise.

"Em, if the warriors corner us down here . . ." Cas looked at her pleadingly. "It's the red key."

She rushed to Cas's cell and unlocked it. Cas stepped out, his fingers wrapping around hers. "I'm so sorry they did this to her," he said quietly.

Em shook her head. "It's not your fault."

"It's absolutely his fault," Olivia said from behind her.

Em turned away from Cas and faced Olivia. "I'll explain later. The Olso warriors are attacking, and we need to get out of here."

Olivia's eyes lit up. "They are?"

Em jumped over the dead guard, running up the stairs with Cas and Galo close behind. Olivia took in a deep breath as they stepped into the parlor.

"That is so much better," she said with a sigh. "Did you smell the Weakling flower down there? They lined the cells with it. I've barely been able to breathe for a year."

The sounds of yelling and swords crashing together echoed through the fort, and Cas began running toward the front door. "Galo, can you help them get out safely?" he called over his shoulder. He disappeared around the corner.

"Unnecessary." Olivia held out her hand, and Galo's feet left the ground. He hit the wall with a loud thud and crumpled to the floor with a grunt.

Em quickly grabbed Olivia's hand, pulling it down. "Don't. He's a friend."

"And that's why I didn't pull his spine out through his throat." Olivia made a waving motion with her hand as Galo got to his feet with a wince. "Run, human. Before I change my mind."

Em cast an apologetic look at Galo. "Go, Galo. We'll be fine."

Fear crossed his face, and he took off after Cas without a word.

"Are there really warriors outside?" Olivia asked, darting across the parlor.

Em caught her arm, pulling her back before she ducked through the archway. "Wait." She pressed her back to the wall, peering around the corner. A guard walked past the front door, his sword drawn.

"Who let him out?" Jovita's voice rumbled through the fortress, accompanied by the pounding of footsteps. She ran down the stairs, jabbing a finger at the guard. "Who let Prince Casimir out? Why did I just see him run into battle?"

Em put her arm out, telling Olivia to stay put for a moment.

"I don't know," the guard said. "He ran by me before I could stop him."

Jovita turned her back to them, and Em gestured for Olivia to follow her. Em carefully snuck around the corner, taking a quick glance at the mess she'd left a few minutes earlier. The only guards in the room were dead, lying beneath piles of rubble.

Olivia yelped suddenly, and Em whirled around to see her pulling a rock off the bottom of her bare foot.

"Hey!" Jovita yelled, running around the corner. "Who's—" Her eyes widened as they landed on Em, and she whipped her sword out. Olivia focused on the guard behind Jovita, sending him flying across the room.

Em raised her sword. "Remember how this ended for you last time."

Jovita's lip curled as she took a step forward.

"Move, Em," Olivia said, nudging her arm. "Let me—"

"The Ruined are attacking!" The yell came from outside, and Jovita's head whipped around.

Em lunged, her sword grazing Jovita's cheek. Jovita gasped, stumbling back as she pressed a hand to her cheek. Blood seeped through Jovita's fingers, and Em lowered her sword. She wouldn't kill a member of Cas's family.

Em grabbed Olivia's hand, but her sister stayed put, pointing at Jovita.

"No, I want to see her spine come out of her—"

"Olivia, no," Em said sharply, tugging her sister away. They broke into a sprint, leaping over the rubble. As soon as they ran outside, Aren was in front of them.

"Aren!" Olivia rushed forward, throwing her arms around his neck.

Aren's face broke into a grin as he embraced her briefly. Two Lera guards were headed their way, and Em took off first, pulling Olivia with her. Her sister wasn't wearing any shoes, but she ran fast, keeping pace with Aren and Em.

The Lera guards weren't chasing them. Em frowned, turning to look at the fortress in confusion. Why weren't they chasing them?

"Let's get out of here," Aren said. "The Ruined are going to take the fort down at any minute."

"The guards aren't chasing us," Em said quietly. She swallowed uneasily.

"Once the fort is down, we can kill so many," Olivia said, ignoring Em's comment. She grinned at Aren. "I can't wait to show you what I've learned. Our powers are so much stronger than we realize. We can—"

Pop pop pop. Olivia stopped at the sounds, turning her head to the sky. Em followed her gaze. Tiny little particles of something floated through the air, barely visible in the light from the torches.

"Don't breathe!" Olivia screamed. She clapped her hands over her mouth and nose, and Aren and Em immediately followed suit.

Olivia jumped like she'd been stung by something, and Em watched as the little particles hit her skin. The Ruined marks swirling around her arms grew darker, spots of blood appearing as the skin began to rip apart.

Em watched as the blue pieces hit her skin. Nothing. She lowered her hands from her mouth and took in a breath.

She knew that smell. Weakling.

Em dove for Olivia first, then Aren. She shoved them both to the ground and wrapped her arms around them as best she could. Olivia had more flesh exposed than Aren, and she pulled her sister's arms in closer, covering them with her own.

She stayed crouched over them until the particles had all mostly drifted to the ground, then pulled them up. "Run," she said. "Run until you can breathe."

Olivia stumbled as she stood, keeping the back of her arm against her mouth. Aren did the same, steadying her with his free hand. They took off together, Em following close behind.

Screams tore through the night, and Olivia came to an abrupt stop. They'd just cleared the Weakling, and she and Aren sucked in deep gulps of air.

"They're killing the Ruined." Olivia clenched her fingers into fists and ran back in the direction of the fortress. Em almost yelled for her to stop, but the air had mostly cleared.

Aren and Em sprinted behind her.

"The Ruined were set up at different points around the fortress!" Aren called. "In a U shape. Over there!"

Olivia glanced back to see where he was pointing, then veered to her left. They ran into the trees, then immediately stopped.

The Weakling was stronger here, clinging to the leaves and still floating through the air. Olivia and Aren took several steps back, letting Em walk into the thick of the trees.

Nic lay on the ground, blood seeping out of the Ruined marks on his neck. His lips had turned blue, and he was wheezing loudly, his red-rimmed eyes fixed on the sky.

Em bent down, grabbing Nic by the shoulders. Maybe if she pulled him away from here, he stood a chance. Maybe Olivia could heal him.

Nic gasped. Then his chest stilled, his head rolling to one side. Em swallowed, dropping his shoulders. She looked at Aren and Olivia, standing several paces away. Olivia was breathing heavily, fury dripping from every pore.

Yells sounded from the fortress, and Em stepped out of the trees to see the warriors charging at the Lera soldiers. It was a bad move, considering they'd probably just lost most of the Ruined they'd put into place.

Olivia stormed toward the fort, her arms outstretched. "You think you can hurt me?" she screamed. "Try again, cowards. TRY AGAIN!"

Four Lera soldiers were in the air suddenly, their bones shifting and contorting in ways that made Em's stomach rise into her throat. They hit the ground, dead.

Killing four people with Ruined magic should have immediately exhausted Olivia, but she didn't even slow down. She charged forward, yelling at Aren to help her. He ran after her.

Em darted into the battle and drew her sword, her heart thudding in her chest as a warrior raced past her. A few more steps, and she would be in the thick of the fight. Swords clashed and yells sliced through the night, sending the hairs on the back of her neck into full alert. The warriors and the Lera soldiers were hard to tell apart in the night, and all she could see was a huge swell of bodies, tangled together and crashing into one another.

Was Cas in there? Was he fighting alongside the Lera soldiers? Had he known they were going to release Weakling right after Olivia escaped?

No. Of course he hadn't. He'd been with her the last few days, and then locked up in a cage as soon as he arrived.

A man was in front of her suddenly, and she didn't have time to worry about Cas. He launched his sword straight at her chest, and she quickly blocked the attack. His face was vaguely familiar from her time at the castle.

"Emelin—" His shout died as she drove her sword through his chest.

She whirled around, finding Iria fending off an attack from two Lera soldiers. Em jumped to her side. She blocked a sword just before it connected with Iria's arm. The Lera soldier blinked in surprise as Em appeared, and she took advantage of the second of weakness. She slid her sword into his stomach, then used her foot to knock him over.

"Thank you," Iria said, breathing heavily as she extracted her own sword from the other soldier's chest.

Em surveyed the scene in front of them. Dead warriors dotted the ground, far outnumbering the Lera soldiers. She desperately searched the crowd for Olivia and Aren, but they were nowhere to be seen.

Panic seized her chest as another soldier came at her. For several minutes everything became a haze of blood, bodies, and swords as she fended off attack after attack and tried to glimpse her sister in the brief moments between.

She pushed a bleeding Lera soldier away from her, kicking his sword out of his hand as he sank to his knees. She took a step back and hit something solid.

She whirled around. Cas.

He lowered his sword, shaking his hair out of his eyes. "Go," he said, wrapping his fingers around her wrist. "Tell the Ruined to retreat now, or they're going to die."

"I think most of them are already dead," she said, fighting back tears.

His face crumpled, regret filling every feature. "I'm sorry. I didn't know."

"I know."

He squeezed her wrist, then let it go. "Please, Em. Get out of here."

He turned away, jumping over a dead warrior as he ran toward the fortress. Iria stood not far away, watching as he went. She looked from him to Em, as if deciding whether she wanted to follow.

"Retreat!" Em yelled as loud as she could. "Warriors, Ruined, retreat!"

Iria echoed her, and the warriors began running. There were so few of them left that Em could count them as they ran down the hill—seven, twelve, eighteen. No more than thirty were left, as far as she could tell. They must have started with at least a hundred.

She spotted Olivia, Aren leaning heavily on her as they staggered down the hill. Em ran for them, sheathing her sword. She took Aren's other arm, swinging it around her shoulders.

Olivia was splattered with blood—her clothes, her arms, her face. It was everywhere.

"Are you all right?" Em asked.

Olivia nodded, her eyes flashing. She turned to Aren. "Don't worry. I'll teach you how to stay strong when you use your powers."

"Yeah?" he asked, his voice full of hope.

"Definitely." She smiled at him, wiping at the blood on her cheek.

They dragged Aren down the hill and through the trees. The warriors had scattered, and the area around them was quiet, still. The silence was almost too much, after the noise of battle.

"Where are we going?" Olivia asked.

"To see if there are any Ruined left alive."

Olivia gasped suddenly, and Em's words died in her throat. An arrow stuck out of Olivia's left arm, and she staggered back, Aren crumpling to the ground without her support.

Another arrow whizzed through the air, so close to Olivia's face that it left a tiny scratch on her right cheek.

Em whirled around. She couldn't see anything.

Olivia yanked the arrow out of her arm. A blue liquid seeped out of the wound. They'd tipped the arrows with Weakling.

A body slammed into hers suddenly, and she realized too late she'd forgotten to look up. Of course the soldiers were in the trees. She knew that trick well.

Arms grabbed her around the waist, the neck, the legs. She twisted in their grasp, desperately trying to see Olivia, but one of them put her in a chokehold, yanking her around so all she could see was forest.

And the queen.

Fabiana didn't smile, but the satisfaction was written all over her face.

She jerked her head. "Back to the fortress. She dies in public for her crimes." She pointed behind Em. "You can kill Olivia here. Bring me her head."

Em kicked her legs, but the arms holding her held even tighter. Olivia was still screaming, and Em was too scared to turn around and look for Aren. Was he already dead?

"Please just let her go," Em begged as the soldiers dragged her behind the queen. "You can have me, but please let Olivia go."

"I already have both of you," the queen said, casting a glance over her shoulder. "Your negotiation skills could use some work."

"Please." Em's words sounded desperate, but she didn't care. "If you let Olivia go, you won't see any of us again."

The queen didn't bother responding to her at all, and tears

and rage swelled in Em's chest. It was hopeless. She'd failed to save Olivia. Failed to save the Ruined. She would die having accomplished nothing.

Footsteps pounded against the ground, and the queen drew her sword as Em looked around hopefully. Now would be an excellent time for the warriors to make an appearance.

Cas's face appeared through the leaves, and the tiny ball of hope in her stomach grew bigger.

He was out of breath, and his eyes bounced from Em to his mother. His expression was wild, and Em could tell he'd come expecting to find this situation.

The queen lowered her sword with a sigh. "Cas, please go back to the fortress."

"Release her," he said, pointing at the soldiers holding Em. They didn't move.

"I understand why you can't do it yourself," Fabiana said. "But someone has to."

"No, we don't." Cas's voice shook, but he stood tall. "There's been enough killing on both sides."

"The damage she's done to our kingdom is immeasurable," the queen said. "If you just let her go, you will lose control of your people. I promise you that. They will see you as weak."

Cas shook his head. "I think you and I have different definitions of weak. I'm not going to be that kind of king. I won't order her execution."

"I know you won't," the queen said quietly.

Em caught the glint of hope from Cas, the way he barely

lifted his eyebrows at his mother, as if asking whether she was going to back down.

For a moment, he looked utterly optimistic.

The queen swung around, so suddenly one of the soldiers jumped.

She sank her blade into Em's stomach.

The world turned black, then red, and black again. Em's knees hit the ground, but she didn't remember falling. Someone yelled, "No!" It was either echoing through her ears or he was saying it over and over.

She started to sway and hit a warm body.

"Please, no," Cas said in choked voice, and she realized she was on the ground, against his chest. She looked down and saw blood on his hands. Was he hurt?

No. That was her blood.

"I'm sorry," he said against her hair. "I'm so sorry."

She shook her head, because she didn't want him to be sorry. He didn't need to be sorry. She couldn't speak, but she managed to find his hand on her stomach and squeeze it.

I could think of worse ways to go. Cas's words from yesterday floated through her brain, and she almost laughed. Maybe she did.

Then there was screaming.

Horrible, terrified screaming.

And a man's head was rolling, rolling, rolling across the ground.

Cas's arms gripped Em tighter, and she blinked a few times,

trying to make her vision work again. There was blood all over the ground. There were no more guards or soldiers, just pieces of them scattered about.

Olivia stepped into the middle of the mess. Stretched her arm out.

The queen's chest swelled outward, an inhuman sound escaping her mouth.

Her chest opened with a crack that made Cas's entire body jerk. Something flew through the air, landing in Olivia's hand. Blood dripped down her arm as she slowly unfurled her fingers one by one, letting the queen's heart drop to the ground with a *plop*.

Olivia turned, her eyes narrowed at Cas. "Move."

He didn't obey right away, but Olivia yelled it again as she came closer to Em. His warmth was gone suddenly, her head laid gently on the ground.

"You're all right," Olivia said, the anger absent from her voice. She put her hands on Em's stomach.

Em sucked air into her chest, the world suddenly coming back into sharp focus.

"Go," Olivia said, glancing over her shoulder.

Em rolled her head to one side to see Cas standing a few paces away from his dead mother. His face was a frozen mask of fear and horror.

"Go, she's going to be fine," Olivia said through clenched teeth.

Cas stared at Em, as if waiting for confirmation. She barely nodded. Her body was weak, but she could feel Olivia's magic working, stitching her back together.

His entire body shook as he hesitated another moment, his gaze locked on hers. Tears filled his eyes when she nodded again.

He took off running.

Em returned her attention to her sister. Olivia's eyes were wide and wild, her mouth stretched into a bizarre grimace. The expression was a crazy blend of happiness and rage.

"You're going to be fine, sister," Olivia said softly. "You and I, we've barely started. When we're done, they'll all be on their knees, begging for forgiveness."

Em fought back tears, though she wasn't sure what she was crying for. It was exhaustion, or defeat, or the look on Cas's face as he stood next to his mother. Whatever it was, the tears leaked out and slid down her cheeks.

Olivia moved her hands from Em's stomach, reaching up to smooth a piece of Em's hair back. She smiled.

"Don't cry, Em. They will fear us soon enough."

END OF BOOK ONE

ACKNOWLEDGMENTS

Ruined was truly a group effort. So many people read, encouraged, or just gave me a good kick in the pants when I needed it. A big thank-you to:

My editor, Emilia Rhodes, who made this book so much better than I thought it could be. *Ruined* has so many moving parts that I thought we'd never get them all working together, but you made it easy.

My agent, Emmanuelle Morgen. Thanks for sticking it out when I could see a thousand ways to execute the story and wanted to try every single one of them.

Jennifer Klonsky, for taking such good care of me with the last book and making sure this one got into the right hands.

Alice Jerman, for all your support on this book and the Reboot series.

Michelle Krys, for the early read and excitement. Thank you for helping me find the best beginning and for the fabulous blurb.

Shannon Messenger, for the early read and character notes. You helped me bring Em and Cas to life. (And thanks for talking me off a writing ledge in Vegas.)

Kiera Cass, for the fabulous blurb. I'm so thrilled to have your words on the front of the book.

Jenn Reese, for the conversations about fantasy and being patient with my millions of questions. Also, thanks to Amaris and Tracy for the epic brunch talks!

Thank you to the design team at HarperTeen for giving *Ruined* such a gorgeous cover. It's prettier than I ever imagined.

A big thanks to the whole team in marketing and publicity at HarperTeen for always taking such good care of me, especially Gina Rizzo—thanks for the early excitement about *Ruined* and always being a smiling face at RT!

My GFA girls—Natalie, Michelle, Amy, Lori, Corinne, Gemma, Deb, Ruth, Kim, and Stephanie—thank you for being there to share the highs and the lows. You're the best writer friends a girl could ever have.

Natalie Parker, for planning the most epic retreats and introducing me to basically all my writer friends.

Michelle Rosenfield, for being a terrific friend, seeing all those movies with me, and letting me vent on more than one occasion. Also, thanks to Ethan for the walks around the lake. Luna misses you.

Sara and Sean, Mely and JP, Nick, Louise, Josh, Chris and Megan—thanks for coming out to events and being fabulous, supportive people.

Thank you to all the bloggers who read and supported the Reboot series, but especially Stacee (Book Junkee), Erin and Jaime Arkin (Fiction Fare), Dianne (Oops I Read It Again), Katie (Mundie Moms), and Sash (Sash and Em). I love seeing your smiling faces at events or in my Twitter feed.

Thank you to my parents and family, with my apologies for the dead and/or evil parents in this book. I promise they're not based on you.

And last but certainly not least—thank you to my sister, Laura, my first and best critique partner and the reason this book became a sister story. Sorry I made the little sister the crazy one.

Read on for an excerpt from

AVENGED

ONE

THE REMAINS OF Em's home sat at the bottom of the hill. The Ruina castle was nothing but a pile of stone and dirt, weeds snaking in between the rubble. One wall remained intact, and Em liked to think it was her mother who had made sure of that. Even in death, her mother had made one last stand.

Olivia sucked in a breath as she reached the top of the hill. "I thought there would be more left."

Em took her sister's hand. Olivia was taken prisoner before their home was demolished and most of the Ruined exterminated. It was her first time seeing the castle like this.

Olivia squeezed Em's hand too tightly. "Don't worry, Em. We'll make them pay."

Olivia kept saying things like that. *Don't worry, Em.* She still worried. *Don't cry, Em. They will fear us soon enough.* She'd said that to Em immediately after killing the Lera queen. Em didn't tell her sister that she was certain everyone already feared them.

"I thought they might have cleared it away," Aren said as he stopped beside Em. He was haggard, his handsome face tight with exhaustion. The Olso warriors had been able to spare a couple of horses, but most of the Ruined made the journey on foot, and they all desperately needed a day or ten to rest.

"At least now we can sift through it and see if anything is left," Olivia said.

"I looked a year ago," Em said. "All I found was your necklace."

"*Your* necklace," Olivia corrected. "I told you I want you to have it."

Em smiled, dropping Olivia's hand and grasping the *O* pendant.

Olivia pointed to the castle. "Are we setting up camp here? We could put the hunters' heads on spikes nearby, as a warning to others."

Em swallowed down a wave of disgust and tried not to let it show on her face. Olivia and Aren had left a trail of dead bodies behind them as they traveled from Lera to Ruina over the past week. Em had convinced them to leave King Casimir and his cousin, Jovita, alive at Fort Victorra, but she hadn't bothered arguing for the hunters' lives. There was no point. Perhaps they deserved to die, after exterminating thousands of Ruined.

That's what she kept telling herself, anyway.

"They know," Em said. "I don't think there's any need."

"Besides, I don't want to smell dead-hunter head while I sleep," Aren said.

"It's your decision where we set up camp," Em said.

"Why is it my decision?" Olivia asked.

"Because you're the queen."

"They voted to abolish the monarchy after I was taken," Olivia said. "And their elected leader is dead. So, technically, I'm nothing."

"They thought you were dead," Em said. "I'm sure they consider you their queen again."

Olivia shrugged. "Let's have a meeting in a few days, when most of the Ruined have found their way back. For now, I say we build a camp right here. Let the Lerans and the hunters know we're not scared of them anymore."

"We're not scared anymore?" Aren asked quietly. A new Ruined mark had appeared on his left hand recently, a white swirl against his dark skin, and he rubbed at it absently.

"Cas promised to leave us alone," Em said, not for the first time.

Aren and Olivia exchanged a look. Em had insisted they'd be safe, that the war against the Ruined was over. Cas had said he wouldn't continue the attacks on the Ruined now that he was king. Em believed he would keep his word.

Olivia and Aren were not convinced.

An icy wind blew Em's coat open. She shoved her hands into the pockets and pulled it tight around her body. She'd taken the coat and the clothes she was wearing from a Ruined killed at the battle of Fort Victorra. She'd needed something other than the blue dress she'd worn to cross the Lera jungle, but the clothes still made her squirm when she thought about it too hard.

Em turned at the sound of laughter and saw a group of about a hundred Ruined emerging from the trees. They were exhausted from the battle at Fort Victorra, and dirty from days of walking, but smiles lit up their faces as they took in the remains of the Ruina castle.

"We'll set up here," Olivia confirmed with a nod.

"It's more brown here than I remembered," Aren said to no one in particular.

Em had to agree. She and Aren had spent weeks in lush, green Lera, next to the ocean with sparkling clean beaches. Ruina did not look good in comparison. The grass was brown and dead, the sparse trees bare. Past the castle was a giant patch of empty dirt where a cluster of shops used to be. They weren't much to look at when they were standing anyway.

She stared at the pile of debris that used to be her home. Maybe she should have suggested a different location. How long was this going to be her view? How long would she have to sleep on the ground while staring at the spot where her bedroom used to be?

The room took shape in her head—the bed with piles of pillows, the full-length mirror on the wall where she used to stand and desperately search for Ruined marks when she was younger.

The worn green chair in the corner where she curled up to read.

She expected tears to come, but a hollow feeling settled at the bottom of her stomach instead. The girl who had lived in that room was gone, and maybe she was relieved that the room was gone as well. They all needed a fresh start. They could rebuild Ruina to be even better than it was before. *Safer* than it was before. Em hadn't slept without a weapon within her grasp in a year. If there was one thing she needed—one thing all the Ruined needed—it was to find a way to feel safe again.

"I'll check on the wagon," Em said. She jogged down the hill. The wagon they'd stolen from the Lera soldiers was slowly making its way through the trees, pulled by two tired horses.

They'd mostly piled supplies for tents and extra water in the open-air wagon, but a few children and sick Ruined were inside as well. A young Ruined man named Jacobo walked alongside the horses. Mariana walked on the other side, her black braids moving as she nodded at Em. Both Mariana and Jacobo had Ruined marks on their dark-brown skin, the white lines curling up their necks and even across a cheek, in Jacobo's case.

"It's—" Em was about to say "clear," when a flash of movement caught her eye. The bush to her right rustled.

She drew her sword, catching Jacobo's eyes and nodding to the bush as she stepped toward it. He walked to the wagon, gesturing for the three children inside to come closer to him. Mariana froze.

Em carefully stepped over a log. Someone sniffed.

She parted the leaves of a bush with her blade. Two men were crouched on the ground. Their clothes were dirty, and one man had so many patches on his coat it was an array of different colors. He had a dagger clenched in his fist, but the other didn't have a weapon. Neither had any blue pins. They weren't hunters.

"Who are you?" she asked.

"We're just trying to get across to Vallos," the man with the dagger said. He stood slowly. His legs shook beneath him. He was staring straight at her chest.

"That's not what I asked. Who are you?"

"We're Vallos laborers working in the Ruina mines," he said to her chest. "Are you . . . are you Emelina Flores?" He said her name in a hushed, almost reverent, tone.

She frowned in reply, unsure how he knew that.

"The circle of vengeance. I've heard about it."

"The what?"

"Your necklace. The circle represents vengeance. 'What goes around comes around,' as they say."

Her lips twitched. Did everyone really think that was what her necklace symbolized?

The circle of vengeance. How fitting. Olivia would love it.

The man with the dagger held the weapon in front of him, but it shook in his grasp. The other had his arms pressed to his chest, fear oozing out of his every pore. She'd earned a reputation, it seemed.

"Go," she said, jerking her head. "Don't come back."

They both spun around and sprinted away from her. Everyone

ran from her now. People whispered her name, as that man had. They said it with fear.

It was what she had always wanted.

It did not feel as good as she had expected.

READ THEM ALL!

www.epicreads.com

JOIN THE Epic Reads COMMUNITY

THE ULTIMATE YA DESTINATION

◀ **DISCOVER** ▶
your next favorite read

◀ **MEET** ▶
new authors to love

◀ **WIN** ▶
free books

◀ **SHARE** ▶
infographics, playlists, quizzes, and more

◀ **WATCH** ▶
the latest videos